John Gives His Wife Hot Adventures
Book 2
in the Servicing the Work Men Series
Ruin Willow and Ruan Willow

Table of Contents

Certified Human Authored by The Author's Guild 4766937.

Dedication

This book is dedicated to lovers who play in and out of the bedroom, those who never stop playing, and those who desire to please their partners and get off on getting their partner off, plus celebrate who they truly are because that's how it should be. Mutual pleasure is mutual bliss. Aftercare matters. Before care matters.
During care matters.
Communication is key.
This book is an erotic romance, specifically an erotic polyamory romance featuring a throuple living an alternative lifestyle who explore sharing of intimate experiences with others, please read and enjoy it knowing this is the subgenre of romance it is in.
Marinate in your sexuality daily.
Enjoy and never stop seeking pleasure.
Pleasure is your birthright.

Chapter 1

L aney woke with images of the group's pleasure flooding her brain. It was lovely, a hot and sexy, overwhelming of images and feelings to wake up to. The most intense sexual experience of her life to date. She smiled before she glanced at John's side of the bed. It was empty, but this didn't deflate her good mood. She'd heard him get up once during the night after his phone had rung with its designated work jingle. So, he was likely working again, unfortunately. He'd been pulled into work problems right before she'd put on PJs, too, and clearly, it had continued on and off through the night. Which meant he wouldn't be able to have morning sex.

She pouted as horniness filled her waking senses. If only Anderson had come home, they'd be having sex. She longed to wake up with him in their bed again. It had been too long since he'd slept at the house, and Laney was worried. Maybe Anderson was losing interest in their union, which scared her. She shuddered at the thought and forced herself out of bed. She was sore after all the work she'd done with the college men on the fence, and of course, from the sex with them, but it had all been worth it. She chuckled at herself, wanting more sex this morning. She truly was insatiable. And she loved that John loved that, too.

She grinned hugely, savoring the lewd barrage of thoughts. That was a really raunchy sex session, and it would likely never get topped. She hoped John would invite them all back again for a sex date reunion, and then Anderson could be the sixth cock. She snickered,'...participant, rather. No, cock. She needed to plant that seed in John's sexy director's brain. He was always open to her suggestions, but he decided what made the final cut. It astonished her to be full in on that plan because, in the past, it was definitely not how it used to be. But John earned it, and continued to, and she had realized how much she loved to follow him. Life hadn't stopped surprising her, and with the recent changes to their marriage being positive ones, she was no longer fearful of the future with him. At one point, she had envisioned herself single and dating, so much so that she'd started doing online searches to learn more. She had tipped her toes into being single just as everything had begun to change.

She stretched and considered hopping in the shower, or should she snag her clit sucker and blast out a big O to start her day? She was torn. She wanted to wait for John or Anderson, but self-pleasure was oh so tempting.

Her phone buzzed. She smiled, and an excited zing coursed through her as she glanced at the screen.

It was Anderson texting: Coming home. Need to talk.

Her heart sank. That kind of sentence never ended well.

With her mood souring, she decided a shower was warranted instead of personal playtime. She slipped off her pajamas and turned on the shower water as worry consumed her. What would Anderson need to say? He was done being their third? They had just found him. On the one hand, he might just have good news, but it felt ominous, and she dreaded his arrival, her excitement totally fizzling. She wanted to stay in her bliss of their unspoken throuple instead.

She stepped into the shower and turned the water even hotter, hoping it would massage her sore muscles a bit. It had been a lot of manual labor yesterday, then the multiple cocks in and on her, plus all their hands fondling, yanking, and torquing her body in different directions, had left her sore and feeling deliciously used. And lusciously satiated. She had loved that the most of all the sex dates John had set up for her, and that thought kept banging around in her head. Not that one could ever replicate such an epic day, but she was so ready to try. She knew Anderson's presence would make it even better. If he were still with them, that is. The thought of him not being there brought the threat of tears to the backs of her eyes. She shook her head to banish the thought.

She sighed as the water streamed down her body. Her libido was not cooperating with her mood as she began to yearn for another orgasm. Maybe she'd just do it, because it would make her feel better. She wanted John's or Anderson's cock, but her toy would likely have to do this morning. It was an efficient little tool. She'd be done in two minutes flat.

She scrubbed her hair as she considered skipping today's workout because of her worn-out body. Her day was starting out rough with Anderson's ominous comment, and the only fix was to climax, with or without her men.

She dried off in a rush with thoughts of her trusty clit sucker overwhelming her brain into mind-numbing orgasmic bliss. She skipped her usual slathering of oil across her skin and opened the door to the bedroom.

With a step into the room, she saw Anderson in the bed, nude, with a sheet strewn over his middle. She gasped. He was grinning so big that it erased her worries. Fuck, this man was the embodiment of sexy times a zillion.

"You're here!" she said, filled with joy and dropping her towel. She squealed as she dashed toward the bed, her tits flopping as she scurried. She launched herself onto the mattress and scooted over to his naked body.

"Hi, baby," he said with a lustful grin, eyes like molten chocolate. "Perfectly washed and ready to fuck, huh?"

He looked extremely scrumptious. She squirmed against his warm, bare flesh as the wafting scent of his manly cologne filled her nostrils. "I'm so excited you're here! I've missed you. You missed an epic day yesterday." She lamented the bit of scolding tone that snuck into her last sentence. The last thing she wanted to do was make him feel bad.

He dropped a kiss on the top of her head and pulled her closer. "I know, but I'm here now and so ready to fuck you."

"Next time, will you come to a group event? Please?" she begged as she wiggled against the hard-on that was nestled against her belly. She wanted every speck of her flesh touching his all at once.

"Yes, of course," he said with a sexy grin. "Wouldn't miss it. I was bummed I missed yesterday, too."

His texted sentence plagued her, though, like a rotten spot on an otherwise nice piece of fruit. Not only did she want to avoid it, but she also wanted to cut it out of existence. She wanted to ask what he'd meant, but she dreaded his response, so she kissed his burly lumberjack man chest instead.

He sighed as he petted her hair. "John's stuck on a work problem, so he told me to come up and fuck you into a multitude of orgasms."

She grinned. He was always thinking of how to satisfy her gargantuan appetite for sex. "He's so good to me."

"He's so good to us," Anderson said as he pulled her into a French kiss. "Because that's exactly what I want to do to you."

He kissed her hungrily, just like she expected him to after being gone. It ramped up her lust even higher, and she grasped desperately at his torso.

"I want you so bad, Anderson. I need you," she murmured against his flesh as his mouth and hands traveled her body. She'd come to realize there was a huge difference between a man who just wanted to fuck her and one who wanted to make her come. Both Anderson and John were thankfully kind.

He suckled her nipples and then chuckled as he traced a bit of leftover paint on her chest. "Can't get all the paint off, huh? John sent me the pictures. That was such a hot set of pics. Let's just say they were well-used last night." He snickered as he traced the paint with his fingers. "I'd like to paint you someday, too."

"Anytime," she whispered as she gave him steamy fuck me eyes.

His phone buzzed. He leaned over to check it, and Laney wanted to throw the phone across the room.

"Might be John," he said, glancing at it.

She relaxed; she could forgive that.

Anderson released a devilish laugh as he rose off the bed. "He wants the monitor on so he can watch us."

She giggled in delight. "That was the most brilliant idea he had, buying that thing." She thoroughly loved the idea of her husband watching them fuck from the basement where he was working. "This will liven up his work."

"No doubt." Anderson switched the monitor on and glanced at the phone, then typed something. He looked up as he neared the bed. "He told me to rail you as hard as I can and make you scream so he can hear in the basement, even without the monitor on." His smile showed he relished the thought, and his expression turned sexy, devilish. He crept to her body across the bed like a predator.

"I love this idea! Good morning, lover," she said, waving to John through the monitor. "Great idea." She gave a thumbs up and kissed the air before Anderson devoured her in a strong embrace.

She squeaked as he grabbed her buns with both hands and threw her head back as he kissed along her extended neck. She caressed his body, savoring all his dips and valleys while writhing herself against this thick shaft. He worked hard at his job, and he had the muscles to prove it.

"Mmmmm, missed you so much," she said breathlessly.

"I missed you," he parroted back. "So much."

It felt good to hear. She had fully expected him to come and say he'd met someone, and they were done, so this was more than welcome; it was a relief.

They rolled across the bed, their bodies entangled as their breathing rates ramped up.

Laney moaned and sighed. She wanted him to know exactly how heavenly he made her feel, so he'd keep doing what he was doing, because it was magnificently wonderful.

He kissed the tops of her breasts while fondling them and then began to tug her right nipple, hardening it further. Once he had it as erect as possible, he took it in his mouth with aggressive passion and sucked hard. He ran his hands up and down her tummy and back as she twisted slightly, trying to get him to touch her pussy lips.

"More," she pleaded.

"Not yet, I want more of this," he said before attacking her other nipple. "I'm not done," he asserted.

It was like her nipples had strings tied directly to her pussy because the more nipple play he did, the hotter she was getting, and the more her wanton hole craved him inside her.

"More," she repeated, noting her own desperation.

He just chuckled with his mouth encased around her nipple. He ignored her demand and continued to maul her body into a heightened state of arousal, while also denying his clear urge to satiate his wants.

"More," she said again with urgency.

"The more you beg, the more I'm edging you until you're a ravenous wench screaming for my cock." His eyes shone like wicked pools of boiling lust.

"I'm there," she insisted as she wriggled inside his touch, nuzzling her body against his.

"You taste so good in the morning," he said with exigency as he reattached his mouth to her tit.

She twisted and clutched his muscle-packed, bulging biceps, whimpering as her lust swelled into blistering seeds of desire, glistening like welts marring her sanity. All she wanted was his cock riding her, fucking her into lucid moments of orgasmic flight.

"Please, Anderson, I need your cock in me, now," she said in a whiny, hungry voice. "Please," she begged.

He denied her and kept feasting on her nipples as she sank her fingers into his arms, but that only egged him on further, and he became even more tenacious in his suckling. Finally, he trailed his fingers down her tummy and danced his fingertips along her hips.

"Pussy," she said in a barely audible voice.

"I love your pussy," he stated in a hot breath against her bosom. "And your tits. All of you."

She was ready to grab his hand and place it between her legs. She released a grunt of impatience.

"Patience is a virtue," Anderson said mockingly while grinning.

"For the non-horny prudes, perhaps," she said as she tried to wrap her thighs around his leg so she could hump it.

He laughed evilly as he pushed her legs off him. "Not yet," he insisted once more.

"Hmpf," she garbled out.

Both men loved to tease her and make her wait. Which she did prefer to the men who wanted to just shove their cock in, then weakly climaxed after like a minute or two, and the sex was over. So, she really shouldn't complain. They liked to make her a raging molten she-cat, frothing at the mouth for their cocks before they even touched her labia lips. It usually worked, and made her come before they even remotely broached penis in vagina sex. There was nothing sexy about a minute man who only wanted to get off and had no burning desire to drive his partner to inferno levels. And she had not only one man who was obsessed with making her come to the max, but two. And it wasn't just one man obsessed with driving her over the edge; it was two. She grinned despite her near-exploding lust. She'd had a few hotwife dates with failing men who couldn't perform, but John had thankfully promptly rectified the situation like a real man after they'd left.

"I see that smile," he said before kissing her on the mouth. His tongue caressed hers for a few minutes of deep tongue loving. "That tastes delicious."

He kept kissing her as finally his fingers caressed her sealed lower lips, then he carefully nudged his fingers inside, parting her swelling labia.

"Mmmmm, yes," she said as she began twisting her body with the new pleasure. "I'm yours, always and forever to fuck."

"I love your body and I love fucking you," he slurred as he pressed two fingers inside her wet folds. "So nice and wet." His lips looked lush and full, wetted with saliva as he penetrated her faster on repeat.

"Mmmm-hmmm," she murmured with a nod. "Like that."

He began to pump his fingers into her at a super-fast speed, then he took her juice to her clit with his fingertips, as he rode her fattened bean.

She cried out as his rapid pace rubbing her swollen external clit increased even more, conveying her approval, urging him to keep going.

"Don't stop," she said fiercely as she rode up her climax. Thoughts of John watching them and stroking his cock flung her even higher on her arousal scale. "John," she cried out, wanting to acknowledge him as Anderson played her body into a crazed state.

Anderson began to wildly spank her clit, and her body recoiled from the intense sensation. She grabbed at his hair. He mouthed her tit while he slapped her clit hard again. He reached behind him and grabbed a vibrating dildo that she hadn't even seen him get, and he pressed it into her pussy. She lurched forward at the full penetration, then, when he re-consumed her nipple in his mouth and stroked her ripe clit aggressively, she launched into a big orgasm that made her body curl toward him and shake like she was being infused with electricity.

"Yessss." She gasped and sputtered her way through the monumental wave of pleasure, fell silent at the peak, then crashed into the rush of the aftermath of the climax. She mewled with relish as she was gifted contraction aftershocks, like little baby bump echoes of her big O. "Mmmmm, that was so good," she said in a happy, lush tone. "More," she said, playfully begging. "Only this time with your cock," she urged.

"Oh, you're getting this cock alright, and you're gonna take it good and deep and hard," he said as he rose up and nestled himself between her legs.

She adored his determined tone. There was to be no arguing with him, and that was such a turn-on.

"Yes, yes, yes, give it to me, Anderson. Give me your big cock, put it inside me. Want your cum painting all along my insides?"

"Your wish is my command, and my honor," he said as a glimmer of love flourished in his lusty gaze.

They hadn't said 'love' yet, but Laney was sure as the sun that she also loved this man. It didn't diminish or make her love for John less special, though, as some may have thought. It was like the love for them both raged it stronger for them. Being a hotwife, some may have likely believed she'd find a better lover with all the men she fucked, but that wasn't possible because these two men always made her a priority, and their chemistry boiled and popped ever stronger instead. They wanted pleasure for her above all, and they got their own pleasure and more with it. It was like what they did fed their love, worshipped her as a goddess, rather than selfishly just taking from her, and their relationship became further solid.

Years ago, she would not have thought all this possible, not ever. But she was small-minded and clueless back then, as was John.

Nothing could have convinced her that her life could now exist and even flourish. It wasn't even a flicker of a possibility. But that was all before she knew about alternative lifestyles, a time when she bought into the culture and the stifling invisible cage her upbringing had shackled her to.

Anderson pressed his meaty mushroom-headed cock against her still-quaking lower lips. She silently pleaded for more as he nudged his way inside her. They both groaned out as the amazing feelings flooded their bodies from the touchdown, a union of their love.

He began to pump his cock into her as her moans rushed out of her mouth like a wave. He groaned his enjoyment of being inside her, and he rocked his body against hers, driving her hips deeper down into the mattress. He pounded himself into her, chasing his own orgasm like a righteous beast. Then he shifted to make better contact with her clit with his thrusts, which he was a master at, and he rammed himself, gifting her another rise to climax.

She pressed his flesh with her fingertips to signal his sexual mastery as he pounded. The skin smacking as their bodies clapped together filled the room. She glanced up at the shiny globe dome above the bed in the middle of the fan and watched Anderson's ass as it bounced in the reflection as he rode her. It filled her with so much excitement that she rocketed into another orgasm. Her body twitched as her back arched, bringing her tits to graze his gyrating torso as he fucked her with gumption.

Her contractions began to radiate out from her womb, crushing Anderson's cock inside her in a series of constricting hugs.

He released a deep man growl, then a groan, then he muttered, "Oh, fuck." His body slowed as he endured his climax, his face spilling into bliss. "Fuck, that was so good."

He kissed her on the lips. As he lifted himself off her, their happy smiles matched.

"So very good. I needed you." She watched him through her partially closed lids.

"And I needed you." He leaned down and gave her another kiss.

Her eyes fell closed as their lips touched. He pressed himself into her body.

"You're still hard," she said seductively. "Let me suck you."

He grinned and rolled off her, waving his hand over his cock. "All yours," he said appreciatively. "Have your way with him."

She scrambled to hover over his fat dick, aligned her body perpendicular to his, and pointed her bare butt in the air. She greedily took him into her mouth. Then she slowed down. It was her turn to tease him. She leisurely sucked their combined juices off his meaty head as he fondled her breasts and nipples. Then he reached to caress her ass as she gently sucked his cock.

She let the head slip out of her mouth and slide across her cheeks. She rubbed her face along his wet, firm flesh, then licked her tongue all around it before taking it back into her mouth. She lay on his thigh and casually played with his dick with her mouth and hands, savoring him rather than charging into anything aggressive. She enjoyed the taste of his cum-soaked manhood, noting her own flavors as well, for several minutes before she took more stern control. She wanted to make him come hard. She rose up on her hands and knees, clasped her fist around his cock, and glided on his thick dick with the seal of her mouth and the clasp of her fingers around his shaft.

She felt the power of guiding him through his helpless pleasure arc. He groaned as she mouthed his freshly fucked hard-on. His body jolted as his hands squeezed her head. His hot cream flooded her mouth, and she barely fought her gag reflex by swallowing his load down her throat. She remained steadfast, keeping her mouth on him despite her desire to pop off. She wanted him fully sunk into the pleasure.

He groaned with satiation as she sucked him dry until every last drop seemed drained from him. He lay limp with a giant smile across his face.

Success.

She snuggled along his body with her own matching grin, and they lay in the heat of their afterglow. She felt sleepy, but didn't want to fall asleep and miss the comfort of his body. She'd been waiting for this; she wasn't about to give it up by succumbing to some weak-ass sleepiness.

He caressed her as he held her close. "That was amazing, Laney, thank you."

"No, thank you. I really, really, really needed you, and I'm so ecstatic that I got to have you." Worry snuck back into her consciousness, and she wanted to ask when he'd meant earlier, but she also didn't want to know. This was too good a moment to think about it being missing from her life going forward. That made her want to cry. She bit back her tears and instead relished her body against his.

They lay there for several minutes in silence, just breathing. The sound of their breaths comforted Laney as she drifted in the golden after-sex aura.

"I suppose you're wondering," he said in a soft voice full of compassion.

"Yes," she said immediately, her heart sinking into an abyss of the unknown. She didn't think she was going to like what he had to say.

"I've met someone," he said plainly.

Her heart desiccated, and she felt unable to breathe, yet she wanted to scream and cry all at once. Her fears were true; he'd leave her and John when they had barely just gotten started. This was dreadful, and she wanted to rewind time and do it all differently, so he'd want to stay.

"She's amazing. I really like her a lot," he confessed.

She cringed further and wondered if John still had his ear to the monitor.

"She knows about us, and she's not turned off by it." Anderson didn't seem sad.

Relief cascaded through her body as her hope grew. "She does? And she's okay with it?" Laney asked with trepidation.

"Yes, she's in the lifestyle too. That's how I met her." Anderson caressed her back.

Laney told herself to relax, but her heart was in flight and freak-out mode. "Okay," was all she could manage to say.

"I told her I was coming here today, so it's not a secret." He shoved an arm under his head.

She knew this was coming. Anderson was too much of an amazing, wonderful, incredible, one-of-a-kind catch not to snag the gaze of a young woman. "And clearly, she was okay with this? You're sure?" She was scared to even ask it, even though he'd just said it.

He nodded. "She has a Dom herself, but they are polyamorous. Hence why she was with me."

This was a relief. It meant Anderson wasn't going to be forced to choose, at least not yet. It also meant they'd likely had sex already, which was his prerogative. They'd never stated any sort of exclusivity or monogamy rules in their relationship and wouldn't go there.

Another woman in Anderson's life might complicate things, though, but she also knew she couldn't claim him as just hers and John's. He was young, and he had his whole life ahead of him. "Have you slept with her?" she asked, not feeling jealous, but feeling relieved that she wasn't some vanilla who would demand him for herself only. She hadn't thought he'd pick such a woman anyhow.

"Yes, that's how we met. We were at a club, and she was there with her Dom. We had sex, and we both felt a connection, so we kept talking afterward." He grinned at her. "Her Dom Muskie watched us fuck. He likes to share."

Well, that sounded hot. Laney's mind reeled, wondering where Anderson would fit into their existing dynamic with the new woman and her Dom. Would he just be a plaything? Or would he become a permanent fixture in their world as he was becoming in Laney and John's? She needn't have worried because this meant Anderson wasn't leaving them for the new woman, so she relaxed. It was all so complicated.

"Don't worry, I'm not leaving you and John," he said with confidence. "I can see that worry in your eyes. I don't plan on leaving you guys, okay?" He held her chin and gazed into her eyes. "I'm having the time of my life with you, too."

She smiled. "Good. And please, don't ever hesitate to speak up. Communication is what will keep us going where we all want to go."

He nodded and kissed her on the lips. "For sure."

They lay together, marinating in their discussion. Laney was relieved that it no longer felt tense. Her dread was dissipating.

"You feel okay about this?" he asked with genuine concern.

"Yes, we don't hold a monopoly on you, Anderson. You are a free agent to do as you please. I'm just so happy you are with us in any capacity because I'm having the time of my life with you, and John is too."

They snuggled, and she released a happy sigh.

"Big sigh," he said airily.

She nodded against his chest. "Big sigh."

Anderson's phone buzzed, and he reached for it on the bedside table. He tapped his code into it and read the text aloud. "John says, 'My dick is very lonely down here, and after watching that, it's hard as a rock. I've been texting Laney, but she's not responding. Can you send her down to suck me off?'"

She smiled. "Oh, I must have left my phone in the bathroom."

"Go suck his cock," Anderson ordered. "I'll shower, then search the kitchen to start breakfast."

She liked him ordering her to go suck her husband. It hit her, getting used to kinks and sub-kinks squarely in the head. He gave her bottom a swat.

"Get going, whore," he said with a wink.

His salacious look made her want to pounce on him again. Her lust increased to a high heat level when he gave her another spank.

"Get going or I'll punish you," he joked.

"Oh, I don't think it will take me that long. That could still happen," she said with a laugh laced in her words. She was sure she might actually like him punishing her, but she scooted off the bed quickly. She snatched her phone from the bathroom counter and made her way swiftly out of the bedroom, her breasts jiggling as she hurried. The idea of sucking John's cock and pleasuring him after he'd watched her and Anderson fuck was very hot indeed. She was so happy John had bought that monitor. Who knew such a thing would work as a sort of sex toy for the three of them?

Chapter 2

Laney zipped down the stairs, her heart pounding. Not too long ago, she'd been reluctant to suck John's cock. It had felt like a chore, not something she enjoyed or sought out to do. And now her heart was blissfully pitter-pattering, and she was clamoring to get her lips around his pole.

This was what their new lifestyle was gifting them; their passion for each other was renewed, the feelings were old ones made new, and they were ravenous for each other. It still floored her where they were in their marriage, not too long ago, versus where they were now. It was like night and day, divorced versus devoted, unhappy versus blissful. She'd like to take full credit, but it was John who changed his approach to her and their marriage, putting her first and focusing on her pleasure had ballooned his own. She loved that he was never jealous; instead, organizing and directing her sex dates had him prospering in his love and passion for her. It was like a magic air had invaded their marriage and was constantly leaving new nuggets of experiential gold for them to enjoy. No one would believe her if she told them.

She descended the basement stairs and heard John talking. She surmised he must be on a call. Her heart sank. She wouldn't be able to suck him off after all. But instantly, she was elated by the fact that she was disappointed. In the past, that feeling had been unheard. Back then, she'd have felt relief at not having to give him a blow job.

She rounded the corner to his office, even though he was clearly deep in conversation with someone. Just before she entered his office area, she froze, remembering she was naked, and if he was on a virtual call, his coworker would see her naked body appear in the background. She hid behind the corner and peeked to see if she could get John's attention. He'd either wave her in or wave her away.

He kept talking, unaware that she was there. She scanned his body. He looked so commanding and sexy, full of confidence and knowledge, so managerial and stoic. He wore different expressions across his face while he worked, and she loved seeing him in this light. It was always very different to see him this way than when he interacted with her. He was all business-like and professional; no one would ever guess they were hotwifing.

What the men were saying was beyond her capability of understanding, but observing him all serious was a turn-on. Likely because she knew all the sexy expressions he made with her, so much so that this contrast ended up being an aphrodisiac, she instantly longed to turn those proper expressions into sheer orgasmic delights.

She tapped the wall with her fingers. He still didn't respond. She considered risking crawling in, hoping she'd be under the viewing of the worker's camera line of vision. After all, John had often worn PJs to such meetings, and no one knew, so, logically, she could perhaps slip in along the side and stay low so he wouldn't see her coming in hot and naked.

She dropped to her knees and began to crawl, her tits hanging like pendulous bulbs of fruit. Her nipples hardened as she imagined the man John was talking to could actually see her. That would be really hot. But it was so hard to know what other people would be okay with, and shoving her naked body in front of his eyes without his permission felt wrong.

She moved along the farthest corner of the room, stealthily crawling like a robber. This was a thrill to try to sneak her way in without being seen, while not knowing whether or not he might actually be able to see her.

She was soundless like a stalking panther as she neared the desk.

John was still talking away as if he had blinders on. He was clearly hyper-focused. She peered at his legs, wondering how she could sneak her way under his desk so she could suck him while he talked to the man. Likely, John wouldn't want this, though, because he'd have trouble masking his pleasure from his coworker. But she wanted the scrumptious challenge to make it so.

She sat like a cat, her butt on her heels and her hands on the floor just like cat paws. She mewled softly, and he turned his head sharply her way.

His grin flashed quickly as his eyes filled with mischief and desire. He swiveled slightly in his chair so his crotch was no longer inaccessible to her. He gave her a come-hither motion with his fingers as he did a quick tick of his head to the right and back over his shoulder.

She crept over, her heart beating even harder, so much so that she felt it could almost make an audible sound outside of her body. This was so taboo, and she hadn't thought John would mix work and pleasure like this. She couldn't wait to try. If he was in, she was too. She wondered if the man would hear her sucking sounds. Was the computer that sensitive that it could pick up little sucking sounds? She devilishly hoped it did. Not that she wanted to get John in trouble, but the danger of it was most definitely arousing. Blowing John to climax while he was in a meeting sounded like the best way to continue a very good day. Most of her days were good days now, though.

John abruptly said, "Alex, can we take a short break? I have something quick to attend to."

Alex's voice came through the laptop. "Yeah, sure. I'd definitely want to attend to that as well." His tone was assured with sexual suggestion.

John cocked his head, clearly unsure of what to say next.

Shit! Laney's mouth dropped into a shocked big O shape. Certainly, Alex had gotten a glimpse of her, and he did not seem turned off or offended by it.

John simply chuckled. "Yeah. Right?" he asked knowingly.

"My wife wouldn't do that for even a million dollars. You're a very lucky man indeed." Alex sounded jealous, but in a good-natured way.

"Sorry about this," John said. He raised both of his hands in apology. "We can finish first, then I'll attend to her."

"Oh, damn. Don't even apologize. And don't you dare. What I wouldn't give to be in your shoes." Alex cleared his throat. "We've known each other a long time, John. Don't even sweat this. I'm more jealous than anything." He laughed at himself, his face humble, but with a twinkle of lust in his eyes. "You enjoy. I'll be here when you come back."

Laney loved this idea. It wasn't a bathroom or coffee break, but a blowjob break. She nodded her head vehemently at John, her hands folded in front of her like in prayer.

"You sure?" John asked sheepishly of his coworker before resuming eye contact with her. He was clearly feeling bad about interrupting their meeting to get some head.

"Positive." Alex's face lit up. "Your wife's stunning, if I may say so. I hope that's not too forward."

"Not at all. I love hearing how a man appreciates the beauty of my wife." John grinned at Laney proudly. "She's the sexiest woman on the planet."

Laney squirmed under his compliment, which made her tits sway a little bit.

"Wow," Alex blurted. "I thought you'd be jealous and tell me to shut my fucking mouth."

Laney chuckled. Their relationship was obviously on a more casual basis than she'd previously thought.

"No, I'm not the type." He shifted in his seat, a new, large mound growing in his groin area. "At all. In fact, actually, we're swingers."

"No shit?" Alex asked while shifting in his cushy-looking chair. "I broached that with my wife a few years back; she still hasn't forgiven me." He snorted. "Nor stopped punishing me for it."

"Ah, damn. Sorry to hear that." John caught Laney's line of sight and raised an eyebrow on his licentious face.

She liked the question that appeared in his eyes. She crawled closer and sat in front of him.

"I'll give you as long as you need. I have nothing going on. My wife and kids are gone for the day, so I'm just here alone." Alex sounded a bit down and desolate, but his eyes flickered with curiosity. "May I be very bold?"

John turned his attention to his computer screen. "Absolutely. We've already crossed a few borders smoothly already here, so go for it."

Laney's heart exploded with anticipation. What would he ask? Would he watch?

"You could certainly...forget to turn your camera off, if you'd like to be so kindly negligent," he said with humor in his tone.

"Really now?" John asked, his interest clearly piqued. "What would you think about that, my lovely little naked sex kitten?"

She rubbed herself along his legs like a cat, indeed, and smiled up at him. Without looking at the computer screen, she said, "I'd love that very much, Daddy." Laney's eyes drifted back and forth between the men as the silence stretched on for what felt like a minute.

Alex guffawed while grinning, breaking the silence. "You lucky mother fucking son of a bitch!"

"She's very obliged," John said with a wicked glimmer in his eyes. "She's quite my little exhibitionist, to be honest."

"Again, you lucky SOB." Alex's double chin bobbed as he heckled, moving in his comfy-looking desk chair.

"So be it, and you, my sexy little hotwife, can do as you please." John motioned for Laney to move between his legs.

"Well, this is a deliciously unexpected development," she said seductively as she rose up, fully intending to allow Alex to see more of her naked flesh.

"Wow, whew. You've got yourself quite the woman, there, John." Alex's horniness was practically leaking through the computer screen.

Laney loved the envy in his eyes, but also his obvious enjoyment. She never imagined someone being envious of her relationship with John, but it felt so good to be in a place where her marriage was envied. Even the college men painters had said such things to her. Dare she say she felt proud of her marriage, which was a breath of fresh air to feelings of pure obligation and being chokingly tethered to a decision she'd made as a younger person. Life decisions had a way of either imprisoning or freeing.

He looked at his coworker and responded, "Yes, that I do. And I'm very lucky." John nodded at Laney. "You can go ahead, baby."

She pressed her tits to his knees and puckered her lips, loving his permission.

"She's also got a power play permission kink," John said with a savoring smile at her.

"Lucky fucker," Alex reiterated.

John leaned down and gave her a peck on the lips, then pulled her into a more intimate French kiss. He grasped her forearms and led her upward to sit on his lap. They kissed, and he swiveled the office chair so her back was facing the laptop. He gripped her hips and fondled her ass as they kissed.

Laney caressed him back hungrily, grabbing at his biceps and then threading her fingers through his hair. She loved that Alex could now see her ass, too.

"Good girl." John gripped her hips harder and pulled her upward, suggesting she get on her feet.

Once she was standing, he pulled her down for another kiss, which efficiently bent her over. He roughly grasped and spread her ass cheeks wide, and she gasped.

"Aw, fuck," Alex exclaimed as her full asshole and pussy were completely open for him to see. "Thank you," was all Alex said. His tone told Laney everything.

John broke their kiss and pushed Laney to stand fully. He turned her body so she faced the camera. Now Alex had a full-frontal view.

"Eye candy for the ride," John muttered to his coworker as he groped her breasts and pinched her erect nipples. He whipped Laney around again and caught her eyes in a lock. "Now, suck my cock, my perfect wench."

She giggled. "Argh, with pleasure, cap'n." And with that, she dropped to her knees as Alex blew out a whistle.

He remained silent, but Laney snatched a quick glance at the screen. She couldn't see his cock, but his hand was chugging and his face was burgeoning with excitement. This was quite an unexpected, saucy, and delicious exchange.

She leaned into the cavern of her man's thighs and undid the button of his shorts. She slowly pulled the zipper down while holding John's hungry gaze.

He leaned back with a happy, lewd grin. "That's it. That's my girl."

Laney savored the exchange for a moment of stillness. Then she rubbed his shaft along both cheeks, stopping for a lip press followed by a lollipop lick. Then she shoved his cockhead into her mouth and as she pumped her hand, riding his shaft with fast strokes, she sucked hard while bobbing her head. She pressed her other fingers around his balls and massaged them. She alternated between lightly squeezing them and adding more pressure. Thoughts of Anderson cooking upstairs with a drained cock spurred on her satiation. She really didn't need to come; she just wanted John to. And now, she wanted Alex to as well.

John groaned as she worked him. She loved being controlled sexually by John, but she also loved controlling him with a blow job, just as she'd done with Anderson. Power wasn't just theirs, but she'd let them think it was. She could take him where she wanted, millisecond by millisecond. His sounds grew more intense as he worked his hands into her hair and scalp. His strong finger pressed into her head, telling her he was not far from climaxing. She slowed her pace, which made him succumb to his urge to thrust into her mouth. She gagged as he did and popped off, laughing at herself before re-consuming his cock.

Alex released a deep groan.

She hadn't considered this type of exhibitionism before, but she was loving the fuck out of it. Hearing Alex's groans added so much to her arousal that she felt she could almost climax while giving head, which had never happened to her before. She really wished she had thought of bringing a sex toy down so she could come as well. She continued to ride him, wishing she could magically poof a toy to John's office. She needed to stock a few of them in his desk drawers for times like this. Then she remembered she could ask Anderson.

She slid off John's cock. "Will you text Anderson to bring me a vibe so I can come too?" she asked sweetly while giving John her vested doe eyes.

"Oh, yes. That's the best idea yet," John said. He reached for his phone to text Anderson, and Laney loved watching his manhood bounce about as he moved.

She glanced at Alex on the screen and smiled. "Hi, nice to meet you, Alex. I've heard a lot about you." It was high time she addressed the man who had been staring at her nude body.

He scoffed. "I guess I haven't heard enough about you!" After his laughter died down, he said, "It's a pleasure to meet you, and thank you so much for allowing me to watch. I don't get much of this at all."

"Oh, my pleasure." She gave him a big smile. "I really get off on it, to be honest."

Once John set his phone down, she went back to lightly playing with his cock, licking it and tapping it to her lips.

Before long, Anderson appeared with one of her favorite sex toys. Laney smirked as he let himself be seen by Alex.

Anderson nodded at Alex and waved. "Hey, I'm Anderson. The pool man."

"And many other delicious things," Laney added in a seductive voice.

"Oh, damn. You've got a whole lot going on, John!"

"Oh, you have no idea. If you're at all interested, let's do a virtual happy hour soon, and I'll fill you in." John appeared to be very excited to share all their stories with Alex.

Laney beamed up at both John and Alex. Then she turned to face Anderson. "Thank you, Anderson. You're truly the best."

"It's all about your pleasure." He started to leave. "Brunch in fifteen if you can make him come by then."

She snickered. "Oh, that will not be a problem." She gave John a primal gaze as she placed the toy in his open palm.

"And he cooks too," Alex stated, shaking his head, his eyes full of astonishment.

"On my lap, facing Alex," he instructed firmly. John turned the toy on to manual mode, the loud buzzing indicating it was set to the maximum power level.

She blushed with delight as she sat on his right thigh. Her lust raged as she spread her legs wide open.

Alex muttered, "Well, shit."

John teased the toy along her lips, then pressed it in. No lube was needed.

She moaned her appreciation and then slid back down on her knees between John's legs. She took John's meaty head in her mouth with purpose and began to bob, taking him as deep as she could. His groans escalated as did Alex's, which made her want to take him deeper. She bounced her head on him while her own climax began to build. The sex toy was quite the instigator for that.

John reached for a titty squeeze, then twisted her nipples with rough tugs.

That did it. She convulsed as her orgasm took over her body. She'd always found it hard to keep sucking well while she climaxed, but her sounds must have triggered John because his cock exploded in her mouth.

Her orgasm kept chugging along, peaking a second time when she heard Alex climax in a rush of groans, followed by sighs.

She swallowed what cum was in her mouth, then swiped the sides of her lips to catch the overflow. She made a production of sucking the extra fluids off her fingers while maintaining eye contact with John. She pulled out her sex toy and handed it to him.

He looked so happy as he took the toy, and it thrilled her. This feeling of full acceptance wasn't that old either. Mostly, she'd wanted the sex sessions with him over as fast as possible back then.

"Mmmmm, that was so good, babe. You outdid yourself. The toy was a good idea." He released a grateful sigh. "Just what I was craving after watching you two." He pressed the toy into his mouth and sucked it, then licked it fully clean.

"Oh, now that you need to fill me in on," Alex said with urgency. "And I don't think my wife would let me do that. Hell, she claims to hate the one dildo we do have."

"Happy hour at six?" John asked with elation.

"I'm free, and yes, hell yes. I'm curious as hell." Alex looked relieved as well and sat perfectly right with Laney. She made a mental note to bring this up with John and make it a regular thing with

Alex. The poor man had a vanilla prude for a wife. She needed a swift kick in the ass and a boatload of orgasms to give her a much-needed attitude adjustment.

"Now I am ready to tackle our problem. You?" John petted Laney's head, which was lying across his lap.

"When she came, holy shit," Alex muttered. "That's exactly what I need in my life. If only my wife were more willing."

"Laney should teach classes." John kept lovingly stroking her head.

That ignited a thought in Laney's mind. That sounded like something she'd be good at and would really enjoy.

She soaked up all his sweet caresses as she listened to them jabber on about stuff she didn't want to understand. John didn't dismiss her as he might have in the past, but let her remain until she felt ready to leave.

Feeling so very loved and satiated, she finally rose after about five minutes. John pulled her into a kiss with adoration in his eyes. She left with the licked-clean sex toy in her hand and climbed the stairs, excited about seeing Anderson making food in her kitchen.

Chapter 3

Laney topped the stairs and immediately spotted Anderson over the sink. He was washing strawberries, now dressed in just khaki shorts. Laney was grateful to see his upper body shirtless.

"What are you making? It smells amazing," she said as she hugged him from behind.

"An egg bake, bacon, and strawberries. Coffee." He leaned his head back toward her. "Get your orgasm?"

"Yes, and it was incredible. Thank you for bringing down the toy. You always come to my rescue." She adored seeing Anderson all domestic. Being so built and brawny, this was a touching side of him. She absolutely adored it when he'd cook for them. It wasn't very often.

"I always will. John, too?" He passed her a strawberry over his shoulder.

She took it and popped it in her mouth. "Mmmm, this is a good batch. So ripe. So sweet."

He motioned to her robe hanging on a kitchen chair. "Not that I don't want you naked, but I brought your robe."

"You really are the sweetest man, you know that?" She rocked him back and forth, still hugging him from behind.

"Thank you," he said with appreciation.

She could hear the grin in his voice.

"I love feeling your tits on my back."

"I love pressing them to you."

"So, John's coworker..."

29

She giggled and then released a happy sigh. "Yeah, that was really hot. And unexpected."

"Oh, I bet. He came, too?" Anderson asked as he swiveled to face her. He embraced her, staring down into her eyes.

"Yup. It was a huge turn-on. I'm going to ask John if he thinks Alex would like to do that again." She smirked up at him in a teasing way. "Maybe he could even watch us fuck."

Anderson grinned. "A live feed fucking, huh? I'm in."

John entered the kitchen. "Well, I'm famished. What have you made?" He seemed very pleased. "I love that you are still naked, babe."

He pressed his body to hers, and butterflies filled her as she was sandwiched between her two main men.

"If we hadn't just all come, I'd say let's fuck," Laney said. Mostly, she still wanted to fuck again, though. But she didn't want to ruin all of Anderson's work in the kitchen.

"Right, that was epic watching you two. I was so horny. I'm loving this monitor." John bent Laney's head back and kissed her on the lips. "Good orgasms today, babe?"

Laney nodded. "Yes, very." Instantly, she wondered how much of the after-sex conversation John had heard. "How long did you listen?"

"I had a meeting, so I turned it off when you guys were cuddling."

"Well, then we have things to fill you in on." Laney wiggled her way out from between them. "And, in truth, I'm famished. Let's eat."

"It's not that ominous," Anderson promised good-naturedly.

"It's not, no. I was afraid it was at first." Laney slipped the robe on and returned to the counter to pour coffee. "Anyone else want a cup?"

"Yes, please," John said as he reached for his favorite Key West mug.

"Yeah, I'll take one too." Anderson began washing a frying pan.

"Should I be worried?" John asked as he caught Laney's eyes in a lock.

"No," Anderson said quickly without removing his eyes from the pan he was washing. "But I met a woman."

John froze before he spoke. "Oh?"

"Yeah, but don't worry, it doesn't mean I'm leaving this." Anderson carried the bowl of strawberries to the table. "Sit, and I'll grab the rest."

There was something extra sexy about seeing a big, strong, muscle man like Anderson waiting on them. She was used to seeing him do manual labor in the backyard. But now, he was a caretaker, not overly self-important, and it was evident in everything he did.

"I can't wait to try your dish. Where did you get the recipe?" She was very interested because she had her new cookbook production on the brain every day.

Anderson smiled. "It was one my mom made all the time when I was growing up. I found most of the ingredients here; it only has a slight variation."

"And she taught you to make it?" Laney was impressed. "I didn't know this about you, Anderson. This is great!"

"Yeah, my mom and grandma both taught me to cook. None of my brothers were into it, so when I showed interest, they went overboard." He paused in thought. "Or maybe it was just because I was the baby and they finally had time for such things."

"Nice to have another good cook in the house," John said as he sat. "And loved how you made her come earlier. She needed that. So thanks for stepping up."

Anderson laughed. "You know that's exactly what I want to be doing."

John joined in laughing. "Yes, true. Maybe I'll consult you about your schedule for the next group date. Laney really missed you when the college group painted the fence."

"It sounds like it was epic. Those pics you sent were hot as fuck. I wish I had been there." Anderson served each of them a piece of egg bake.

"Now, tell me what's up with this new woman." John took a sip of his coffee, a look of intrigue plastered on his face.

Anderson sat down and placed his hands on his head. The silly expression left him before he spoke. "I don't know. We met, her Dom was there, and we fucked. And..." He paused. "We like each other. That's about it."

"Ah, she's in the lifestyle too. Nice. Well, she's more than welcome in our play dates, right, Laney?"

"Absolutely. I love cocks and men, but I'd play with a kitty." She gave a sly smile.

"Now that's something I'd want to watch. Anderson?" John cut the corner off his piece of egg bake and shoved it into his mouth. "And this is very good."

Anderson gave a single nod. "Thanks. And, yes, I'd love watching you and Darcy, Laney. What I'd really love is to be the meat in the sandwich between you two. She's very sexy too." Anderson's grin was zesty. "You'd be up for that?"

Laney nodded her head. "Yes, I definitely would, especially if you're involved. John, what do you think?"

"Oh, I'd love to host it!" His exuberance was contagious.

"I told Laney, this doesn't mean I'm leaving you guys." Anderson shoved an impossibly big piece of egg bake into his mouth.

Laney giggled as she cut a dainty piece off hers and brought it to her lips. "This smells so good."

"Good," John said. "We know we can't cage you here with us, but we're happy to have you in any capacity." Then he added, "And any of your extras."

"Anderson, John, and I have talked about this, and if you want to save money, you could just move in here and get rid of your place.

Then you could just save up money rather than wasting it on a place you aren't at much." It wasn't meant to be a hooking of Anderson, but it felt a little bit like it.

"Serious?" Anderson looked back and forth between Laney and John. "You guys would have me like that?"

"Absolutely," John said. "We wouldn't charge you rent."

"Well, I'd want to pay something. Or maybe take care of the pool for free. I wouldn't feel right living here and not paying, and still charging you for your pool service."

"Well, I like this idea. You can help out around the house, maybe mow the lawn, do handyman stuff, cook, if you want, though that's what Laney likes to do."

Laney clapped her hands. The thought of Anderson here all the time was decadent. She was elated by the idea, plus the potential for more sex. "I love this! And we could even cook together. Maybe you could help me with the cookbook." She nodded her head. "Though I know you still have all your other jobs."

"I like this arrangement very much. I'll be your worker bee on call for whatever needs to be done." Anderson's grin showed he was all in.

"Oh, me! I need to be done!" She laughed at her own ridiculous joke, but in truth, she was right.

"And Lancy, yes, of course." John looked even more relaxed. "Thinking of that really would relieve some of my stress of getting stuff done around here. I've been so busy with work lately. I feel like I'm neglecting the house and yard. Honestly, Anderson, it would be mutually beneficial. I think it only makes sense to have you move in." And with that, John made it final.

"I'll clean out the spare bedroom closet today, and you can have it. But I want you in our bed." Laney touched his arm. Never in one million years and all the ages of the stars combined did she ever think

John would be okay with another man sleeping in their king-sized bed with them. Yet here he was, the one encouraging it.

"Okay. It's a plan. I'll move in. And I'll invite Darcy over. She's twenty-three years old." He stopped and then frowned. "But we will have to clear all this with her Dom, of course. He'll have to be okay with it." He winced as his face turned skeptical. "He may even want to come along."

"I think he should come along, if he wants. I'm willing to share that space if he's good with it." John set his fork down and looked Anderson in the eyes. "I'd want to go if it were Laney."

"Right, good point," Anderson agreed. "I'll bring it up and see if they're interested. Might be one hell of a party!"

"Might be? Oh, it definitely will be!" Laney exclaimed with pure glee. "This is the most exciting day ever!"

What started out as a day with dread had blossomed into a bigger, more exciting development than she'd ever have dared to dream up. And two Doms? In the same sex date? She wasn't sure how that would go, unless they were just watching, or took turns somehow. But that wasn't her problem; she'd let them sort that out.

They finished their meal, making plans for the move-in process. Laney was jittery with anticipation and so pumped that nothing could dampen it.

MOVE-IN DAY WAS THE next day. They all figured there was no reason to wait. Anderson set about finding a subleaser for his place and found one immediately, likely due to his place being near the college campus. John made room in the basement for Anderson's workout gym equipment, which Laney was excited to now have access to, and Laney gutted the spare bedroom so Anderson could make it his own space. John needed to clear out the garage and the area in the loft for some of his stuff. He didn't have a lot, but it still all needed a spot. He figured he'd keep his bed, stick his recliner in the living room, and store his table and chairs in the loft. But then there were also all his kitchen supplies to be assimilated into the house, too. It was no small chore, and it would be a while before it was all neatly stored.

Laney grabbed Anderson's hand as they stood in the hallway. "This will be your room, and I'll understand if you want to sleep here, but please, please, pretty please sleep in our bed." Laney was wearing a bikini because she'd just done a swim workout in the pool. She jumped as she silently pleaded.

"I'll definitely be in the bed with you two," Anderson said with a wicked grin. "Having lots of sex with you."

She nodded exaggeratedly before gripping both of his biceps. "I can't believe this is happening!"

He chuckled as he pulled her in close for a kiss and a big hug. "I can't either. Never thought I'd be sleeping in a bed with another man there."

"It's a good thing we have a king-sized bed. I'll sleep in the middle as the border for you two."

He laughed. "I'm good, but yeah, I like you in the middle." His gaze was impish. "John working?"

"Yes," she said before she kissed him back.

"I don't think we need to disturb him now, but I'll need his help carrying some of it in."

Anderson started moving in while she was swimming, but once she'd caught sight of him, she'd scurried out of the pool to help him settle in. No workout time was important enough to trump Anderson officially moving into the house.

"I'm getting you all wet."

"That's my line," he said with a chivalrous bow.

"Yes, it is, and I'm ready whenever you are." She pulled her bikini top off her breasts to give him a nip peek.

"Careful, or I'll take you in my non-bed and fuck you until you scream," he joked.

"Oh, please do!" Laney desperately wanted to fuck him, but she also wanted to wait for John. Part of her wanted their first official fuck after Anderson's move-in to be with all three of them present. She was loving this all-out fuck-fest streak that had begun with the college guys and hadn't let up since.

"We should wait for John, though." He ran a hand through his dark, lush hair.

She loved that he had the same thought. "Agreed. But I can help you move small things. Let me just go change."

"I guess, if you have to," he said, pouting.

She loved his tenderness because it was so in contrast to his rough modes of sex. His full package was deliriously sexy. She scampered to the master bedroom and slipped on some clothes she didn't mind getting dirty. It was work time, and if she wanted to get to sex, the work must be done first.

She helped him move in, taking all the smaller loads, and soon they were both exhausted and lying on the couch for a break. While they were sipping ice-cold water, Anderson got a text.

"It's Darcy," he said with a saucy raise of his left eyebrow. "She sends me nudes every day."

"Oh, she's smart," Laney said, loving the fact that he was sharing this, rather than hiding it.

He flipped his phone toward Laney and began to scroll through the naked pics. She had dark blond hair that in some pics was curled and in others it was straight. She had what looked like maybe C-cup breasts, a tiny little waist, and a big ass. Her eyes were a piercing green, and she had a sweetness about her expression when she wasn't giving the camera a seductive look, but her cuteness never left, even as she was clearly being provocative.

"She's very sexy. A cutie, too," Laney cooed.

"I made a file just for her pics. I'll have to show John." Anderson's cock began to grow into a mound as he gazed at Darcy. "She's adventurous. Wait until she tells you some of the stuff she's done. It will blow your mind."

"Oh, really?" Her interest was definitely piqued. Instantly, Laney wondered if John would want to fuck Darcy. It wasn't something they'd done yet, where John fucked another woman, but she also didn't want to deny him the pleasure; after all, Laney would be fucking her, so why not John too? She made a point to think about talking about this with him, but without Anderson around. And how would Anderson feel about it, too? There was so much to talk about, but that was part of the fun for her and would build up the anticipation, too. She was giddy for it all to happen.

"Yes," he pulled Laney onto his lap. "She's into rough stuff, too."

Now Laney saw her appeal to Anderson. The rough stuff. She was intrigued by it, and in fantasy, it was great spank-bank material for her, but how would she react to it in real life, though? Of that, she wasn't sure. She was all good with spanking, but beyond that, it was a black hole of uncertainty.

"I like rough stuff too," she said, biting her lip.

"Yes, you do. But she does really rough stuff." His eyes were flaming with passion as he spoke.

"Like what?" Laney pressed as she ground her pelvis against his hardened cock.

"Fuck, I'm getting so turned on," Anderson said with a hot and horny look blistering across his face.

"Tell me one thing," Laney insisted as she pressed her hands on his shoulders for more leverage to grind on him.

"Aw, fuck, that's driving me crazy," he said as he leaned his head back. "Okay. She wanted to be hunted. So her Dom asked friends to come to a space of land he had asked a friend to use. It was in a forest.

She wanted to be hunted like prey and fucked by whoever caught her."

Laney's eyes grew big. She'd masturbated to such a scenario before, but never told John. "Wow, that's incredible! And so, she did it?"

Anderson nodded. "She did. She said it was the most intense experience of her life. She spent considerable time in subspace and came way too many times to count." He grinned with a lewd sheen in his eyes. "She wants to do it again, and she wants me to participate."

Laney was a little jealous of this woman, but she knew, if she asked, John might consider this for her, too. But she wasn't entirely sure if it was too far. It wasn't likely something one could ever erase from memory, and would that fear translate to a turn-on for her as it had for Darcy? "She really liked it?"

"Very much so. They have quite the dungeon in their house."

"Oh! A sex room. This is something we should bring up with John."

Anderson nodded aggressively. "And I could build it."

"Build what?" John asked as he sat on the couch next to them, reaching for Laney.

She shifted to sitting on John's lap, her legs in Anderson's. "His new sex toy, Darcy, and her Dom, Muskie, have a sex dungeon room in their house. Could we do that? Maybe like converting the basement bedroom into one?"

John's face turned into amusement. "Well, now there's an idea. And something Anderson could do."

"Oh, I'd love to do it. You tell me what you want in it, and I'll design and build it." He looked like someone had just gifted him a sex toy shop and told him he got to try everything in the store for free. "This is the best idea yet."

"Lots of fun could come out of that. Think of the three of us, of sex dates. Of this new Darcy." John looked like he liked this whole

Darcy development. His cock was filling against Laney's thigh as they talked.

"I have pics." Anderson flipped his phone and handed it to John.

"Oh, that's you," John said, showing the cock pic to Laney.

"Yeah, I reciprocate pics." Anderson looked surprised. "I didn't think you'd be able to pick my cock out."

John lowered his reading glasses and peered at Anderson. "I've seen it a few times," he said, his words heavy with sarcasm.

Anderson released a curt laugh. "True. True."

Laney watched John's expressions change from excited to amused to wanton. "Well, with you on my lap and these pics, I think it's high time we fuck to christen this young man's move into our house."

Laney was tired from the move, but not tired enough to reject sex. "I'm in." Her heart began to pound. She was legit living with her two men, her two lovers, and there were so many exciting prospects on the horizon that she wasn't sure she could even imagine them all at once.

"I'd sure love to pound your backside right about now," Anderson said with an inviting jeer. He began to caress her legs that were strewn across his lap. "How about you, John, what do you want right now?"

He still deferred to John, no matter how dominant Anderson got with Laney, he still let John lead.

"I'm liking that idea. Why don't you start and get her nice and cummy for me so I can slide right in my wife after you, and finish her off?" Anderson pulled Laney to stand, and John pulled out his cock. "Get me a beer, Laney? Naked." He turned his head. "Anderson? Care for one?"

"I'd love one."

"Do the honor of stripping my wife for me?" John lounged on the couch, putting his feet up on the lounge section. "Fuck her nice and hard and make her come, then when she's nice and wanton for me, I'll fuck her until she's a floppy mess."

Laney's insides shrieked with jubilation at hearing John's plan as she waited for Anderson to strip her.

He did it fast and rough, giving her bottom a nice, hard smack before saying, "Get us beers, beer wench."

Her clit did a little dance as she dashed to the kitchen to get their drinks. She was so ready to be fucked, used, and pleasured into a sloppy, wet, obscene mess.

She hurried back and handed a beer to each of them. He laid his on the couch unopened and pulled her into a bear hug in the middle of the living room. John put on some rock music with a strong beat, setting the mood.

Laney glanced at her husband, who looked very comfy, and he returned her suggestive smile.

"Let me see you two get raunchy," he demanded with a racy glare. "Hardcore."

Anderson's hands traveled her body aggressively, and her aroused state bloomed.

"I want you," she murmured as she massaged his biceps and chest. "Let's fuck."

"I'll fuck you until you scream, you horny slut." His intense gaze made her lust boom. He took her right nipple into his mouth and further mashed her breast in.

She squealed as he roughly ate at her breast. He pinched the other one and then moved to kiss her neck while groping her ass.

He was still clothed, and she loved that she was naked. Their mauling of each other grew more amorous and ardent with each second, their moans giving proof.

"Now, fuck her doggy, rough," John pelted from his cushy spot on the couch. "Make her scream."

Anderson gripped her hips and swiveled her body so fast that her hair flew and her head lagged. He palmed her scalp and pressed her head into the crack of the couch. "Head down, ass up, whore. You're mine."

He slapped her bottom, and she hollered, the sting lingering as he rubbed his erect cock against her naked ass.

"Yessss," John slurred with appreciation. "Again."

Anderson backed away and spanked her once more, making her flesh seem as if it were screaming from the hard smack. He leaned over her and grabbed at her breasts, squeezing them brusquely in his strong hands.

She squirmed and belted out a mild complaint. But she couldn't deny this was titillating her clit as it announced its hardening with a lurch.

He lined up his cock at her slit, sliding it around for a tickle, and then plunged inside her body.

They both groaned at his penetration, and he began to press himself into her further and further with each subsequent thrust. Deeper and deeper he pressed himself until he was in right up to his balls.

Her tits flopped with each relentless ramming, and her insides were ready to spill as little explosions pelted out from her clitoris to her body. The blasts of sensations felt like mini orgasms, like rungs on a ladder, each burst carrying her closer to the top of her climax.

She huffed as he pounded, his breathing getting even more labored than hers as he rammed his thick cock inside her.

"Yes, get that G-spot nice and tender. Laney, rub that clit, baby, rub it hard and good and come for Daddy."

Anderson pounded her like the sex tool he was being portrayed as, loving every slam into her, and he chugged himself into her like he was a racehorse, not stopping even as her body began to curl with her massive climax. He climaxed, too, and still kept thrusting like a champ.

"Oh, fuck," she said as she pulled her hand away from her clit. "Too much."

"Don't stop, babe." John rose and rushed toward them. "Let me," he insisted as he took over, riding her clit with his fingers.

Anderson growled like he was coming, but kept on pounding away into Laney.

She screamed as she roared into another peak, her body succumbing to being powerless to her almighty clit. "Shit," she sputtered as she tried to push the men off her sensitive parts—that hollered at her as every nerve ending lit her euphoria further on fire.

"Now, switch," John said with determination.

Anderson pulled himself out of Laney and stepped to the side so John could enter Laney's core. He moved quickly to engage her clit as John entered her. He boosted her arousal, amplifying her ecstasy with his high-speed thrusting. That, combined with Anderson aggressively rubbing her bean as if whetting a knife on a grindstone, hurled her into one of those orgasms that were almost intolerable in intensity. She screamed again, whapping her hand against Anderson, but her weak attempts did not stop their reign over her body. She gasped and fought for breath as her bodily reactions were maxed. She collapsed onto the couch, and John allowed his cum to spurt inside her.

John crashed down next to her.

The panting of the three of them filled the living room, with John's phone still playing the music in the background.

"Wow," Anderson said, and being the first to speak, his voice sounded jarring to Laney.

Her breathing started to normalize, but her body was still crumpled into a discombobulated state. She rolled onto the couch, placing her head on Anderson's lap and her feet on John's.

They remained still as they all descended their highs.

"Holy fuck," Laney finally whispered. "That was incredibly hot and intense." She released a sigh. "You guys fucked the piss out of me."

Both of the men laughed at her admission.

"I didn't pee, but I definitely feel drained."

"Good, and same," John said as he began to give her feet a massage. "I think Anderson did most of the work."

"Oh, and it was my pleasure," he iterated. "Believe me." He caressed Laney's face, and their eyes met. "Good for you?"

She scoffed. "Good? How about spectacular? Monumentally mind-blowingly amazing!"

"Excellent," Anderson stated happily.

Aftershocks blessed her clit, and her body twitched. She was lovesick for them both, and her libido was a slave to it all, very happily so. "I'm the luckiest woman on the planet," she said with exuberance. Their warm, tender touches were so inviting that she rolled into a slice of the bliss looming to come. "Mmmm, this is the life."

"Welcome to our home, Anderson, now your home as well." John beamed them both a grin.

"Thank you, I'm blessed to be here." They lay on the couch, relaxing in silence until Anderson insisted, "I'll order pizza to celebrate."

"And a movie," Laney suggested.

As he shared his slightly warm beer with Laney, he ordered the pizza on his phone as they soaked in the yummy afterglow of another satisfying three-way fuck, which was now blooming as a glory, a very real promise to be their new way of life. If Laney had anything to say about it, it would be their permanent way.

Chapter 4

Laney sighed as the sun heated her flesh. At least she was wearing a bikini and was ready to swim once she was done hanging up their wet clothes.

"This sucks," she muttered as she hung up Anderson's undies. "Such drudgery."

John and Anderson had strung up a makeshift clothesline in the backyard. Instead of letting the laundry pile up while they waited five whole days for a dryer repairman to come fix the dryer, by day three, she'd decided it was better to keep up. But now she was stuck making their backyard look like some relic housewife dungeon from the 1960s with a damn clothesline. Who has clotheslines these days? No one!

She kept working her way through the pile of wet clothes with thoughts of dipping into the pool to cool off. It was a hot August afternoon, and both Anderson and John were working, so after taking her pictures of her dish for the day for her upcoming cookbook, she'd taken to dealing with the mess of clothes piled in the laundry room. She loved having Anderson live with them, even if it meant her taking over his laundry. She didn't have to do it, but she loved doing it because having two men living with her who were her lovers was about the best way she could imagine living, especially because they loved to share her with other men.

Doing Anderson's laundry, in addition to hers and John's, made it all very real, and she did it out of her desire to take care of them both, not that either of them implied it was her duty. That would ruin it.

She hung up John's pajama shorts, and the basket was finally empty. John had taken to wearing shorts to bed after Anderson had fully moved in, which was odd to her because the three of them had sex every day. The change had puzzled her. Both she and Anderson slept naked, but John wore shorts. It was weird, and she made a mental note to ask him why. Honestly, it didn't matter, but it was a quirky thing.

She tossed the empty basket on the back step of the house and dashed toward the pool. This was her chance to get wet and relax for a bit. The descent into the slightly cool water was heaven right from the first tip of her toes entering. She sighed as she descended the stairs and released a louder one as she immersed her breasts in the pool water.

"Heaven," she stated softly as she glided about.

"Heaven to watch you," John said soothingly from the edge.

"Oh, I didn't hear you come out," she said, noting her surprise was not tinged by anything negative, as it would have been several years ago. She no longer felt invaded when someone suddenly appeared unbeknownst to her. It was an air of freedom she had become aware of recently.

"I saw you place the laundry basket down, so it triggered me," he said while uncrossing his arms. "You always look so beautiful in the water, babe."

"Aww," she said, truly enjoying his compliment.

"Good news, the repairman called; he's had a cancellation and he's coming today," John smirked as he glanced at the hung-up clothes. "So, we can get rid of this eyesore."

She stood up and clasped her hands together. "Oh, serious?" She was so happy that her days of old-fashioned housewife hanging up wet clothes in the sunshine were about to be over, but she also couldn't help but wonder if she'd get sex too. Would John go there this time? Repairmen at the house had come to mean she'd get to exercise her hotwife bone, and so, of course, her brain went right there.

She gave John a coy look. "Will I get to enjoy him?"

He laughed with glee. "What if it's a woman?"

She waved her hand at him dismissively. "You already said repairman, so there's a cock."

His face morphed into huge amusement. "Yes, a cock is coming, babe. And we shall see."

Her lust swirled inside her, heating up her thoughts. "I'd love to." Just in case he was wondering, she was all in with stating the obvious. She snickered as she dove beneath the water. When she emerged, John was still staring at her with the same expression.

"I adore you, Laney. Anderson is on his way home in about an hour. Been thinking about asking the man if he'd like to give us a live show while Anderson and I enjoy an early happy hour cocktail on the couch."

She couldn't stop her hopes from rising with that statement. She really hoped it was the same man who had come to fix their washer about a year ago. This had been way before her hotwifing had begun, and when she and John were still stuck in their misery. It was often hard for her to even put herself back into that scene with how happy she was now.

She pictured the repairman from her memory. He was tall, with droopy brown bedroom eyes, complete with a dreamy, sexy gaze, no matter what he was saying. That man must seduce women with his gaze alone. Then there was the rest of him. He was toned and strong, not overly muscular, but definitely fit and firm-looking. He had nice lips, and the day that Laney had opened the door for him a year ago still lived in her brain as a yummy image. She'd found him so sexy that he'd been a regular in her self-pleasure fantasies. He always did the trick.

But no matter if it wasn't him, because she'd have fun with cock regardless of who ended up showing up. The point was, it was a new cock. A new cock attached to a new man she'd get to play with, and if both John and Anderson watched as they played, she'd love it more than ever. It would be new to have both of them watch at the same time as she played with another. Then the after fun would be otherworldly, more so than ever before, because she'd have them both.

"I see your wheels turning. I will broach the topic and see if there's any interest." John smirked, then turned to head back into the house. "I have a little more work to finish before he's due to arrive. That's in about half an hour, so enjoy your swim for a bit, then get ready."

She nodded his way, even though his back was to her. She swam for fifteen minutes more, then left the pool. She wanted to be dressed rather than in a wetsuit this time. Having a repairman take off her clothes was somehow hotter, being that he worked on things that laundered clothes every day.

She dried off, enjoying the sun on her wet, cooled flesh, then scurried inside. The air conditioning was blasting strongly in the basement, making her shiver and her flesh pebble with goosebumps. She waved at John as she stripped off her bikini. She gave him a mischievous look before opening the sliding door.

He widened his eyes as a salacious look combatively took over his previously stern work face. He was on a work call, but spread his legs to put the hardened lump between his legs on display.

She smiled at her husband before stepping back outside. She tossed her wetsuit onto a patio chair to dry in the sun, then skittered back into the house.

John motioned to the lump at his groin.

She squeezed the air with her outstretched fingers while sporting a saucy grin. She then swiveled and bent over to give him a view of her underside as she scooped up her sunglasses. She straightened up her body, then made flirty eyes back at her hubby. It felt so good to genuinely want to do it. They were so good these days that their relationship was now even better than when they had first started dating. She could see it in her husband's eyes. He was happy. She was happy. And Anderson was happy. Three-way bliss was more than she'd ever thought possible. Communication flowed freely between them, and judgment bore no weight.

She zipped up the stairs as she pondered what to wear when the repair guy appeared. She entered the walk-in closet, scanning for potential options. Her gaze zoomed in on Anderson's button-up jean shirt hanging next to her pink silk robe. She smiled. Perfect. She snatched it off the hanger and hurried to her bathing suit drawer. She wanted to be ready when the repairman arrived, so she quickly fingered her way through her bikinis, settling on a white strapless one. It would look sexy beneath the jean shirt. She zoomed through a quick shower, dressed, got her makeup on, and dried her hair. She made it downstairs to find Anderson had come home and was enjoying a beer on the couch.

She smiled at him as she approached. "Hey, so happy you're home." She leaned down and gave him a kiss on the lips.

He pulled her onto his lap, his eyes full of fire and lust. "Me too. I hear we are having a visitor for you to play with."

She held his head between her hands and touched her nose to his. "Well, I sure as fuck hope so."

John sauntered into the living room with his own beer. He smiled down at her and kissed her forehead. "You ready for this?" He handed her his beer, then reached down and unbuttoned her shirt. "I think this will help you feel cooler." He kept unbuttoning the shirt until he reached the bottom. "Plus, it gives him a better preview of you than just looking at you pants-less." He cupped her left breast and ran his thumb across her nipple, which had pebbled up against the fabric to announce itself. "I want you to wear as little as possible. I'd prefer you were nude." His tone was serious, but his eyes were playful and brimming with fiery mischief.

"I agree. I'd love to see him walk in and see you naked." Anderson continued playing with her other breast as John took over her left. "No need for a pesky swimsuit. It just gets in the way."

Laney was sure they were about to give her a warm-up of something sexual or strip her when the doorbell rang.

John leaned over to whisper in her ear, "Why don't you answer that?"

She loved the idea of opening the door and letting the repairman get a glimpse of her in the bikini right off the bat. She hoped he was an open type of person, and single or a swinger. She really wanted to do this. She jumped off Anderson, and John gave her bottom a swat to get her moving quicker. She giggled. Her heart pounded as she rushed toward the front door, the slight wind of her hurrying making the open shirt flap against her flesh. Her lust seethed with the imminent suggestive seduction that her answering the door with so much flesh showing would surely give the worker.

She flung the door open. She was delighted. It was indeed the man with the sexy eyes from last time. Oh, well, shit. Those eyes could sweet-talk her right into bed with him with very little effort, not that she needed much convincing. He had jeans on despite the heat. Such a workman thing to do.

He held a toolbox in one hand and his phone in the other.

"Hi," she said, a bit shy as she hung onto the open door, her right foot on tiptoe so she could rock herself.

"Trouble with your dryer?" he asked, all businesslike, but his eyes roamed up and down her body, trying but failing to be subtle, before settling on her face. The slow, simmering grin that grew as she maintained a spicy look of eye contact with him was very promising indeed.

She remained speechless as she made sexy eyes at him, so she was thankful for John coming up behind her to take charge.

"Yes, come on in. This is my wife, Laney. And yes, we have a broken dryer she'd very much like fixed." John motioned for the man to enter the house. "We appreciate your ability to come earlier than scheduled."

The repairman averted his eyes from Laney in John's presence, and her heart sank. She gave John a desperate look, and he nodded his reassurance, making it seem like he understood her disappointment and would fix it. Of course, the repairman was just being respectful, which was to be expected in the vanilla world, but Laney wanted his lust-filled eyes roaming over her again and showing his desire for her. To be gifted a glimpse of that, then have it ripped away, was most certainly disheartening. But she understood. In most houses, he'd need to behave that way. Culture deemed it a rule. But she couldn't wait for John to inform him that this house was indeed different, and that they didn't play by those kinds of stuffy, restrictive rules.

Laney watched as John led the sexy man to the dryer. He was taller than John, closer to Anderson's height, and nearer to his age, too. His movements only served to inflame her lust as she put her hands behind her so she could restrain them. She was in a grabby mood; her lust had a mind of its own, and it wanted to grab the repairman's butt and ask what position he was craving. She chuckled silently to herself as she imagined actually asking him that before John prepped him. Would he smile or shrink back in denial? She adored surprising men with sexual promises when they didn't expect it. It somehow made it more satisfying and delicious when things progressed.

John began to explain to the man, whose name, 'Jefferson', was stitched on his shirt in dark blue thread. Such a distinguished name for a plaything. Laney snickered silently as she watched him assess her broken dryer. Jefferson bent over and opened the dryer door, looked things over, and then stroked his chin.

"I'll check some things, check the belt, and we'll see." He straightened up and glanced at Laney. His attention to her was more than a casual, accidental glance.

She knew she was hovering, but she yearned for his eyes hungrily eating her up again.

John met her look and smiled, a feisty twinkle in them. "Anderson, could you help Laney with the clothes in the backyard?"

She perked up. This meant he likely wanted alone time to talk with Jefferson. Practically tripping over her own feet, she scrambled toward the door, where Anderson swiftly joined her. He looked dashing in a salmon t-shirt and beige shorts. The perfect summer outfit on his fit, sexy body. Clearly, he had changed out of his work attire while she showered, which made her wonder why he hadn't joined her in there, like he usually did.

"After you," he said, motioning with his hand through the open sliding door. He pulled the door closed behind them and pulled Laney into an embrace. "A quick kiss before the repairman gets his hands on you."

She melted into him and stared up at him with doe eyes. "Well, I certainly hope he gets more than that from me."

He laughed, and then he French kissed her deeply.

She reciprocated his kiss hungrily in the relentless blast of the sunshine. A slight breeze strolled by, matching the soft sigh she released. "How am I the luckiest woman in the world?"

"I think luck is endemic in this house." He smiled down at her before they separated.

She walked down the stairs, loving hearing Anderson descending behind her. She had half a mind to entice him into a quickie before John finished his talk with the repairman. He looked unbelievably irresistible, and she was fully cocked to the hilt with horniness. Her breath caught as she imagined all the scenarios that could happen. She could be getting railed by the repairman while Anderson and John watched, be sandwiched between the three of them, or John could watch Anderson and Jefferson take her. All the possibilities titillated her sexual creative juices and announced themselves as a flood of passion in her veins. She was so charged that she didn't even notice she had forgotten her shoes. No matter. Anderson could check the clothes over the rocks to see if they were dry yet.

"I can't imagine living this way. Rustic life. It would suck. Everything is so crispy and rough." She pulled down stiff shorts, shirts, and undies while Anderson grabbed the clothes over the rocks without her even asking. He was always noticing things without her having to point them out. She really loved that about him. He paid attention and just got things done. John had never been that way, but was more so now than before. Maybe Anderson was rubbing off on him.

"Yeah, agree. I love a soft shirt." Anderson crushed a crispy shirt between his palms.

"So, any dates with your new hottie coming up?" Lancy had been dreaming about that hookup, too.

"Yeah, tomorrow we are." He scooped up a few more items from the clothesline and followed her to the patio table, where they began to fold the clothes side by side. "We need to talk with John about a group event. Maybe for the weekend or next. I think they prefer a weekend day, last time I discussed it with them."

"Ah, got it." She was very happy to find out he'd been chatting with them about a round-robin of some sort. "Well, I can't wait." She paused and leaned forward as a flirty expression overtook her face. "It will be my first experience with another woman."

He scoffed as a giant grin smothered his calmness. "Oh, I can't tell you how excited I am to watch you two. I'm getting the biggest woody on the planet right now thinking about it."

"I noticed you already had that when we kissed," she teased.

"True. I'm pretty ready to watch that tall repairman rail you. Let's just say I'm pretty fucking hot at the moment."

She sighed heartily. "Same." Her brain ticked closer to deciding to seduce him for a quickie before John appeared. But instead, they continued to fold clothes, chit-chatting about the weather and what Laney had planned for dinner. Within ten minutes, John appeared on the patio, looking quite proud of himself.

"He is about done, and our man is in." John raised his eyebrows at Laney with a devilish gleam. "And I mean all in. You should have seen the joy on his face. It was priceless."

Laney hopped up and clapped. "Serious? I'm so excited!"

"Love to see you sexually satisfied, baby. Then Anderson and I will reclaim you. And you'd better be ready for a cum drunk brain fog for the evening." He snickered. "Maybe we'd better order dinner in because you may be asleep after all this."

"Well, I do have dinner planned, but I guess we can play it by ear." She was so ready to be flying high from being fucked to a body-floppy state after as many orgasms as she could tolerate.

"I've given him the rules, and the two of us will be right on the couch watching, so there's nothing for you to worry about. I'll grab him by the ear and kick his ass right out the front door at the slightest violation." John's face was stern with no nonsense. "I guarantee it."

Hearing this made Laney feel so safe, protected, and well taken care of. She really felt she was perhaps getting ready to consider the idea of visiting sex clubs, but the streak of workmen to the house was working out so well, she wondered if she would ever even need that. She also knew John liked full control, and at the house, he had that. There were no extra people floating around to muck things up. It was a sacred microcosm at home, whereas out at a club, it could be the wild, Wild West.

"When?" she pleaded, with hope overflowing from her eyes.

"Soon, just sit tight, and I'll let you two know when to come in." John turned on his heels and disappeared into the house.

"Oh, I can't believe it's going to happen!" she shrieked. "I remember this guy coming to our house before. I thought he was mega sexy back then." She adored how she could say such things in front of Anderson, and he never got jealous.

"I can't wait to watch you in the throes of passion, then to reclaim you with John after." His eyes told her he meant every word to his core. "I'm really getting into this reclaiming stuff. Now I see what drew John into it."

She found the reclaiming part of their relationship so hot, too. It was a reaffirmation that she was theirs, that John was in charge of her sexuality, to the extent that she deemed, and Anderson was second to John. So far, they'd melded together in their dominance/submission like sticks of melted butter, seamless and indistinguishable one from the other. She was lucky. Really lucky. She was also looking forward to meeting Anderson's new side toy, giving her another woman to talk to who was living life the way she was. That held promises she'd never considered before, but she was finding she was yearning for lately.

Chapter 5

Laney sat back down in the chair, but felt too electrified to simply sit still. She was jittery, and her heart was pounding. It was like how she felt right before John reclaimed her, like she was on the brink of something epic. That same adrenaline surged in her, which was in part mixed with a very much desired fear to be taken in a storm of lust. Nothing piqued her interest more than what she was about to do. All. Of. It.

Her musings on how best to prepare dinner were ghosts before the vibrant parade of impending debauchery of male passion dancing through her brain. This was going to be the most excellent and topmost experience for her. She just knew it. Well, it was pretty tough to top the college fence builders. That day was basically unstoppable, but it didn't derail her from being excited about being fucked by the dryer repairman. Not in the least.

Anderson's expression was one of amusement. "I can see your brain's gears going on high right now. And I love you thinking about sex so intensely that you seem consumed by it." He folded his hands on the patio table. "I'm right there. Thinking about all this is a rush. A total turn-on. Taking you back, I mean, most of all."

She was succumbing to the wiggles and couldn't sit still. What was taking John so damn long? She should already be in there, and Jefferson's cock should be out. "Maybe I'll go in. Just to check."

Anderson gave her a stern, skeptical look. "John said to wait, I believe."

She dismissed his admonishment and entered the house. If John didn't like it, he could deal with her. She ran up the stairs and found Jefferson still working on the dryer. No matter. This was a chance to interact with him before the sex began. John would just have to understand that she needed this.

She glanced around for John, but he was nowhere to be found. She approached Jefferson and timidly spoke. "Hi." Not sure where the shyness was suddenly coming from, but she still stood her ground.

He turned to face her, and a smile spread across his face that spoke a million words. Words that Laney liked very much. "Well, hello there, Laney." His demeanor was pleasant, with the fierceness of a wolf lurking, hungry for something. What she saw in his eyes indicated John had spelled it all out. And he liked it very, very much!

This pleased her immensely and added more weight to her lust for their interaction to start.

His eyes were so dreamy, she felt weak as she took more steps toward him. She had been right. This man could likely seduce her with his eyes alone, let alone all the other sexiness about him. He was doing it already. He was perfection on multiple levels. His lips were full, and his smile was a lazy, flirtatious one. His hands were large, corresponding to his height, and his muscles were certainly a match for the rest of his fine self. He'd make a fine bull any and every day. If she didn't move in now, she knew John might appear and ruin her plans, so she kept walking until she was just mere feet away from him.

"Almost done?" she asked innocently as she tried not to glance down at his groin, the mound of which was growing right before her eyes. There was no ignoring it. Needing something to do with her hands that wasn't touching him, she grabbed two lemons off the counter, which looked like John had been readying to cut into wedges, and rolled them in her hands. She didn't mean to seem nervous, but she had to touch something, so lemons it was.

"Yes, and I hear we're going to get to have a bit of fun." He smirked as he made eye contact, showing his full desire for her in his gaze. "I must say I've found you very sexy every time I've come here."

She dropped her jaw as surprise filled her eyes. The 'every time' rolled around in her head, exciting her further.

"Oh, I'm sorry, was that too much? John said you were open to compliments and..." He paused. "Even more."

She doubled over with laughter. "Oh, don't worry. That's right. I just didn't expect that." 'Every time' is still stuck in her head like a blinking light. So, he'd been looking lustfully at her for a long time, just as she had at him. That was beyond sexy and hot, and she loved it. "You have? I mean, like other times?"

"Every time," he said with emphasis. "I go into a lot of homes, but homeowners don't look like you."

She giggled with glee at the excitement of having been desired by him over a period of time. She had figured he hadn't even noticed her, so he had certainly masked his attraction to her very well. Too well. "I had no idea."

His phone buzzed, and he answered it, holding his finger in the air toward her. "Hey, yeah. Just about done here. Then I'll just go on a lunch break. Yup. I can do that. Okay, bye." He shook the phone at Laney. "Head office, just checking in. Turns out this is perfect timing because I'm about to go on lunch."

She set down the lemons and hopped up on the counter next to him. "Mind if I watch as you finish up? I really like looking at you, too." She bit her lip as he gave her a lewd grin.

"Only if you don't watch me too closely. I might make a mistake being distracted by such a magnificently sexy woman watching me." He grinned, making his flirtation with her bloom further. "Especially one I know I'm going to get to fuck in a few minutes."

Thrilling zings of glee bounced about inside her. She laughed lightheartedly and put the lemons in front of her eyes. "I promise, I won't look." She paused. "Too much." She moved the lemons so she could peek at him.

He chuckled and settled himself back into finishing up his work on the dryer.

"Is it working?" she asked coyly.

He guffawed as if it were the most ridiculous thing ever. "No, my dick is a brick."

She released her own exasperation in a quick sigh. "Well, I like...bricks." She burst into laughter. "They rhyme with dicks."

He belly laughed so hard he had to sit down on the kitchen floor, a hand over his gut. "Why aren't all women like you?"

"I'm special," she stated with conviction, licking her lips. She loved being able to flirt with him before the sex. It was exactly what made her desire burn even brighter.

"That you are." He shifted in his pants, making his erection shift across the fabric.

"So, almost done? I'm kind of ready to play with your cock. Well, make that ravenous." She smirked. "You look rather uncomfortable with full pants on like that."

He once again burst out with a laugh before replying, "I'm pretty much done. I just have to put this back together." He patted his cock. "Then it's all yours."

"Do you have reservations about doing this in front of my men?" She knew only a confident man would agree to such a thing, so she figured he must fit the bill, or this would have been done long ago.

"Oh, I have no problems with them watching me fuck you. Hell no." He cleared his throat. "I'm quite looking forward to it."

She gave him her sparkliest smile as she crossed her legs. "Me too."

The door coming from the garage opened, and John entered, carrying a brown sack. He didn't look rushed, but calm and pleasant.

"Oh, hey, babe. I see you've found Jefferson." He strode toward her and set the bag down on the counter. "I had a hankering for some nice scotch to sip on while I watch you getting pumped full of Jefferson's cock, so I ran to the liquor store quick."

Jefferson coughed as if choking on his own spit. "Holy fuck," he muttered. "Wow!"

John cackled. "It's true. But I must say my favorite part is afterward, when I reclaim her as mine after she's orgasmically drunk from all your hard work on her, that is."

"Wow, just wow! I've never met people like you," Jefferson said in a voice full of wonder and shock, but appreciation.

"Oh, we exist. I like my wife to be fully spent sexually, as much as humanly possible. So don't hold back. She can take a forceful pounding like a champ."

Laney shivered. John's words ramped up her desire for this all to happen at the maximum level. She was ready to explode if they didn't start soon.

"Right, babe?" he asked as he pulled her off the counter and held her thighs, so she was straddling his middle.

"Yes, that's right," she mewled in agreement. She hummed and purred as she gazed into John's eyes.

They kissed deeply as Jefferson watched.

John looked down at Jefferson, who was digging for something in his bag. "I'm going to take her to the living room so you can finish. Then come on over, and you can take my wife. Remember all I said. Fuck her good and hard. She likes dirty talk and being treated like a whore, but precious at the same time." He paused. "Making her come a lot is non-negotiable."

Jefferson nodded in disbelief as John carried Laney to the living room. "Oh, for sure, sir. It will be my extreme fucking pleasure to do so."

"Good." John kept walking, carrying Laney toward the living room. "I'll get you a cocktail while you wait, babe."

He plopped her on the couch and returned to the kitchen just as Anderson was coming up the stairs.

"Scotch, Anderson?" John asked. "Jefferson? Are you a scotch drinker?"

"Sure, I'll take one," Anderson said as he strode into the living room.

"Yes, but I have more jobs this afternoon, so perhaps just half of one."

"You got it," John said, already pouring.

Laney watched as John set about mixing all their drinks.

Anderson sat next to her, then pulled her onto his lap. He met her lusty gaze and yanked down her bikini top to expose her right breast. He took her nipple into his mouth and began to suckle aggressively.

She loved the exhibitionism of Anderson doing this with Jefferson in view. Though it hadn't seemed that he'd noticed yet because he had his head down finishing up the job. Anderson's cock beneath her was a solid rod, and she was sold on the idea of double penetration, but she already knew that wasn't John's plan. She loved submitting to John. She was just along for the ride he created. Her sexual and emotional submission was full with John, and she loved it.

Anderson's sucking was arousing her to the max, and she began to moan as she played with his hair. He mouthed her nipple and squeezed her ass cheeks as she writhed in his lap. He slid his arms under the shirt above her shoulders and slipped it right off, tossing it across the room.

When John entered the living room with a tray of four drinks, he set them down on the ottoman. He looked as excited as she felt.

There was an electrified energy in the room that was as thick as the air on a humid summer day. It was unmistakable.

"Want the other one?" Anderson asked as he exposed, then finger-teased, her other breast.

"No, I'm enjoying watching you. I'm saving up all my energy for after." John settled in on the couch and checked his phone before zoning in on watching the tit sucking. "You're the pre-show."

"And the post," Laney piped in.

"True, babe. True." John's voice held a lusty leer, one that she loved because it meant he was really extra horny and would perhaps get a bit rough and aggressive later. It sparked her passion into a high blaze as Jefferson lumbered into the living room. If someone didn't put a cock in her soon, she might launch into the sky with craziness.

Anderson quickly covered up her breasts with her bikini top. "I'll re-wrap to let you unwrap."

"Thank you," Jefferson said with a snigger before snagging his half glass of scotch. He downed it in one gulp, then handed Laney a glass.

She took it with a smile. "Thank you." She sipped the drink as she watched Anderson get comfortable on the couch next to John. She had no adequate words for her combustive excitement at having them ready to watch her imminent live porno with Jefferson. She wondered if John would bark out orders or let Jefferson do his thing. Let her do her thing. She was open to either scenario, of course, and she loved that she knew John knew that. Anderson would fall in with whatever John deemed worthy, but Laney could notice Anderson shifting a tiny bit into more dominance in his own right. It was fascinating to watch.

They sat sipping their drinks in silence. Jefferson just watched. The air in the room was alive and moving; even in their silence, it was not static.

"Can I get you another half, Jefferson?" John asked, his voice full of cordiality.

Laney had had enough of this fake politeness, and her hands twitched in response on her lap.

"Nope, I'd better not. I have to drive to my next house in a bit, so that wouldn't be a great idea. Though if I were done working for the day, I'd say yes." Jefferson was pretty calm for a dude about to fuck a woman in front of her two men. She was impressed.

"This is kind of a late lunch break," Laney mused.

"It is, but I didn't get one earlier because a job went long, so I asked to take it late, and the schedule opened up and allowed it now since your job actually went quicker than I expected." He grinned. "Until now. But I only have about half an hour because my intern is meeting up with me at the next house." Jefferson didn't sound impatient; rather, he sounded grateful. "So, I'm ready whenever you are." He looked so happy and lit up that it made Laney smile.

Laney was thrilled he was shoving the scene along. "I'm ready too. I've been ready for a long time."

John smiled. "Okay, then."

She took one more sip from her drink and then rose off the couch to place it on the tray. "For after," she announced. The drink was going to her head already, so she was happy to stop sipping. It was likely because she had eaten such a light lunch.

Jefferson approached her with his arms outstretched, his palms up, walking around her, sidestepping in a semicircle like a wrestler about to start a match. He was muscular, but didn't look like a gorilla as he moved. He shook his head as he said, "I'm ready, just come to me. I'll catch you."

She found it to be an odd approach, and she always loved something different. It flared her up, and she flew into his arms.

John whistled.

Anderson said, "Nice. That's hot."

Jefferson began to run his hands up and down her back, ending by cupping her ass cheeks. "Mmmm. A nice handful of butt."

She skittered a laugh, throwing her head back.

He devoured her neck with an open mouth and voraciously sucked her flesh. He pressed his pelvis to hers, and his manhood was a beefy, firm mass.

"Oh, fuckyess," she said, rolling her body as he held her.

He held her head and kissed her deeply, his tongue twining with hers. He was a hungry kisser and groaned as she attacked his tongue.

"I want you, Jefferson. Fuck me in front of them. Please." She knew she sounded desperate, but that was because she was.

He squeezed her as he rocked her back and forth, first kissing her open mouth, then down her neck, getting closer to her breasts. He reached behind her and undid her bikini top clasps. The small triangles of fabric stuck to her breasts, so he plucked them off and threw them toward the front door.

He gasped in a deep groan of surprise as he stared at the spot where the suit fell. "Oh, shit!" he shouted as he stepped back from Laney as if she were on fire.

She almost fell but caught herself as she followed his line of sight. She was bewildered to see a young man standing in the long window to the right, beside the front door. His mouth was open wide, and his face was filled with shock.

"Oh, fuck. It's my intern!" Jefferson ran toward him and flung the door open. "Max. What are you doing here? I thought you were meeting me at the next house."

Max shook his head with a confused expression. "Um. I'm sorry. They told me you were still here, so I just came. I'm sorry. Shit. I didn't mean to see that. I'll leave." He began to back up, looking sheepish.

John's face shifted from momentary panic to calm as he hopped up and ran over to the front door. "I think we can fix this," he said with confidence.

How?

Chapter 6

Laney watched as the men talked in hushed tones, which wasn't really necessary, but whatever. She connected with Anderson's gaze, and he, too, seemed to be genuinely curious about how John was going to 'fix this'. The intern had legitimately seen Jefferson remove her bikini top and do things with clients he knew were big no-nos.

What transpired next totally depended on the kind of person the intern was. If he were a rule follower, tattle-tale kind of guy, that would spell big trouble for Jefferson. If he were laid-back and a sexual being, there might be a chance to gloss things over. But one thing was for sure: sex with Jefferson would not happen. There was no way they could continue. And it was before any naked private parts had touched, so there was at least that. Maybe Jefferson could convince the dude that this was a harmless mistake and not something he goes around doing all the time. She would absolutely hate to see Jefferson lose his job over this.

John looked pleased. How odd. This wasn't the face of trepidation or dread. He released a laugh and spread his arms toward the living room. "Come on in, Max. We are happy to have you as well."

What was this? Had John actually said, 'Have you as well?'? Did this mean double workmen? If so, her joy poked its head into the possibility, and she got her hopes up in a heartbeat.

"Laney, Max would like to join in the fun." John gave her a pointed look, a dominant look that sent chills down her spine. This wasn't really an ask; more of a tell. But he also knew that she wanted these types of things, so being told to do what she already wanted to do was extraordinarily luscious to her.

Max was a medium-sized man with a goatee and a gruff-looking one. He had piercing gray eyes and sandy blond hair. The look of amusement on his face told her he was more than in; he was thrilled about the prospect. He had on jeans as well, the usual workman attire, and tan leather boots that he began to remove. His socks were white and clean-looking, and that gave Laney confidence. She glanced at his hand but saw no ring. He was trim and lean in his body shape, but not with bulging muscles. He was shorter than Jefferson by a good foot.

No one spoke, but glances flipped back and forth.

Laney giggled, shrugged, and then said, "Well, sure. You know me, the more the merrier. I guess I'll be busy."

That broke the awkward silence, and both workmen smiled and chuckled.

"Bet you didn't expect this on your third day," Jefferson said with a snicker to Max.

"Ummm, hell no. Are you kidding me? But this is literally like my dream. I've always been turned on by older women."

Laney laughed gregariously as John mirrored her reaction. "Now I feel quite old!"

"Oh, I didn't mean it like that," Max said quickly, in an apologetic tone.

"Well, you are in your twenties, I'm guessing? So, it's true. I am about twice your age."

"Twenty-two," Max replied.

Jefferson guffawed heartily. "You're a baby."

"Aw, come on. You can't be much older than me," Max protested.

Laney's eyes fell to their crotches, and both men were sporting erections beneath their jeans. She was pleased their banter wasn't killing their libidos.

"Twenty-five is light-years older," Jefferson teased.

John watched the two men exchange their razzing as he settled back on the couch next to Anderson, who also looked amused.

Laney was dying to ask John how he finagled this scenario. He was a good negotiator, but this was pure magic.

"So, we just go at it?" Max asked, perplexed, as if this was too good to be true. "I feel like I've fallen into a porn flick."

"You did," Anderson stated with a laugh. "And we're your live audience."

"Not to be put on the spot," John insisted with a cordial expression. "Just have fun. I won't yell at you too much, I promise. Just let loose. I've given you both a quick rundown of her boundaries, and you know her safeword. Anderson and I will be watching closely, so there's nothing to worry about. Just have fun."

Laney loved that her tits had been bare through all this, and both of the workmen's eyes kept drifting down to her bare chest. It was delicious to be on display in the safety net of John and Anderson. At the slightest indiscretion, she had confidence that John was grabbing their ears like disobedient subordinates and tossing them out the front door. But she surmised these two weren't stupid enough to mess up a fabulous opportunity like this. Pussy was way too irresistible to men.

Max deferred to Jefferson, actually taking a step back from Laney. It made sense, and she smiled. Though she was topless, her vulnerability felt tolerable in front of near strangers under John and Anderson's watchful eyes. It was a safety feature in an otherwise potentially dangerous playground. She imagined their cocks must be filling, and she relished the thought. It fueled her already swollen lust.

"You have perfect breasts," Jefferson stated with his eyes glued to her bare chest. "I'm ready as fuck to play with them." He reached up and cupped her right one gently in his hand. His expression was one of awe and wanton lechery. A perfect combo in Laney's mind. His other hand cupped her other. He rubbed his fingers across her hardening nipples, and she simply stood there, letting him feel her up. Being on display for four sex-hungry men was feeding her fire like lighter fluid. His bouncing her breasts in his hands this way felt naughty as she suppressed a giggle. It was almost innocent in nature as he bobbled her breasts about in his fingers.

He dove for her right breast with an open mouth. Clearly, the slow savoring was over, and he took her left nipple in a full, devouring feeding. He played with the other one as he suckled her.

Max moved around to her backside and grabbed both butt cheeks, rubbing his fingers along the hem of her bikini bottoms. His grip grew stronger, and he released a seething breath through his teeth in a whistle. "Fucking amazing ass on you." He brusquely fondled her cheeks.

She allowed them to maul her as she made eye contact with Jefferson, then John and Anderson, who both looked very pleased that she was getting such assertive attention.

Max pressed his hard manhood to her buns on her backside and lightly began to hump her butt. This made her body gyrate and bounce against the pressure Jefferson was exerting on her front side. Her body bobbed back and forth as each man did as he pleased, which was seemingly arousing all five of them, Laney most of all.

Jefferson grasped her face and went in for an intimate, deep kiss, running his tongue into her mouth to caress hers. She responded, and they were locked into a tongue tango that lasted several minutes.

Max had a hold of her hips from behind as he ground his erection into her ass crack. There was something hot about humping. It was reminiscent of her younger days with her first boyfriend when humping was all they'd done for months, edging each other as it drove up their passion for days on end. Making out and humping were such simple, pure acts of lust that the seduction of it lulled Laney further along the course of her arousal. There was something extra seductive about it when the men knew they'd be getting their dicks in her, anyway.

The workmen seemed to be following the same wanton spiral as her as their hands squeezed her more aggressively, covering more ground in caressing her back, arms, hips, ass cheeks, and breasts. Jefferson's hand slid into her bikini bottoms and grazed her clit, making her gasp and writhe into his arousing touch. He broached her lower lip and pressed a finger along her slit, not going in, sufficiently teasing her.

"Feeling wet, are you ready for more?" Jefferson asked as he tickled his fingers along her slit.

She moaned and nodded. "Yes, that feels amazing. Please, keep going."

Max slid his fingers into the bottoms, covering her backside. "Let's make her naked," Max said with a lusty snarl. "Butt naked."

Laney wondered if Max was more of a butt man or if he was just there because Jefferson had claimed the front of her first. She longed to know.

"Together," Max stated. "One, two, three."

The men tugged her bikini bottoms down at once, not stopping as they dragged the skimpy bottoms down her shins, past her knees, and down to her ankles. It was a ceremonious undressing, having them both bare her bottom and pussy at once. She was putty in their hands as they felt her up from her shins to her tits, to her face, and kept going. Max nuzzled against her hair as Jefferson took her mouth in a kiss again. Having both men's hard cocks pressed to her drove her wild as she twisted in their continued grabbing of her body.

"Please, I need you two to fuck me." Her voice sounded weak and needy, and she didn't give a fuck that it did.

Neither of them responded, which made her smile because they were too busy suckling her flesh and playing with her curves to respond. Of course, they knew she wanted them to fuck her, but saying it was always so satisfying and raised the arousal for everyone.

Max moaned in her ear before pushing her hair off her neck, where he proceeded to suck her flesh as he thrust the bulge of his cock against her ass.

Jefferson kissed down her neck as he held her biceps and made his way back to sucking and nipping at her erect nipples.

"Gonna need your two cocks in me," she repeated.

Jefferson glanced up at her from where he was feeding on her, and grinned around her pink peak, loosening his lock on her flesh. "Umm hmmm," he moaned as he then flicked his tongue along her nipple, still inside his mouth.

Jefferson was definitely a tit man because he couldn't leave her nipples alone for long.

Jefferson grabbed both her nipples and twisted them, making her squeal as she leaned back against Max. He tugged on them roughly, and she squawked. The devilish look on his face told her he adored getting a reaction out of her, so she made more sounds as he tugged and pulled on her titties.

Max reached around and fondled her breasts as Jefferson pulled them away from her body by her erect nipples. This was more tit action than she usually got, and she wanted to smack them away from her tits, yet she wanted them to keep going at the same time.

"I need a tit in my mouth," Max pleaded with gusto.

Jefferson grasped her shoulders and spun her around. "We can trade."

She settled back against Jefferson as she was loose as a floppy rag doll between their strong touches and aggressive grabs.

She loved all the foreplay, but her pussy was screaming for something inside her, even a finger. "Please, I need something in me. Please." She was shocked at how desperate she sounded when she knew very well that this fuck was a sure thing, but nonetheless, hearing her own yearning voice added to her arousal.

Neither of them gave her what she wanted, which made her wonder if John told them to drag it out and tease her because most men would have entered her pussy by now with how she'd been pleading. When she got this hot with John and Anderson, the penetration was always even more satisfying when it finally happened.

She opened her eyes and made eye contact with John. He looked smug, as did Anderson. She smirked back at them and raised an eyebrow. They certainly had planted such seeds of slowness in these young men, who were clearly eager to fuck her and would have likely already been pounding her to oblivion if it were of their own accord. John had a hand in it, no doubt. And of course he did, he always did. But that's also what she loved about their life. He always put her first, and her pleasure was of paramount importance, even if she was too impatient now to appreciate it.

The men continued to play with her body, and she grew weaker with desire, wishing she could lie down on the couch because standing in this wanton state was a challenge. Laney mused how they'd double-team her. Would they allow their cocks to touch? They seemed pretty new to each other, so that might be too far for them. Would they simply take turns in her pussy, the other kissing her or at her breasts? Or would they spit-roast her? Would John and Anderson hop up and charge into the scene, or would they simply stay back and watch the show put on for their hungry pleasure? The mystery of it was exciting!

Whatever would happen, she needed it soon. She let a scream of frustration and desire fly out of her mouth, and this made both John and Anderson snicker. They were loving this, and she was ready to pull into full brat mode if someone didn't put something in her pussy pronto.

"Please," she grunted as Max took his turn at tit sucking, while Jefferson played with her butt.

Jefferson snickered in her ear and then bit it. "Soon. Soon we'll fuck you speechless," he promised in a breathy whisper, the commanding tone sending shivers down her back.

She shuddered slightly as Max bit down on her breast. She grabbed his head and squeezed. "Fuck!"

He released her nipple with a pop before he chuckled. "Too hard?" he asked, in a not very apologetic voice. "Couldn't resist. You have such yummy tits."

Jefferson pressed her forward, and she fell onto Max, who moved quickly to the side, so she fell partially onto the couch. He pressed his fingers against her entrance from behind, and she gasped.

"Yes, please," she said as she waited with so much anticipation she might finally explode.

Yet he still didn't press his fingers into her.

She released a disgruntled groan, which ended in a disappointed bemoan.

"Now," John said firmly.

Jefferson pressed his fingers into her pussy, and she groaned out, John's permission making it even more exquisite. She twisted her body slightly, arching her back at the pleasure of finally being penetrated. Jefferson rode her pussy with his fingers hard and fast from behind, and she buckled, fully crashing onto the couch.

She was so overcome that words wouldn't form, but she let her verbalizations fill the room in their place.

Max sank to his knees and reached under her. He pressed his fingers to her clit, and she curled into the sofa, her mouth open in nonstop vocalizations. He played with her pussy roughly, not letting up for a second. She soared into the peak of a climax, her body shuddering its way through the high. They didn't stop, but worked her over even stronger, which sent her into a second peak. She was helpless to their relentless fingering and slumped fully to the floor, spent from orgasms.

Jefferson pulled his fingers from her and dragged her up to stand, then bent her over.

"Sit," Jefferson commanded.

She wondered if he meant her until she saw Max sit.

Jefferson pushed her top half over Max's lap. "Titty fuck or blow job?"

Laney thought that was her decision, but she also liked them controlling the situation.

Max nodded and said, "Yes."

Anderson and John laughed, and this whole scenario fleshed itself out as a full-on use of her body, satiating her getting used to kink quite well. She wanted to relax and lie limply on the couch, but she was to be on her feet, being crevices for the men.

She let them place her body appropriately between them, without any muscling or resistance or any verbalization of complaint. She braced herself by resting one hand on the couch cushion beside Max's thigh.

Jefferson grabbed her hips, then pressed his cock against her pussy lips.

She was wild with warmth, her body raging in elation, now blissfully saturated with hormones. She reached back and fingered her own swollen labia lips with his cock tip at the ready to enter her. They were profusely puffy as she perused them.

He bumped her butt forward, and her face landed in Max's lap. Her cry was muffled against Max's hairy groin. Both of them laughed, and that sent her being used kink a tick further.

Max pressed her face sideways on his thigh and tickled his cock head with her lips.

Jefferson pushed himself inside her, fully entering her within seconds. He began to pump himself inside, getting his cock in deeper with each forceful thrust.

She groaned as Max played with his tip along her lips, tapping it around her jaw, cheeks, and nose. She opened her mouth to indicate she'd take him inside it, but he just tapped as he played with her breast with his other hand. The man was not in a hurry, and she appreciated that now that she had a cock inside her pussy.

She smirked at her wrong assumption, jumping to conclusions just as he fed her his cock so fast, she couldn't even gasp.

Jefferson was shoving himself into her at a rapid, hard pace in doggy, which made her mouth slip and slide around on Max's packed cock. He held the back of her head to try to steady her, but it was useless with the hard pounding she was getting from Jefferson. She kept her mouth ready and went slack and firm with her lips in tune with the fucking she was receiving, as best as she could.

She moaned, as did Jefferson, who seemed really close to climax with the man's growls and grunts he was releasing. The skin-smacking sounds increased as he obliterated her. She struggled to stay standing as he beat himself inside. Her face and top half rubbed on Max's lap violently. Nope. There was no chance of a BJ as he rode her like a ravenous beast.

Max held his cock, stroking it as he tried to get it somewhere that would give him a good time.

Jefferson yelled out, "Fuck." He dug his fingers into her as his voice went raspy. He was coming. He yanked himself out and came, the jizz landing on her ass and back.

As his breathing and sounds settled, his cock still hard, he continued to fuck her but at a slower, more sensual pace. This allowed Max to get his cock back in her mouth. She sucked him as

Jefferson thudded his pelvis against her backside. This went on for a while, and Max's hands moved around from holding her head to playing with her breasts.

"Hey, can I titty fuck her, then we switch?" Max asked, clearly not afraid to ask for what he wanted.

Jefferson pulled out and stepped back. "Sure."

She knelt on the ground and pressed her breasts together to make a cock cave for him, her eyes twinkling impishly like a true slut. In truth, it felt like a rest to kneel on the floor and use fewer muscles.

He slid his cock between her breasts, and she bounced, but quickly he held her shoulders to keep her still, and he thrust himself between her smashed together boobs at a gruffer pace.

Anderson clapped and hooted, which made Laney chuckle. He was always up for a good titty fuck, too.

"Okay, switch," Max said with earnest excitement.

He and Jefferson switched places. Max was entering her doggy within seconds, and she had to play catch with Jefferson's cock with her mouth this time. Max was a beast from the get-go and ravaged her pussy like a fiend. Laney yearned to bless his horniness.

She reached back and tried to rub her clit, but it was too much of a challenge with Jefferson controlling the front half of her body. She gave up trying to climax, though the whole scene had her riding the edge, which was damn good.

Max gave a guttural cry and then slowed his pumping before pulling his cock out and splattering her ass with his cum. He pressed his tip to her right ass cheek as he released relieved sighs of pleasure. "So fucking good, shit."

She sucked Jefferson's meaty mushroom head as he stroked her hair. She knew he'd already done his spewing deed, but she couldn't stop herself from wanting it again.

"That's a good nympho," John said as he patted her head.

She released the cock in her mouth and smiled up at him. "Hi," she said with a voice full of sleepy-sounding satisfaction.

"We'll take it from here, guys. But thank you for giving my wife pleasure. I thoroughly enjoyed watching, but we'll take over from here. You can see yourselves out."

They didn't seem upset by being dismissed. They both looked happy, and that made Laney happy.

John sat on the couch and pulled her into his lap, immediately cuddling her face to his chest and caressing her hair. Laney smiled, loving that he had taken his shirt off already. Skin to skin was what she always craved after sex, and the rougher the sex, the more she craved it.

Jefferson and Max dressed.

"That was amazing. Thank you, Laney, thank you, John." He nodded toward Anderson. "Anderson."

"Yeah, thank you. I never expected this." Max rubbed his cock, which still looked like a lump beneath his pants. "Ever need someone to give her dick, text me." He handed John a card. "I'll come in a flash."

"Same," Jefferson said as he searched for something in his pocket. "Let me get a pen."

"On the counter," Laney said, opening her eyes. "And thank you both. I really enjoyed it."

Jefferson snatched the pen and wrote his number on the back of Max's card. He handed it to John, who set it on the couch cushion beside him.

"Thanks, and have a great day," Jefferson said as he and Max started for the door.

"I hope you liked your tip," Laney called after the men with a giggle.

"Oh, fuck yes, I did. Thank you again. You're an awesome woman. You guys are very lucky."

"Yes, we are. Thanks again."

And the repairmen left the house with their balls nice and drained.

"Now, for finishing that orgasm you were just denied. We're going to fuck you into as many as you want, babe."

Laney smiled at him, sleepiness threatening to steal her good time, but she forced her eyes to stay open. "You'd better start stimulating me before I conk out."

Anderson stood up, and she knew it was game on.

Chapter 7

Laney scooted backward on the couch as John motioned her to settle in further back on the soft cushions. She was quite grateful for the rest after the repairman duo.

"All the way, baby. I want you fully comfortable and stretched out." He stroked her thighs. "I'm going to make you come so hard you scream until you can't anymore."

"Yes, please," she begged with a grin that was unmistakable in intention. "I'm so ready."

John pressed her thighs apart as she relaxed all her muscles. Melting into the couch, she sighed loudly as John descended open-mouthed between her thighs. Watching him ready himself to pleasure her sent her already chugging up that orgasm hill. It was so hot to have him ready to eat her out after the repairmen's cocks had been coasting past her lower lips for so long.

Anderson appeared over her top half with a grin that told her he was ready to pleasure the fuck out of her, too.

"You two are truly amazing," she said, biting her lip as Anderson knelt beside the couch. He traced his fingers along her cheek with a look of love smoldering in his eyes. She wasn't sure what to make of this new way of looking at her that he'd recently begun, but it made her so happy.

Anderson took her face in his hands and kissed her, slowly tasting each of her lips before diving in deep.

She bucked as John aggressively sucked her clit, her hands grasping Anderson's hair. Kissing while being eaten out drove her wild. She'd be coming in no time at this rate. Anderson released her face to explore and tease her left nipple with his fingers while still kissing her. This sent her sky high, and she moaned. She was losing control of their relentless dual oral stimulation. The peak of the orgasm was going to be so good!

Anderson kissed down her neck on his way to her nipples. He took her taut right areola into his mouth and sucked hard while playing with her other one with his hand.

She thrashed and gripped Anderson's scalp hard. She launched into an orgasm that traveled her body, making her arch her back. Anderson and John followed her body's movements without letting up their suction, and she burst into a second orgasm. She clawed at John's head, trying to get him off her as she shrieked. It was one of the more intense Os that were almost too much to tolerate.

"Please," she said with an overtaking gasp. Releasing that word was not enough information to get them to stop the oral pleasuring of her. In fact, they'd likely think she wanted more. She forced herself to ride the almost unbearable sensitivity, and when the next big O came for her, it was an avalanche that made her scream and then go silent as she lost total control of her flopping body.

John pulled his mouth off her as she panted so hard. That set of climaxes had wiped her out even more, but she still wanted her men to come. There was no way they were done yet.

Anderson came off her nipples and squatted next to the couch with a smile.

John wore a proud smile on his moist mouth, his cheeks wet with her juices, too. "Epic? How many?"

She gasped and spoke through labored breathing, "Three, and oh," she said panting through, "my gawwwwwwdd!" She lay slack as her eyes fell half closed.

"Perfect," John said with satisfaction. "I want you so satisfied and cum drunk you can barely speak, and I'm thinking that's right where we are."

She nodded, but her protest belted out. "But I want you guys to come too."

John smiled. "And this is why I love you, this and a million other reasons." He had an erect cock that looked larger than normal. She wondered when he'd pulled his bottoms off because he had been on her with his mouth the whole time.

Anderson stood up. "Maybe a missionary since she's so worn out?"

John nodded. "Yup. Let's do that. Why don't you go first? I'd like to hold her head as you fuck her and caress her hair and face. Watch her cum again."

Anderson looked pleased. "Oh, I'm in."

They arranged themselves, and Anderson settled between her still quivering thighs. She wondered how she was feeling so weak this time, but the multiple-peaked climaxes always seemed to zap her energy, and she'd had several. She rolled in the woozy feeling of a flood of hormones coursing through her veins as Anderson entered her. He wasted no time and began to pump into her at a steadily increasing pace.

John held her head in his lap and caressed her face. Looking into John's eyes and then into Anderson's was special in a way she'd never experienced before. Perhaps it was because she was openly acknowledging that she was in love with both men, and their absolute dedication to putting her first had her heart and soul in a bear hug like she'd never felt before. She was rolled up, feeling cozy and loved by their expressions, lulled to a place of absolute freedom that also held unlimited, unadulterated, and magnified pleasure.

They loved her, too.

John snuck a hand to play with her nipples, and Anderson shifted so his penetrative thrusts hit her clit just right, and she launched into another orgasm while being held between her two men. She surpassed elation and ecstasy as comfort and stimulation were pervasive, and fear didn't exist. The orgasm carried her to waves of unspeakable joy, and she twitched as Anderson came inside her.

He leaned down to kiss her smile before switching spots with John.

The dedication to joint pleasure made even the air feel luxurious as John fucked her missionary until he came inside his wife, too.

Afterward, the aftercare had her sandwiched between both men on the floor, amidst the couch pillows. They lay together as they entered the after-coitus calm. A peace settled upon Laney that she wondered if she'd ever broach again. It didn't seem like something she'd ever be gifted in the future. It felt incredible. That's special.

John was the first to speak. "I know this may seem like a bad time to bring this up, but I need to talk about it. I'm worried."

Laney was startled out of her reverie at his words, her heart jumping. She couldn't possibly fathom what he could mean. She was in the best place of her life. "What do you mean, John?" Her voice wavered as fear snuck in.

"I'm worried about abusing you and your open nature. I don't ever want that to happen," he blurted. He sounded so concerned.

She laughed with relief. "What? No. That's just silly. I loved today." Well, that was a lot of fright for nothing, yet her heart was still pounding.

"I'm serious. I have a fear of abusing you or it slipping into abuse." He fell silent.

She caressed his face, hoping to swipe the worry off it.

"I'm not following you either, John," Anderson piped in as he stroked Laney's hip. "I think she'd say her safeword if she felt overwhelmed or threatened."

John rose up on his elbow. "Here's my fear. I don't want you to do something just to please me, and do something that you feel is too far. Like today..." He paused, "When Max showed up. I just pulled him in, assuming you'd be okay with two men."

She guffawed. "I loved it, John! You're worrying for nothing." This was pointless. He knew her likes and dislikes.

"No, hear me out. I fear you love pleasing me so much that I might push you too far, or you yourself. I don't want any regrets or trauma brought onto you because you want to please me. Cause you think I want you to do it."

Laney reached up and stroked his cheek. "You are the most considerate man, husband, lover, and friend. You aren't just my partner, you are part of me. I love to please you, yes, that's true, and it's becoming a stronger kink with me as we go on, but I promise to use my safeword when necessary. I thought you knew this."

"I do, but today had me worried. I guess it's a fear of mine to push you too far and accidentally abuse you." His eyes held legitimate concern.

"I think that shows how much you revere her safety and comfort, and that's awesome, John. I believe what would help you is talking to another Dominant. Not me, because I'm not at your level, but remember my friends? We need to set that up, and you two need to take some time to talk separately from us."

John settled his body down to the floor, and his face fell into some state of relaxation. "Well, I think that's a wonderful idea. And I think I need it. Today had me worried. I just dove right in making plans to incorporate Max, and it felt, I don't know, like I was pushing it too far."

Laney shook her head with exaggeration. "No, you didn't, but I really appreciate you worrying about me like this." It didn't feel smothering. However, John was wrong about pushing her too far, although she appreciated his thought process. It made her feel even more loved by him.

"I think perhaps you might be worrying that the turn-on of sharing Laney is taking over Laney's pleasure in it. Is that it?" Anderson asked in a kind voice.

"Yes, that's it. Your safety is the most important thing to me, and I felt my own kinky desires were possibly overriding it, and it made me uncomfortable."

She snuggled into his flaccid body and kissed his chest. "Well, you don't need to worry about that. I loved it. And I love you directing the sex scenes. You're amazing at it. I don't think you could ever abuse me, John. You're too conscientious."

"But what if I did it by accident?" The worry returned to his eyes.

"You couldn't. As long as I can signal, we're good."

"Okay. Well, maybe I just need confirmation from you that you won't go against yourself for me."

She nodded aggressively against his chest. "I won't. I promise."

Anderson snuggled up behind her, spooning her.

She was safe, even in a world of sexual exploration, a world some may call exploitation, but it was her kink, their kink, and the safety net of their love and presence was all she needed to feel more right than ever before. His worries were nails in her belief that he really was for her; he put her first, and her pleasure and safety were more important than anything else. If this wasn't bliss, it didn't exist. She lay between the warmth of her two men as time passed. The passage of time was longer than a single breath, but easier than one.

Chapter 8

L aney shifted in the seat as her insides popped in bursts of excitement. She was fidgety. She couldn't help it. They were charting new waters in their hotwife way of life, and she was ecstatic about their plans for the day. She glanced at her husband. His eyes were shielded by sunglasses, but his little smile told her he loved this impending adventure just as much. His determination to help her continue to explore her kinks was actually starting to repair even the deepest damage he'd piled on her heart in the past, an unlikely and treacherous trek back from that she hadn't expected to succeed. She counted herself lucky. Where her friends in similar positions had taken the next step to divorce, she and John had bravely stridden into being more open. Apparently, midlife sucked, but not for her. She smiled, biting her lower lip.

"John, I'm so excited I could burst!" She shifted her legs and pressed her palms to her thighs. Her mind spun with hope as she imagined what kind of man they'd find to play with at the gas station. She'd shared her taboo fantasy with John last week, and immediately, he sculpted out an opening in his work schedule to take Laney on this escapade to fulfill her secret desire of stranger sex in a gas station bathroom. It was raunchy, wicked, and taboo, and fantasizing about this scenario had made her come alone on many late nights with her toys.

But now John knew, and he was doing something about it.

"I'm very excited too. And I'm still thrilled you decided to share it with me." His tone was happy. She glanced down and could see his erection at full peak in his pants.

She reached over and stroked his full cock beneath his shorts.

"I'm going to help you find the ideal man to fuck you, then I'm fucking you right after, so be ready for my rage. I'm already near peaking, so I'm going to fuck you hard." He grinned. "Gotta claim my little wench back now, don't I?"

She shuddered with glee as her mind dared to imagine both parts.

John had chosen the large gas station that truckers frequented at the highway rest stop, just three exits away from their town. She wondered if she'd get an older man, or a gruff, horny biker dude, or would she get a sex starved divorced guy who would rail her like his life depended on it. She wanted someone so desperate for sex that they'd go a bit overboard. Those were the most delicious men. She literally couldn't wait. The other fantasy she'd often used, that she hadn't shared yet with John, was knocking on the truck doors of sleeping drivers at such a gas station and offering to fuck them. She'd hop truck to truck, making her way down the line fucking all the men. But that was a fantasy for another day. Today was already claimed.

"And you'll tell them the full fantasy?" she asked, though she already knew the answer; she just liked hearing him say it. It solidified to her that he was okay with it, and she wasn't a total freak. Well, that was subjective, of course. In her old vanilla life, she'd probably have called herself a freak, but that was before she became enlightened to strut about the world as a bona fide hotwife slut. Her every sexual whim had become John's mission in life, as long as he was in charge. That's just how she wanted it, too.

She tugged her sundress up her thighs as her clit screamed to be touch, but John had strictly said no action could happen down there until she was in front of the stranger and bared naked for a fuck.

John's grin was lecherous as he met hers. "Don't you touch," he warned. "I want you ripe as possible. Are you going to make sound?"

She'd been nervous about his request that she be loud while she got nailed in the bathroom. She liked the attention of onlookers, but she didn't want to go to jail today. That would ruin a perfectly good hookup, not to mention throw her in a jail cell where there would be no dicks. She wanted her dick fix, not some butch dickless mama jail cell mate.

She snickered, wondering what that would be like, to be a husky woman's bitch with bars for walls. That was another avenue to explore with her toys that she hadn't mounted, but certainly worthy fodder for her next alone time session, though. She'd most certainly need a dildo involved to finish.

John pulled into the giant truck stop gas station. There was a sea of semis parked behind it, and Laney mused how many men were in the truck beds of their cabs, jerking off to porn. She mused that most were. That was a hot thought, and it stoked her libido further. Thinking about lots of horny truckers inside the privacy of their trucks, like so many little nearby realms chock-full with primal sexual activity, charged her up. She clenched her hands into tight fists as he parked.

They were inside the large gas station store in a flash. John pulled her along as they casually walked up and down the aisles. Her heart thudded like she'd just run from a lion. Some kind of nasty sex-hungry beast of a man would fit her perfectly right about now. She was randy as fuck. John had made her go twenty-six hours without climaxing, and she was a damn righteous bitch in heat; she deserved this. She was ready to present her holes to a series of dicks whose faces she may never even see. But she reminded herself that this wasn't to be a group event, but a single man's. Denying that request over breakfast had made John a bit of a party pooper. No matter, she'd get hers anyhow.

Laney spied a young man over by the soda pop fridge. She nudged John, but he stopped cold in his step when a young woman joined him.

John made eyes with her and shook his head.

They continued their trek around the store until Laney spotted a leather-clad biker carrying black leather gloves, a bag of Cheetos, and a Dew. She froze in place as her jaw dropped open. He was muscular with thick, firm-looking thighs, tallish, but shorter than John, and his expression held the right amount of scowl to make Laney's clit jump. He had strong-looking hands and didn't seem to have a wedding ring. She instantly imagined him slapping her ass with the gloves, and she released a slow breath, which did nothing to tame her nerves that were in a tangled mess of jittery excitement. He moved with a grace his size defied, and his firm buns in the smooth sheath of the leather called to her fingers. She craved caressing the tight fit with her hands while kneeling before him.

He had tufts of gray hair sticking out of the scarf tied around his head, with a bountiful handful of curls rimming the base of the makeshift hat along the nape of his neck. His hair didn't reach his back, but there was a nice handful to explore while French kissing him for sure.

John met her gaze and tilted his head to the side while raising his eyebrow. "Him?" he whispered.

She nodded heartily as her pussy lips flared, begging for his cock already. "Please, yes," she cooed. "He's perfect."

She would love to be fucked doggy while draped over his bike, but that would certainly land them in jail.

John pointed to the ground. "Don't move." He hurried over to the man who looked ready to check out.

Laney watched as her hubby conversed with the biker. His face registered in alarm first, then shifted to contemplation, then quickly bloomed into a lewd expression.

Laney's lust seethed.

John turned toward her and pretended to grab something invisible in the air, and rapidly jerked his hands upward.

She giggled as she grasped the hem of her sundress. She glanced around and saw no eyes peering her way, so she obeyed John and flashed them.

The biker's eyes flared wide as she lifted the dress past her bare pussy and all the way up to her braless tits.

John swiveled his hand in a circle, and she spun around, baring her ass to them as she slightly bent over.

She didn't stay that way for long and righted her dress, wondering if she had just been on video in the station's surveillance system, which was another hot element that stroked her horny bone even higher.

She squealed quietly to herself as both John and the biker started making their way toward her. The biker looked excited, his brown eyes filling with more lust with each step. As he came closer, Laney noted the stranger was likely just a touch older. That also made him ideal.

"Laney, this is Bruce." John's gaze was direct and full of unquestionable dominance, as if he was commanding her that this was the man she was to submit to without question.

She swayed as she played with the fabric of her dress, her submission quaking in her gut like a lit fuse burgeoning to express itself to both men.

Bruce's skin was grizzled with a layer of beard scrub, which she instantly desired to feel brushing her shoulder blades as he had his way with her from behind.

"Hi," she said, not hindering her sudden desire to be seductively demure.

"Bruce is interested in fucking you. I've filled him in on everything." John's intense gaze filled her with confidence that this was going to be an epic hookup and that Bruce legit fit the bill of her fantasy to perfection. Her spouse could say so much to her with just his eyes these days.

"Hi," said Bruce, his straight white teeth offset by a single crooked tooth that jutted out, as if in belligerence to the rest of his nicely aligned teeth. His lips were plump and seemed roughed up, likely from riding the highways in the rushing wind for hours on end. He had the air of a loner ready to fuck her into a wild blistering of skin smacks, his pelvis colliding relentlessly against her backside. Well, that was her hope anyway. "Pleased to meet you. Yes. I'd love to fuck." His chuckle unfurled like he'd just won the lottery and was ready to cash it in.

"Let's go," John said, motioning toward the back of the store.

Bruce set his chips and drink on the shelf and boldly reached for her ass, giving it a slight swat. He continued to give her light spanks as the three of them walked, as if to hurry her along.

She loved a sexually impatient man; they always unleashed the most commanding and juiciest passions. She squawked with each butt smack as she followed John. An older man, perhaps in his seventies, caught sight of the slapping and smirked, but then turned away. Laney instantly wished he were following Bruce in their little parade to the bathroom, too.

John held the door for Laney and Bruce as Bruce gave Laney a harder spank to usher her into the men's bathroom. He wielded his hits and his domineering glances with a brute force that tickled Laney's urgency for his cock.

"This is the best surprise of my life," Bruce stated, his libido evident from his swagger to the nuances of his tone.

John locked the door and checked the stalls for feet. "We're good."

Bruce smiled at her, and her heart dropped to her toes. His eyes shifted into a hard glare. One she'd expect of such a virile man who drank his way to beast mode frequently in biker bars, then fucked the waitress rather than paying his bill, slipping out the back with drained balls and a brain full of wicked memories.

"John is a very lucky man." He slapped his gloves into his left hand on repeat. "A little rough is your taste today," he stated as if this was his choice, too.

She nodded as she looked at his gloves, then met his eyes again. She couldn't keep the libidinous grin from filling her face. She felt it was her place to remain silent.

He smacked the gloves harder against his palm, the harsh sound filling the otherwise silent bathroom. "That's no problem, it's my usual go-to."

Laney didn't doubt that for one second, his calloused knuckles and meaty palms telling her he had years of manual labor under his belt.

"Ass and tits, but nowhere else," John instructed firmly. "Max of five."

"You got it, my man." Bruce held John's gaze, and an air of mutual respect coursed between them, which was evident even to Laney, confirming her notion that Bruce was a dominant too.

The desire for a threesome was born in her, but she knew that wasn't John's plan, which was fine. Her mind always veered off into new fantasies on these sex dates. It was wild with its bold, primal offshoots, no matter how hard she tried to keep her brain on the current one. But that was also something John had come to love about her newfound open sexuality. It had become a favorite part of their post-play debriefings.

Bruce took her face in his hands, and she quivered from his grip, bracing for the unknown. With the cool wind-kissed leather of the well-worn gloves pressed to her cheeks, he kissed her on the lips so gently that it surprised her. His eyes told her of the sexual aggression he harbored, ready to unsheathe on her. "I never fuck a lady I haven't first kissed on the lips," he said gruffly. Then his grin grew greedy. He pulled her into a full embrace, pressing first his lips to hers, then his tongue to explore the inside of her mouth.

He smelled like sandalwood and Ivory soap, like the kind her mom had bought when she was a kid.

His hands mauled her back as they kissed. Kissing in the bathroom wasn't supposed to be romantic, but his insistence on kissing her before shoving himself into her had an odd but welcomed thread of romance to her, which was a ridiculous thought because this was to be nothing but raw, unadulterated sex, without even a whisper of romance. She'd let her naive feeling sit, however, because she liked it.

He stepped back, and she caught sight of John's gaze. He looked proud and anticipatory, and wanton as fuck.

Bruce grabbed her cheeks again, then slid his hands firmly down her neck and onto her arms, as if claiming her. Never had Laney felt such a claiming caress in her life. It sent a shiver down her torso and a spasm through her clit.

After a leering trip of his eyes up and down her body, he grabbed the skirt part of her sundress and yanked it upward, which rendered her naked so fast she forgot to breathe. His growing lascivious gaze gave him a predatory air that ticked her arousal even higher. "You're mine for the next fifteen minutes," he chortled. "Or less." He collected her naked self to his leather and grinned down at her.

His janky smile filled her with a scrumptious unease. What would this reckless man do to her if John were not present? She shuddered in his arms, dreaming of it.

"I love a woman who shows me exactly what she's feeling," he said, kissing her again before pushing her backward. "So don't hold back," he instructed.

His shove made her bottom smack into the counter's edge. The bright lights of the bathroom, which generally made everyone look ugly as sin, only showed more clearly the illicit thoughts that were obviously coursing through his brain. He raised his gloves and slapped them on her right tit.

She cried out upon the impact.

"One," Bruce stated, his eyes never leaving her face. He smiled, his smile confirming for her again that she was his toy. He slapped the gloves on her other tit. "Two."

She released a louder cry.

His ogling of her was poignantly evil as his grin deepened. He gripped her shoulders, spun her around, and pushed her forward, which put her tits right into the cold porcelain sink. She cringed, having her boobs upon such a germ-filled surface.

She gasped as he hit each of her ass cheeks once with the gloves. "Oh, fuck," she cried out.

"One left, I'm reserving." He chuckled like only the wicked can and caressed her bare ass.

This man was surely the cold, hard steel of sex in human form.

He leaned on her bare back and crushed her to the counter, the rod of his erection pressed in the crack of her ass. He fondled her breasts as she squirmed in his arms.

John remained silent as Laney watched him in the mirror. He maintained a licentious expression as he watched Bruce maul her body.

"Look me in the eyes," Bruce commanded as he thrust his clothed hard-on in the crevice of her buns, crushing her body against the counter. "You don't want anal, but that doesn't mean I'm not imagining it," he slurred.

She met his eyes in the mirror, getting more of a full taste of his brand of possessive wildness. It struck her with terror and ecstasy at once, the taste of both building the steady rise to her big O.

"Aw, yeah, that's it," he murmured, his breath making her hair flop as he spoke. "You'd take it if you were really mine."

She'd melt into a pile of ardent mush if it weren't for her devotion to remain standing so she could feel his cock sliding against her G-spot, which she hoped was imminent.

He reached between her legs and tapped her thighs. "Spread your legs for me."

She widened her stance as he tickled her lower lip with his fingers. Her arousal skyrocketed when he stroked and rubbed her clit. He pulled his fingers back and pressed them into her wet slit. She moaned and writhed in the constriction of his hold on her. She couldn't have gotten away if she tried.

"Good girl," he muttered after she released a particularly loud moan.

He pumped his fingers in her at a rapid pace, smacking her clit with his thumb. He then pulled himself off and swiveled her to face him. He pressed her to lean back and kept on pushing until the sink handles jabbed into her back. She grimaced, but he didn't stop. He spread her legs apart roughly as she teetered uncomfortably on the uneven backrest of the sink. He raised his gloves and smacked them down square on her clit.

She lurched forward as she cried out, the stimulation both jarring and arousing, strangely at odds but cumulative. She curled further around his hand at her crotch as the aftershocks of the sensation caused her clit to throb.

"I'd do more of that," he said without remorse as he stroked her clit aggressively.

"Three more like that," John stated, a curious appreciation in his voice she couldn't wait to hear more about later.

Bruce grinned devilishly. "Excellent choice." He glanced back at John. "You own a leather pussy slapper? I know a woman."

He brought the gloves down on her clit with a force that made her yell out louder each time. Bruce chuckled wickedly. "Like that, don't you?"

She nodded as the reverberations in her clit gave her an urgency she had only felt when she'd been serviced by multiple men. "Fuck me," she pleaded.

"Again," Bruce said as he undid the top button of his pants.

"Fuck me," she said with more gumption.

"Good girl," he said, unzipping his pants.

He gripped her hips, his fingertips pressing deeply into her flesh, spinning her to face the mirror once more.

She gasped as he went straight to finger-fucking at such a rapid pace, she knew she'd come quickly.

Bruce rode her cunt with his large fingers, making a barrage of wet squishy sounds. He was a skilled lover, managing to also properly accost her thickened clitoris.

Her moans hit a crescendo, and then she fell silent as she hit the peak. Her orgasm took over, and she curled further into the sink as her body twitched, riding the euphoric climactic wave. With her face against the porcelain, she gasped and sputtered, stunned from the strength of her orgasm.

"Aww, that's right, that's a good girl," Bruce muttered, his hot breath bathing her.

He rose off her back as she continued to twitch through aftershocks.

Her breathing rate accelerated as she met John's eyes. He smiled with so much satisfaction that it thickened her satiation.

Bruce rubbed the meaty head of his cock along her pussy lips and then brusquely penetrated her.

His groan as he entered her tanked her arousal again, and as he began to ride her from behind, smacking his pelvis into her ass at an ever-increasing pace, she bought into his passion. She was going to come again. She loved it when a man enjoyed her body, especially when he made it very clear.

He rammed himself into her, rocking her and deftly filling the air with the sounds of their bodies smacking together. He pounded her hard, her butt jiggling voraciously as he rode on.

Laney was getting off on John watching Bruce use her just as much as they both surely were.

Bruce growled. His sounds of enjoyment as he caressed her internal walls held some legit promise of her climaxing again. She was so close.

He grunted as he roughly shoved himself in. "Fuck toy," he muttered as he took her as easily as he would a fuck doll, his strong arms trapping her tightly.

After a few more aggressive jabs, he pulled his erection from her body and sprayed his cum across her back and ass. "Aw, yeah, that's it," he sighed. "So fucking good."

He spread his cum all across her flesh as far as the fluid would go. He caressed her hips and bottom, his hands sliding less easily as the cum thinned out.

"Nicely done," John said with approval laced in his words. "I've got a few new things to try with her. Thanks for that."

Bruce chuckled. "Happy to help." He put his cock back in his pants and zipped them up. "All yours, my man."

Laney righted her body and spun around to face the men. She felt dazed.

"Thanks for the ride. It's better than my bike any day," Bruce said as he stepped back and out of John's way. "So, you still want me to watch?"

John stared Laney in the eyes, his passion mimicking a lion's gaze on its prey. "Yes." He unveiled his thickened cock with a tug. It swung in the air as he moved closer.

Laney's yearning for her husband rolled luxuriously in his lubricious stare back. "Fuck me," she said to John, her voice dripping with want.

"Always," he said as he forcefully pulled her to him.

They kissed deeply as Bruce watched from about four feet away. "I might just have one to rub out as I watch," he snickered as he unzipped his pants once more.

John kissed down her neck, his hands claiming her back as he pinned her to the counter. Laney watched as Bruce stroked his cock, his jerking off sounds meeting John's mouth smacks against her right breast. John suckled her erect nipple as she finger-combed his hair. He had a few more strands of gray in his locks that the harsh lights of the bathroom revealed.

He finished his tit sucking and then fingered her freshly fucked pussy. "Nice and moist," he said with a shitty ass grin.

He spun her around and pressed her to the bathroom counter once more. He lined up his cock at her womanhood and entered her with ease. His fucking of her started slow but quickly grew with ardent urgency.

She flicked her gaze from watching Bruce jerk off in the mirror to watching her husband's face as he enjoyed using her body.

John reached under her and stopped thrusting while he played with her clit. He masterfully roused her, as only he knew how to do, and she rose rapidly to another blessed peak. She wiggled as she tried not to come yet, but she felt her grip on stopping it waning. The seconds were an eternity as she closed her eyes in an attempt to make herself less stimulated. She craved those special words from him and would try her damnedest to wait.

"Come for me, babe," he commanded.

She allowed the orgasm to birth, and the waves radiated out of her vaginal walls in delectable eruptions of pleasure. She lost count of how many contractions launched as she opened her eyes in the final winddown of her orgasm.

"That's my good girl," John said, his tone full of praise.

He straightened up. It was his turn. He banged himself into her in a hurried rush until his body jerked with his climax, his cum spewing inside her.

She was panting as she glanced at Bruce. He had another happy grin on his face as he secured his limp penis back into his pants.

"That was hot," he said, wiping his hand down his leather-clad thigh. "Thank you. Best joy ride of my life."

"Thank you for pleasuring my wife," John said as he helped Laney off the counter.

"Oh, that was nothing. My pleasure." His grin was the biggest she'd seen yet.

"Yes, thank you. I really loved it." She beamed a smile back at them both. "Epic."

"A true goddess you have there," Bruce said, pointing at Laney. "See you next time." He turned, walked to the door, unlocked it, and left.

John snagged her sundress off the floor and handed it to her.

She slipped it over her head, despite her distaste for adorning clothes that had rested on a public restroom floor for twenty minutes. But she really had no choice in the matter. "I can't believe no one knocked on the door to come in."

"Oh, they did," John said with a laugh. "You didn't hear it?"

She shook her head and joined him in a laugh. "No, I totally didn't. I guess I was otherwise occupied."

"That's for sure." He pulled her close and kissed the top of her head. "Let's go home, you deliciously promiscuous slut. I can't wait to hear all your thoughts."

He let her go, then grabbed her hand, pulling her out into the hallway.

"Let's find a diner on the way. I have a hankering for a big burger with fries as we talk about it."

He nodded. "Sure thing, babe. I'm in."

They left the gas station store, the breeze of summer gracing their plastered grins as they strode along.

Chapter 9

L aney finished loading the dishwasher and planned to start on the next dish she wanted to take a picture of for the cookbook. The time of day was right, as was the weather. She really loved using the natural light for food photos because the pics always came out so perfectly. She had just enough time before lunch to make the dish and photograph it. Then John would be home, and they'd be into the lunch routine.

John rarely went into the office these days, but he had an in-person meeting, so he had left early at seven, before she'd even gotten out of bed. The house had been quiet for her morning workout, and she had enjoyed blasting her music instead of using earbuds while on the treadmill. Anderson was out doing his list of pool care visits for the day, and he had a very full roster, but he often stopped in for lunch. So, she had a tentative lunch planned for the three of them, as usual. Her meal planning had taken on a whole new level with Anderson around for most meals because that man could pack away the food. She figured it was due to his physical job and the fact that he also worked out. Their grocery bill had doubled as well. She liked their throuple life very much, and she was so happy.

She walked to the office to snag a bill she knew was due. As she walked past the floor to ceiling windows by the front door, she noticed a man walking down the street. She rolled her eyes. Another solicitor. She hated to turn them away, but she and John rarely made decisions for services because someone stopped by. It was more of an annoyance than an opportunity, and she considered hiding when he rang the doorbell. Why answer the door when she had no plans of buying whatever he was selling?

She sat at the desk and wrote out the bill. It was a rare one, and she wrote out a check for it rather than paying it online. Movement outside caught her attention. It was the man selling stuff door to door, and he was walking down the driveway of the neighbor's house two houses away. He looked fit and had dark hair. He wore black shorts and a sage green shirt. His shoes were tennis shoes, and he walked with a stride that spoke of confidence. She guessed selling door to door required such a personality that was full of it because he'd have to keep going despite all the overabundance of expected rejections. She didn't envy anyone doing that job. From a distance, she couldn't tell his age, but she liked the shape of his body.

She prepared to hide as he moved on to the next neighbor's house, which was to her immediate right. That was the man she wanted to fuck, the one who often played peeping tom on her and John having sex. For some odd reason, John had not approached him yet to fuck Laney, despite her bringing it up every so often. And he'd never shared why he avoided this man as her play date. He must know something she doesn't. She'd have to press John for his reasons.

Getting a closer look at the guy as he walked up the driveway of her neighbor's house, she could tell he was young. He looked to be in his twenties. He looked sexy from afar, so she reconsidered answering the door when he came, just so she could ogle him. Too bad John wasn't home to arrange some sexy fun for her with this tasty-looking morsel. But an idea struck her. She'd secured her own sex dates before, and with John's encouragement. John just liked doing it, so he was the usual instigator.

Her neighbor either wasn't home or didn't answer the door because the young man swiftly walked back down the driveway. It was interesting to her that he didn't walk across the grass. But then some morons are particular about their grass, when she couldn't fucking care less about the lawn. She'd have happily strolled across it rather than go down a driveway. She didn't like to follow other people's ridiculous rules.

She rose from the office chair and glanced at what she was wearing. She was still in her workout outfit and probably was stinky, too. A visitor was not what she'd expected this morning, but he'd likely not even notice her stench because they wouldn't get that close anyhow. He was just eye candy for her morning, and perhaps fodder for a good masturbation session. Whenever she was alone in the house, she often took the opportunity to rub one out, or five. It was often fun to indulge and watch some porn while she used her toy, without either of her men chiming in with their two cents or joining in. Solo play was something she'd never give up, and both men knew she did it because they always wanted her to tell them about it. They thought it was hot.

She smiled as the man walked up her driveway. He was very sexy and cute. He looked like he was possibly lower to mid-twenties, which she suspected meant he had a healthy libido and a hungry cock to match. It would be incredible to feel him slapping against her body, but she wasn't getting her hopes up. Her brain was salivating at using him for her fantasy, though. She always had the best orgasms immediately after a workout, too. It was a great setup.

The man was already smiling as he came up the front steps, a dimple playfully adorning his right cheek. She loved a man with a dimple, or two. He had touchable bulging arm muscles, and his pecks beneath nicely shaped his shirt. He looked congenial even from fifteen feet away. He quickly ate up those steps in a swift hop up her front stairs. She was acutely aware that he could see her watching him.

She opened the door, and he started to reach for the doorbell. A playful grin was on his face as he met her gaze.

"I'll save you the finger press," she said in a flirty tone.

He was indeed incredibly sexy, and she instantly craved his pelvis pounding against her backside in a stolen moment featuring a doggy quickie, maybe as she held onto the railing of the staircase going upstairs. Yes. That would do very, very nicely. She drew in a slow breath to try to quell her desire for him to do just that.

Her lust seethed as she scanned his face, his plump lips, and his slim torso tapering to his hips, which made him appear like he could fuck like a machine.

She wanted to ride that machine.

"I bet you've seen me around the streets the past few days," he said coyly, but his words were laced with flirtation. He was confident, even cocky. His eyes were filled with saucy interest. So, his elevator pitch was to flirt with a woman twice his age to get the business. Interesting.

He didn't know it yet, but he just hit the perfect house.

She dropped her jaw to speak, but the words came out delayed. "Um, no, I haven't."

His teasing smile slightly waned, and she instantly regretted not playing along despite not having seen him. "Oh, well, I've been washing your neighbor's windows all week." He paused, and his expression returned to the initial suggestive flare, as if the years she had on him didn't matter one bit. He clearly aimed to charm her into a sale, but she'd more likely be charming him into entering her cunt for a nice, hard, and fast ride. "You in need of some window washing? You have some high windows I can take care of for you." His grin flashed even brighter. "I'm quite skilled at reaching tough-to-reach spots."

Oh, well, that had a delicious interpretation she wanted to focus on. "Is that so?" she asked with interest and a raised eyebrow. "I definitely have hard-to-reach spots that could use some attention."

He turned away slightly as astonishment crept across his face. He clearly caught her drift. "I have all the equipment to do it."

"Oh, I just bet you do," she said with relish, unable to keep the suggestive tone out of her words.

This tickled him, and he turned even happier. "I can do it anytime. I have an opening now, but I need to be down the street in two hours. I could certainly start now, and if I don't finish, I could come back afterward." He flicked his eyes to her face, then dropped his gaze very slowly down her body. "I certainly wouldn't mind coming back here."

"My husband usually takes care of this stuff, but I can't imagine him caring if I bought a day pass for nice and shiny clear windows."

His smile flattened to a grim expression. "Ah, okay, got it." He looked defeated.

Oops. She needed to fix this. She'd just have to reignite him.

"Oh, he certainly wouldn't mind. He's very open to whatever I want," she bragged, then gave him a seductive smile. "And that includes men." Why not be blunt? She wanted to fuck him, so why not make it obvious?

"Men?" he asked with an incredulous look. "As in work getting done by men?" He looked confused, and it made him even cuter.

"Yeah, work getting done by men, on me." She was getting so turned on in her pursuit that she began to pant. Breathlessly, she stated, "You see, I'm a hotwife."

He stared at her as the clear realization of what she was saying took hold in his eyes. "No shit?"

She liked the interest blooming in him. "Yes, he lets me fuck who I want, and I'm thinking I need you to come in and wash my windows. You can bounce yourself against my ass as I show you which windows to start with." Her nipples were stiffening, and his eyes dropped to her chest.

"Holy fuck," he muttered in awe. "Bounce myself..." he repeated, dumbfounded. He glanced back and forth across her body several times in quick bursts. "You're being serious, aren't you?"

"Yes, and no, most neighbors don't know, but the house you just visited, he does know, so don't worry if he sees us."

"He's not home," the young man said quickly.

"Ah, don't be so sure." She pointed to the front window where there was a possible shape of a human shrouded in the semi-darkness. "Don't worry. He watches us all the time." She snickered. "And we let him."

His jaw dropped, and his eyes widened. "I think I just fell into living porn."

She laughed. "You're not wrong. Come in..." she paused, "I guess I should ask your name."

"I'm Tyler."

"Nice to meet you, Tyler. I'm Laney." She stepped back and waved her arm inward. "I hope you aren't going to mind that I just worked out."

"Not one bit," he said with a laugh. "In fact, I think that's hot. You're hot. I don't mind sweat on a woman."

"Feeling is mutual." She shut the front door, but not before she made a pointed glance toward her neighbor's window. He was likely wishing they'd have done it right on the porch. Sorry, dude, not this time.

Tyler looked awestruck. His look of bewilderment transformed quickly when she ran her hand over his chest.

"You look like you work out, too," she said in a seductive slur. "It shows."

"Yeah, I do. Plus, I lift." His expression turned into one of someone who had just won a giant prize. But he also looked a bit skeptical. "You aren't playing me, are you?"

"Nope, not in that way, perhaps in another way," she slurred as she placed her other hand on his chest. "I bet washing windows helps you stay fit."

"I will have to get my truck to get my washing stuff and ladder."

"First things first. I need to show you which windows I need you to tend to." She grabbed a fistful of his shirt and tugged him toward the kitchen. Her cougar energy was striding along to five-star fire alarm status. "I have a drawer for you to pick something from."

"A drawer?" he asked in confusion.

She loved confusing men. She dragged him into the kitchen, looking back at him every now and then. "Be a good boy and pick your sleeve." She stopped him in front of the kitchen drawer nearest to the fridge. "This is our play drawer. Pick your favorite color."

She yanked the drawer open, and several condoms shifted inside from the force.

"Oh, my, holy fuck," he said as he stared wide-eyed at the open drawer. "I have fallen into a film." He glanced around quickly. "You're alone?" A look of panic flickered across his face. "I don't need some angry husband pummeling me."

"I don't think you'd be the one taking a pummeling, you look pretty damn strong to me," she cooed. She caressed his cheek with the backs of her index and middle fingers as she made eye contact with him. "Now pick. I'm really horny for you. As you came up my drive, I knew I wanted you. And being a hotwife means I get to have you." She was laying it on thick, but he clearly needed the guidance. "Fuck me, Tyler. I need you to fuck me. Then I'll pay you for the windows, and you'll wash them later."

He snapped his head at her in shock, then a full grin slid across his handsome face. "I will, and with absolute fucking pleasure."

She pointed to the drawer to refocus him, then bent lower to open another. She pulled out her pen vibrator, which she had just charged. "This will do."

He chose a neon yellow condom and then stood still with the brilliant coin-shaped rubber in his open palm.

She snickered inside. A horny man who was so surprised he was frozen in inaction. "If you don't start taking action, I will," she said with determination. He needed a hot poker to stab his butt to get moving.

He shook his head and smiled more deeply. "Just kind of in shock that this is really happening." His demeanor shifted to mischievous, however.

"That's much better. Now let's go over to the first window I need you to attend to, and you can put that cock of yours to work on pleasuring me."

He grinned devilishly and grabbed her by the arm, but followed her lead on where to go. As she stopped him in front of the first window in the living room, she felt a surge of empowerment. This was so exciting, and John was going to be so proud of her for taking the initiative in his absence to get her lusty yearnings met.

"I'm trusting this is the window?" he asked jovially. "Oh, it looks very dirty."

"Yes," she said as she leaned in, pressing her full front to his. "It's filthy."

He grabbed her head between both his hands, the condom in his palm now pressed to her cheek, and he went in for a deep kiss. They entwined, and their dive into each other erupted into mouth smacks and moans. They kissed, feverishly.

His erection popped stronger against her abdomen as he crushed her fully to him. Gone was the little timid boy, as he raged fully into his manhood, showing her his desire for her as he mauled her back down to grope her ass. His hands rode back up her back and slid into her tight workout top. He threaded his fingers between her flesh and the stretchy fabric, then firmly grasped it. He peeled it off her, forcing a break from their kiss so he could get it off over her head.

He gazed down at her bared breasts with a look of need and devoured her right nipple while cupping it for his feed. He did the same on the other side, not slowing the strength of his suckling one single bit. He sucked longer than she thought he had the patience for, given how big his erection appeared through his shorts.

"Fuck you look so good," she muttered.

She went straight for his cock and squeezed it with her hand.

He groaned out as his body shifted in response. "Aw, fuck."

He leaned back, and the fierceness in his eyes sent an electric thrill through her. There he was, a virile beast of masculinity, mere inches from her with a libido hungry for impromptu sex at the drop of a hat. She loved that fierce insta-lust of younger men; it matched her natural state as well.

"Fuck me, Tyler," she repeated with emphasis. "Fuck me good and hard. Take me how you want me. I want that." She was struggling to hold on to her toy; she felt erratic, but she tightened her grip on it like it was her anchor. This guy likely had no idea how to stimulate a clit, so she was packing her preparation. Popping a boner easily didn't mean he also understood how to pleasure a woman.

He slid his fingers into the waistband of her workout shorts, and in one swift tug, her bottom half was naked. There she stood nude in front of her window, but it was to the back of the house, so only by chance would someone on the path see her nudity.

He whipped her body around so fast her hair flew up.

She gasped as he pushed her to the window, her hands smacking the glass. Pride swelled in her as she grinned; she'd managed to keep hold of her toy. "You're adding more fingerprints to the window."

He snickered haughtily but said nothing. He pressed on her head, efficiently bending her over. And just as she suspected, he was already lining his cock up to penetrate her. There was no foreplay, no clit play, and no commitment to wanting her to come. She knew this would be the case and smiled at his selfish eagerness. His immaturity was kind of cute. She wanted him to use her and pound his way into her to take his orgasm. She was using his cock and his desire to satiate her hotwifey wants, so it was only fair. A hard boning was just what she sought, and he seemed more than ready to deliver.

"Use me like a beast." She stiffened as she thought of the condom. He needed full direction. "Do you have it on?"

"Oh, shit, no. I forgot." He stooped to the ground and snatched up the little package.

He tore into it, and she watched him hastily slide it down his hard cock. His hands shook, and he was panting heavily. He moved urgently back into place with a grunt.

"It's on," he confirmed.

She turned on her toy and placed it on her clit. This might just teach him something about female pleasure, and that by itself was gratifying, too. His future fuck mates would thank her. She turned it to the max level and pressed it to her clit. She moaned instantly, squirming in front of him.

"Oh, fuck that's hot," he muttered. He pressed her top half to the window, smashing her tits against the glass.

She allowed a burst of laughter to escape. "That's it, lover. Make them dirtier so you have something more to clean, huh?" She laughed harder. "Ever had to clean tit skidmarks off a window before?"

He laughed in a sudden outburst. "No. But that's the plan."

He had entered her quickly and slickly because she was aroused and wet from the little toy. It buzzed away, sending her into the throes of pleasure instantly. Little did he know that his cock was just an adjunct.

His cock head felt wide, and she'd noticed during a glance back that he had a nice, healthy girth to his dick. As he slid in and out of her, going deeper with each thrust, her arousal launched.

"Ohhhh. Fuck that feels so good," she whispered, struggling to maintain the toy on the right spot on her clit as he slammed into her.

"Fucking incredible," he responded between panting.

The skin smacking filled her ears, and when he grunted and then hammered himself into her while digging his fingers into her hips, it sent her flying. She pressed her toy against herself as best as she could, and it was enough to trigger her vaginal walls to contract. She was flung into her orgasm in a blissful hurry. Her body quaked as she clenched him deep inside her.

He groaned heavily, his body curling over her as his must be spewing into the condom, hovering just above her back. He kept fucking her, though, since he was still hard, and she was gifted another peak to her climax.

"Aw, fuck, fuck, fuck," he spat as he took another turn for his pleasure in another frantic set of pumping.

Her body was rocked viciously as he fucked her hard and steadily.

She gasped, crumpling further into the window, loving the fact that her bare tits were squished against it. Her body rubbed along it as he slowed his thrusts. She hoped at least one person had seen her body chugging along the glass.

"You're sure making good titty skidmarks," she said saucily, her words coming out quiet in between her pants. She just wanted to say that again.

He burst into laughter and drew away from her with a guffaw. "Now that's funny. One to tell the friends."

"Please do." That was satisfying. She smiled as she straightened up and spun to face him. "I'll get my checkbook. Unless you have a way for me to digitally pay you?"

It felt more like she was paying him for the cock ride than for window cleaning, and that hit her naughty target right in the center.

"You can send two hundred dollars to this," he said as he reached into his pocket for his phone. He opened it and held up a QR code.

"Two hundred with a forty-dollar tip for the extra windows," she said with a wink.

"Extra windows?" he asked as he pulled up his shorts.

"Yeah, well, I just got this one extra dirty for you, so it will need the most wiping." She laughed at her own joke. Her shower oil had made a smeary mess.

He glanced at his phone. "Oh, damn. I got another call and missed it while we were..." he said as his voice trailed off. He smirked. "I was having too much fun to notice the buzz." He pocketed his phone. "I have to go do this, and then I'll be back. That okay?"

"Sure, no problem. I'll be here all day."

With that, he grinned big and skedaddled out the door in a flash.

She sighed as she collapsed on the couch, her trusty pen toy still clasped in her hand. She cradled her body against a pillow on the couch as her own version of aftercare and dozed off.

Chapter 10

The garage door into the house slammed shut. Within seconds, John appeared before her. "Hi, babe, oh look at you," he said as he swooped low to kiss Laney on the head. "Miss me?"

"Yes." She smiled back, her dopamine high still coursing through her veins. She mustn't have been asleep for very long.

"Did you just play or something?" He smiled at her, his expression appreciative and amused. "You look flushed and satisfied, sleepy. Just the way I like you."

"Not exactly," she mused with a wiggle of her fingers. "I had a visitor. And he was incredible. I mean, really, really incredible. A sexy young window washer showed up and, well, things led to more things." She snickered as a laugh grew. "Let's just say he was very good with windows, but it was more about the ride during the view that he gave me more than anything." She hugged her naked body and closed her eyes slightly as she savored the memory. "I'm feeling pretty good and floaty now."

John's face erupted in anger before the thunderous words came. "You did what? With who?" His hands twitched as his body jolted in a shake. His eyes filled with thunder.

She stared at him, jarred. What was this? She wasn't used to him shouting in such extreme anger at her, and definitely not from fucking another man. It almost didn't feel real. But in truth, this was a glimpse of the old John she hadn't ever wanted to revisit. He was lashing out and unraveling right before her. He was transforming into something evil, and it sent a fearful chill through her.

"You had sex with a stranger without me here?" he boomed the question at her like a drill sergeant on a testosterone high.

"But..." She quivered, her voice faltering as she careened into the unknown from his tone and angry face. "Yeah, but, John, I've found men on my own before." She was confused, and rightly so; she'd been fucking tons of men, so why was he acting like this now?

"Over my knee, right now. This must be punished." He looked so angry.

Punished?

She cowered.

It was true John had been present for the others, but she hadn't realized he felt this way.

"Now!"

His tone was so commanding that her stomach dropped, and she obediently crawled over his lap. Her brain wasn't working right, though she wanted to obey him. She liked to obey him, but this was shaping up not to be their usual play spanking. The tears were threatening to spill out of her eyes, and he hadn't even slapped her butt yet.

"But John, why?" She was not against him disciplining her; it was a bit of a kink she harbored, but watching their good jive crumble from this was more heartbreaking than anything.

He said nothing, and he roughly positioned her over his lap, pulling on her hips so her butt pointed higher in the air.

"Ass up."

The hits came hard and fast, one after another making her cheeks rock. Confusion swirled all throughout her as he laid the barrage of hard spanks across her ass. It hurt, and she wanted it to stop. She was all for a sexy, dominant spanking session, but this felt different. She was getting spanked and not in a good way. There was a cold brutishness in what he was doing, an almost uncaring aggression that torqued a dark urge in her, but there was also something else lurking, a deep-seated desire that she struggled to name but that she also abhorred. Part of her loved the humiliation of being corrected. The domination he was delivering to her had an edge of something she desired, and she liked submitting to him, but she was wading through his unexpectedly explosive reaction as if it were a mucky swamp. His launching into this was shocking. Why would he do this when he'd been fine with her finding and fucking men before? Jaxon, the garbage man, came to mind. That seduction and arrangement had all been hers. Their new way of life was getting partially dismantled as he kept on pounding on her like a primal, brainless beast.

She was on the verge of saying her safeword for the first time.

The garage door slammed, and within seconds, Anderson appeared before her tear-blurred eyes. And he looked enraged.

"What the fuck is going on here?" he demanded, his eyes set in deep concern, and his expression aghast. "What the hell are you doing, John? This looks way too far."

But John hit her once more despite Anderson's protest.

The sting was even worse somehow with Anderson in the room.

Anderson came close and grabbed John's arm. "Stop this now, John," he said with so much power, she shuddered.

Anderson helped her to her feet and pulled her close. Her ass was on fire, so she was afraid to sit, which was just fine because the wrap of Anderson's arms around her was so comforting. Some of her usual feelings of safety returned while she stayed wrapped in his arms. She was aghast by what had just happened, and she had no idea how to navigate it.

"I..." was all John said. His face fell, and he sank into an expression of deep shame. "I..." he repeated, but nothing else came out.

"This is not okay." Anderson rocked her slightly, his big, strong arms cradling her. "I don't know what's going on, but this is not okay."

She gasped with a sob and turned her face into Anderson's chest. John's betrayal was threatening to bring up all the bad things from their past, and she didn't want to let it overrun her. She'd certainly crumble in a ball on the floor without the strength to even stand.

"I'm not here all the time, but as far as I know, we haven't really talked about that kind of thing. Did Laney give her permission for this? If I'm to be a part of the three of us, I need to be a part of every conversation. Nothing left out. You at least need to update me." Anderson was angry, too, and he very rarely, if ever, seemed this angry. "I'm fine with being debriefed, but there was no debriefing about this kind of discipline." Anderson's coming into his own dominance, and in the direct face of John, was an amazing sight to behold.

"Oh, fuck, what have I done?" John said in a devastated voice. He was silent for almost a full minute, his discombobulation flickering, freezing him in place. He stared at Laney, seeming consumed with guilt and pity in his eyes. "You're right." John dropped his head into his palms. "Shit. I was so angry. So angry. I just lost it. I wanted to punish you, so you don't ever do this again, but I was wrong. You're right, Anderson." He raised his head to meet Laney's eyes. He looked sorry. "Laney, I made a huge mistake. I lost total control, and that's not okay. Can you please forgive me?" He shook his head, not waiting for her answer. "I was thinking if I spank you, maybe you'll never do this again alone." He looked as dazed as Laney felt.

She was legitimately baffled by his reaction to her fucking Tyler. A myriad of emotions swirled in her head, giving her no break from the fog the brutish spanking had put her in. On the one hand, she yearned to berate John for going hog wild on her. His anger reminded her of some events of the past when he'd angrily lashed out at her, memories she'd happily have left buried deep in her gut for the rest of her life.

However, she loved John. She adored her new life with him and Anderson. She wavered in how to respond as she watched her man fall apart and almost weep right in front of her. She could perhaps extend the olive branch, but Anderson was spot on. They hadn't talked about this explicitly.

John knew she liked having a spanking kink and being dominated, but playful impact play with only a tint of seriousness to remind her of his dominance was one thing, and discipline was another thing altogether. They'd never set rules or boundaries around punishment spankings. It was too real-world, and she was too stunned by what had just happened to really formulate her full thoughts on it.

She stared at John. "Yes, of course I can forgive you." Her voice came out almost like a knee-jerk response, her tone meek and subdued. It sounded inauthentic. She was not scared anymore, and that helped. "But we do need to talk about this. Anderson is right. I'll admit, I'm confused. I've had so much sex with so many men, and you never reacted like this before. I'm very confused."

John looked lost, too, like a little immature boy thrust into a scary scene, like someone had shaken his world to a shambles, and there was no offer to help him pick up the pieces. "I don't want you to do this ever again. Not alone. It's not safe, Laney." He transformed into a serious mood, his eyes loaded with concern. He held her gaze intently, not reaching for her. "Laney, imagine if I came home and found you all bruised and bloody? What then?" He shook his head as a disgusted look took over. "It's not that I don't trust you, Laney, I don't trust men." He was scared, and it jarred her. John never looked scared, not like this. And, he was saying he didn't trust his own gender. And that was somewhat horrifying. "I fear for you with us not here to protect you. That's all I was thinking about. I'm not mad you fucked him." He snorted. "Hell, look how many men you have fucked." He stared at the ground. "I just overreacted. I turned into a monster. Just like I feared..." He didn't finish his sentence, leaving the air so full of tension that it felt like a turning point. "Maybe I'm no better..."

His confession seared through her chest like the stab of a knife. But John was partly right. She hadn't been thinking. The young man could have seriously hurt her, and she couldn't have stopped him. He could have beaten her up or even killed her. She had played with fire in the worst way, but instead of getting burned, she'd gotten pleasure and satiation. She'd gotten lucky. She should not have blindly trusted he'd do what she wanted.

She stared right into John's eyes. "I deserved that spanking. I was being careless. You're right. I really didn't even think about any of that happening." When she'd laced her keys through her fingers, walking alone at night, it wasn't because she was scared of women.

"That's my point, honey. You're having so much fun fucking all these men, but we're here with you, watching and making sure you're safe. You really were careless fucking that young man on your own." He still felt like a demon, even though he was justifying his actions.

"I want to make my own decisions," she stated plainly.

But for the first time, she realized that this was all their kinks in unison, but John and Anderson's direction wasn't just them living out their domming kinks, it also served as a safeguard for her. If one rapist got hold of her unfettered, the damage he could do to her was frightening. The brutal reality hit her like a brick wall.

John's face cleared with compassion. "Honey, I want that, too, but you can't keep yourself safe from a man who wants to really hurt you. They will win. And I don't ever want to come home and find you seriously hurt like that. I'm sorry I let my anger get the best of me, and I went too far. But you went too far, too."

She could see his point.

He reached for her, and she moved closer to him, but then paused. She melted as she empathized with him. They had both gone too far, and none of it could be undone. He truly looked sorry. She wasn't scared of him, and his words made sense. She could understand why he'd lost control. He was only human, and she could accept his apology. Many times, more than she cared to count, she'd acted impulsively without thinking, as well. She also feared she was being too forgiving by going into his arms. But she loved him, so she did.

He pulled her into a hug and kissed the top of her head. "Do we have a deal? No fucking anyone without myself or Anderson around. If you do, I will spank you again to teach you a lesson. I won't hesitate to correct you when it comes to your safety." He held her tight. "But we indeed need to talk more about this to frame this out fully, but now isn't the time."

She nodded against his shoulder, trying not to weep.

Anderson slid closer. "I agree with John. And I'm really glad I walked in at the right time." His look of sympathy and confidence endeared her heart to him even more. "Honestly, spending time with my new friends has taught me even more about this kind of thing, and I didn't even realize it until now." He smiled. "It's like immersion learning, I guess. Osmosis."

Laney tucked into John's shoulder tightly as he turned his head toward Anderson. "I'd really like to meet them. I still have so much to learn, clearly." He sounded disgusted with himself.

Laney couldn't help but be amazed at his growth. Before this, his arrogance would have won.

"We all do," Anderson said.

Good for him, giving John a chance to fix this without a huge fuss.

She glanced up at John, and he looked sheepish. It helped her feel better, though. It was proof he cared, loved her, and truly did want her consent, despite him slipping into rage mode.

"Honestly, being totally honest, here. I'm ashamed of getting so brutal like that. I lost control, and I'm not okay with that." He shook his head. "I really need to talk to your new friend honestly. I need to do better."

He sounded so defeated, but that helped her ease the pain of what she had just endured.

Anderson nodded. "Muskie's really great. Can't say enough good things about him. He's been in the lifestyle for like fifteen years or something. I've learned so much from him already." Anderson cleared his throat. "Being a dominant is not without its challenges."

"Well, you're way ahead of me despite being so much younger." He sighed deeply. "I was being arrogant. I kind of shocked myself." He sighed again. "I guess I need you to teach this old dog new tricks."

Laney sat up and made direct eye contact with her husband. "Okay, stop. We're all new to this, and we're all still learning. John, you made a mistake. Given past partial discussions and actions, things I've been okay with before, meaning spanking, I can let this go. And, as long as we're being honest, I fully admit I made a mistake, too." She shrugged. "Well, I've made two. I fucked that guy without thinking about my own safety, and I didn't speak up to stop you when you were spanking me like that. But we've talked it out, and now we can do things differently going forward. So, please, stop beating yourself up over this, Daddy." It warmed her heart to extend more courtesy to the man who had changed so much. But she also felt disempowered by the fact that she almost safeworded, but didn't.

"You're the most understanding partner in the world." He caressed her cheek. "But we are nowhere near done talking about this. We all need to do better. And I broke something I fear I can't ever fix." He hung his head. "I don't deserve you, but I already knew that a long time ago."

He wasn't entirely wrong. She was unsure, at best. He'd done bad things way back in their history, though nothing like this, but things that had hurt her emotionally, how they'd become now as a couple had taken time, and they'd gotten to such a good place. This was a setback, no doubt, but she didn't feel trapped by it. Maybe it was a growing pain, and she intended to focus on it in such a way rather than let it ruin what they'd built. Communication was proving to be everything.

"I think I need to go be alone for a while and think." He patted her thigh. "I fear I've done more damage than any of us realizes."

"John, you're human. You have emotions. You're allowed to make mistakes. And you've already apologized. And I believe you. Please stop beating yourself up." Her heart hurt. And watching him hurt magnified that.

He stood up, and his expression remained distraught. "I appreciate that, but I got more aggressive than I ever thought I would. I'm terrified I've broken something I didn't think we could even build together, and now I have to forgive myself for almost demolishing it beyond repair." He sighed as he dropped his hands to his sides. "I have to figure this out. Somehow."

He looked forlorn as he turned away from her. The silence was too heavy for him, having apologized so genuinely.

She also knew she couldn't fix this.

"I'll be in the basement." John left.

"Wow," Laney said. "I didn't expect things to turn out like this kind of a tragic disaster from a simple casual hookup."

"I can understand where he's coming from, sweetie. He feels like he violated your trust, which is something a dominant should never do. It can cause irreparable damage."

True.

They'd come so far from what they had been. She didn't want what Anderson said to be true, though. And in fact, she was often shocked that they had gotten to the safe place they had in their relationship. It was nothing short of a miracle. It just wasn't done. Their existence was the exception, not the rule. With their wretched past, she'd have never seen this goodness being possible until she was legitimately living it. She didn't want it to die, though, and she didn't have to.

"I think where you and John are at has more to do with you than him: your forgiving nature and generous heart. I'm an outsider coming into your marriage. Trust me on this. Your success has to do with you both, but you, Laney, you're the one who decided to give first and more freely. John truly is a lucky man, maybe he's realizing he's even luckier than he originally thought."

She let that sink in, not fully buying into it, but what he said kind of seemed to fit. She'd genuinely wanted to divorce John, and more than once, as recently as a few years ago, so what they'd come to be honestly was nothing short of unbelievable.

"He's now going to have to find a way to forgive himself in order to move forward." Anderson was blunt, and he was right.

"I understand my perspective, but I guess I have a lot more to learn, too." She sighed. "I'm not a dominant." She yearned to be better as a submissive, too.

"Come here, let me hold you. I suspect John is going to need to hold you, too, but for now, I'm going to." He pulled her close and snuggled her tightly.

She didn't feel abused. But had she just been? Her mind couldn't quite wrap around everything properly. She just knew she felt amazing being wrapped up in Anderson's arms. She shifted because the flesh of her ass was still tender, and there was no hiding from that. She wasn't sure she was fully opposed to stronger impact play, or real discipline, but she hadn't worked out in her own mind what that really entailed. That would be something for her to work through at another time, though. Right now, she intended to enjoy being close to Anderson.

"Did you have a good workout? You worked out, too, right?" she asked as she traced his nipple through the fabric of his workout tank.

"Yes, I reached a milestone in lifting, so now I have a new one."

"Nice," she said. It felt good to have an easy conversation after all that heavy shit.

"I'm starving, though. Does anyone have a lunch plan yet? If not, I'd love to make that salmon recipe I bought groceries for the other day."

"I'd love to try the salmon. You're really quite incredible. Amazingly so."

He leaned back and gazed down into her eyes. "Now what did I do to deserve such a declaration?"

"You being you, Anderson. That's all." All the strong emotions had her slightly worn out, so his offering to cook was so welcome.

"How about you go take a shower, and I'll start the food. Then you can help me when you get back down here."

She nodded as she sat up straight. "Yeah, I think that's a good idea. Might clear my head a bit." Alone time was something that sounded exactly like what she needed, too. She stood and made her way to the stairs.

Anderson didn't move from the couch but kept his eyes on her. She was loved and safe and had two amazing men in her life. That was what she intended to focus on.

As she climbed the stairs, ancient bad feelings bubbled up in her, despite her trying to crush them to a pulp. She tried desperately to stop the memories from erupting, but she was unable to keep them from breathing inside her again. She'd been punished, spanked by her father. Many times. Maybe her kink stemmed from that? She didn't know. In truth, what John had done to her was not unlike what her dad had done. She wasn't sure how to process that. At best, she was conflicted.

Part of her didn't want an impact playing kink at all because of her past trauma, and yet other parts of her, some deep dark parts of her, brought her right into the thick of being intrigued by it, and turned on. Maybe the primal parts of her did somehow want that type of thing, the parts that had somehow become innate, like a natural trigger or response she had no control over.

She couldn't change her past; all she could do was reframe her future with her past there as a stain she'd never be able to fully remove. Perhaps what her dad had done had unintentionally laid the groundwork for her current kinks, and she'd have to figure out how to proceed. Though she'd not asked for her sexual garden to be sown that way, either, she'd been seeded by what she'd experienced, regardless. She shrugged, hoping to shirk away from such darkness. It was all a gray area to try and define better.

The cleanse of a shower was calling her name. She turned on the water and slipped inside, not waiting for the water to feel warm enough. She grimaced from the cold, then turned her body so her reddened bottom was immersed in the frigid spray of water. It wasn't only John who had stuff to work through; it was herself as well. She felt it in her bones that this day would change everything going forward. All the things that had seemed set from the past were in flux. What was just sexual play had turned very real in a hurry.

Chapter 11

After dinner that evening, Laney went for a swim, leaving John and Anderson alone at the table. Alone time was something she still craved after the dramatic events of the day.

"You know, I think it was almost like it was for me. Like I was doing the right thing to keep her safe." He shook his head slowly. "So, I was justified in doing it. But I have to admit, I didn't like the feeling of losing control. It was like I was outside myself, which was weird." He hesitantly made eye contact with Anderson, wondering if he truly understood where he was coming from. He felt so much the villain as their eyes flipped through emotions on and off through dinner.

"Yeah, I can understand wanting to keep her safe, at all costs. She's a pure-hearted woman, but she's also very innocent, or maybe naïve is a better word." Anderson smirked. "Too trusting perhaps. And she's very confident. But we both know she'd be in trouble if a man decided to overpower her, even with her groin kick plan and all."

"That's exactly it. And while I love that brazenness about her, her impulsiveness in fucking that young man scared me. And I snapped. She could have really gotten hurt and not been able to stop him if he had turned on her." He was tired of talking about it, but he knew they were nowhere near done needing to talk about it.

Anderson nodded, a grave expression on his face.

John was aware that Anderson had very strong feelings of love for Laney, which he clearly did not have for John. He wasn't opposed to Anderson in their threesome; he was even delighted about it. Anderson was there more for Laney, though, and John was just the element to collaborate with when it came to Laney, not that they didn't have camaraderie, though, because they did. But he also understood that Laney was his full focus as well. They shared that perspective, which was why they got along. John, like Anderson, would always get off, but pleasing and protecting her had become his top priority, which was also why he was so upset with himself for potentially compromising all of that with the act of discipline spanking her, without a discussion beforehand. It was his major bad, and he'd have to deal with the aftermath of it and repair it, somehow. He only hoped he could. It had become his worst fear to harm her, and he'd stepped into that realm because he'd been blinded by anger. He saw red, and he hadn't stopped. It had been careless of him, and he had vowed not to be that way.

Laney bounded into the kitchen, all sopping wet and looking sexy as fuck. Her glistening skin begged to be caressed.

The men looked surprised that she appeared, and she feared she had interrupted something important.

"I'm so excited. As I was swimming, I got the best idea ever. I've been seeing on social media some sex and relationship coaches, and along with that, I've now come to see offerings of a certification to become one." She was bubbling over with energetic hoopla.

"Oh, nice," John said, looking relieved. "Are you moving on from the cookbook idea?"

She was happy to see he was smiling again.

"No, I'll keep working on that, too. And it works because we have to eat, right? I'll keep doing what I've been doing. Developing recipes, redoing them to make sure they work, and taking pictures. But this takes a long time. Alongside that, I'd like to do this." She wraps the towel tighter around herself as she shivers. "It's freezing in here!"

"I think it would be a great idea. What would you do? Like counseling people?" Anderson leaned back in his chair as he watched her intently.

"Yeah, and I could even do it online, like take appointments and talk with people, maybe even make courses to sell." She squealed as she clapped. "I'm really excited about this idea!"

"So, how long would it take to get the certificate?" John asked with interest.

"It depends on the route I'd go. But it would mean I have to take classes and study a bit. But I think I could do it just fine." She peered at both men in turn. "What do you think?"

"I say go for it," John said quickly. "If it's something that interests you, do it."

"Agreed. And you'd be great at it. You might even consider teaching lifestyle courses to help couples."

She scoffed. "Maybe, but I need a bit more personal experience first before I delve into the realm. But honestly, that sounds really fun."

"Maybe Darcy could be your coauthor," Anderson said with a wink.

"Ah, yeah, except that we haven't even met yet. I can't just meet her and then ask her to work with me on a huge project like that."

"Well, keep it in mind. It's definitely a possibility." He raises his eyebrows. "She'd make the perfect consultant, if nothing else. Plus, I think she'd like it."

"Maybe. Well, I guess you'd know. If she and I mesh, I'd consider it," Laney mused. Her eyes were lit, and her excitement was contagious. "We need to meet first. When will that happen?" she demanded.

"Saturday." Anderson nodded with a sly grin. "Their place. Get your brains, and your libido, ready."

"I'm so ready. I can't wait to meet Darcy and talk with her." She squirmed in the chair. "I'm going to start researching certifications and pick one."

"I can't wait to see what you will do," John stated with a happy and satisfied grin. He reached for her arm and patted it. "I have the utmost faith that you can do it."

She felt her vibrant force brighten; that it could not be dimmed from what had happened was a relief. John didn't seem to desire to dim her, either, nor control her chaos. She latched onto her belief that he simply wanted to protect her enough that the violence of the world didn't destroy her.

"I CAN'T FATHOM WHAT could be wrong," John muttered as he walked into the living room carrying his laptop. "It's got to be the router."

The morning coffee made her feel awake and ready for the day. She checked her cup and was disappointed she didn't have one more swallow left. The whiff of the sweet cookie creamer made her want to get another mug full of coffee.

"You're experiencing it cutting in and out, too?" She partially closed her laptop and met his gaze. "I'm getting extremely frustrated."

"Yeah, me too. I think our router is the problem, but didn't you just get it replaced? Or did you not do that yet?" He sat on the couch next to her.

She felt particularly sexy in a little pale yellow sundress with white flowers.

"I did get it replaced. Last month. So the dang thing isn't that old."

"Well, it's faulty. Or there's some other issue. I hate to say it, but it might be time to get an IT guy in the house to fix it." He smirked.

Her face lit up. "An IT repairman. Well, dare I say, my lovely husband, that is the best idea to try in this case." She batted her eyelashes at him, and her expression turned seductively coy. She was suddenly feeling right back on track for her hotwifing way of life.

He laughed at her. "Another potential playmate."

"I wonder if he will be deliciously nerdy." She rubbed her hands together. "This could be really fun."

"So, what are you working on that keeps getting interrupted?" He glanced at her laptop, but the screen had gone dark.

"Porn," she said plainly. "Research."

"Most people don't put those two words together," he said with a chuckle.

"I'm not most people," she said in a sassy tone. "I want to get a grip on the popular trends. If I'm getting ready to become a sexuality and sexual health expert, I need to know these things, you know."

"That's the best excuse yet. I have to watch porn for my work."

"Technically, it's for my schooling," she said haughtily, but her serious expression broke into jubilation.

He looked amused. "Well, I hope you learn something."

"Porn is entertainment," she suggested. "But that doesn't mean you can't learn anything from it, at least some kinds anyway."

"Did I hear the word 'porn'?" Anderson asked as he strolled into the room. He was wearing his work clothes, and this particular shirt had a smear of white paint across the front of his chest.

"Yeah, I'm watching it, but the internet keeps cutting in and out." She patted her laptop. "Fun research."

"I'm in and can I help?' he asked with a jovial expression. "This is one of my favorite topics."

"Have you been experiencing internet issues?" John asked with a tilt of his head.

"Nope, but I was just working out. I was using the playlist on my phone." He leaned back against the soft couch cushions and stretched his arms up. "I have to work in an hour. A client is having a party, and they want a special extra cleaning before it." He flashed a sexy grin. "But I definitely have time for porn."

John laughed. "If the internet cooperates. I'm afraid something is messed up, so I'm going to have to call a technician to come out."

"Oh, well, I'm hoping I'll be back for that." He gave Laney a knowing look. "I'd love to watch you and a tech nerd get it on."

"I'm going to call, but I'm not sure if they'll come out on a Sunday." John pointed to Laney's phone. "But you can keep up your research using your phone. I wouldn't dream of stopping you from doing that." His expression was wicked, but he seemed thrilled.

She loved how much he enjoyed teasing her, especially when it came to anything sex; she swore he loved indulging her every whim.

He smiled at her affectionately. "At least the phone should work out all right for you. I'm going to put in an order and see what happens. Maybe we'll get lucky and someone will come out today." He stood up and cleared his throat. "If not, it will be tricky to work from home tomorrow. I'll have to go in if it's not fixed by then."

He wandered into the kitchen to call, then he rejoined Laney and Anderson in the living room. They were huddled around Laney's phone with juicy smiles.

"What you got going on there?" John asked as he peered over her phone screen.

"A hot MMF threesome," she said with an excited gleam. "I would love to act this out. Think we have time?" she asked as she glanced at Anderson.

"I think so," Anderson said happily. He patted his groin. "I'm ready when you are."

"I'm always ready for that," Laney said with electricity jolting in her eyes.

John's phone buzzed, and he pulled it out of his pocket. "Well, I'll be darned. They have weekend service and a guy can come out in two hours." He smiled. "We got lucky."

"Oh, shit. I need to get going then, so I can be back for this. Hold that thought on the threesome, Laney. We'll do it, but I want to be back for this."

"Okay, I can totally understand that. Maybe after he leaves." She shrugged. "He may not be up for playing. We just never know."

"True, but I'd rather be here in case he's on board." Anderson hopped up, gave Laney a quick kiss, and zoomed out the front door.

LANEY HAD WATCHED ADULT videos for almost the full two hours while they waited for the technician. She was pretty fucking horny and ready to pounce on a cock. John had periodically joined in to watch with her, but he had tried to get online to do some work here and there without much success.

"I'd love to see how freaky you might get with the IT Tech."

She hoped the guy would be in. John had such good luck scoring dates for her, with only a few turning the fun down. Mostly, those had been married monogamous dudes who were committed to their lives the way they were, and didn't want to risk losing their wives or girlfriends. She could respect that. John himself had often said, "A place I'd never expected to land is exactly where I want to be."

The designated time window of the technician's arrival was approaching. Laney was jittery and couldn't stop moving around the house, fixing this and that, things that didn't really need attention. She had her lust bank jacked up and needed a place to exercise it. If the tech wasn't a hooking-up kind of man, no matter, once Anderson was home, the three of them could enact the video. She'd get her release and bathing of pleasure hormones one way or another. But she hoped she could get both. Why not be a greedy bitch about her own pleasure? She smiled happily.

The minutes dragged on, and finally, halfway through the time slot, he got a text. The technician was on his way. It said, "Derek will be there shortly."

"Derek, huh? Nice name," she cooed as she dashed to the front door. She peered out as if he'd appear any second.

"It will likely be a bit of time, hon," he said, a dose of amusing humility in his tone.

"Oh, I know. I just want to see him approach. Do you think he'll be in his own car or a company van? I can learn things about him at first glance if he's in his own car." Her antsy behavior had her almost jumping up and down.

"I bet it will be a company van." He stifled a guffaw. "I've seen their vehicles around town."

"True. But I can hope." She paused and stared at him. "You find this amusing, don't you?" She was aghast, but not angrily so.

"Yeah," he said in full teasing. "I kind of want to call him and tell him to take his time so I can keep watching you fidget."

She put her hands on her hips, then charged him. Landing on his lap with a thud, her body fell on him with full heaviness.

"Oof," he exclaimed as he wrapped his arms around her. "Well, I certainly like this development."

"You like teasing me?" she asked coyly, her flirtation mode consuming her like an animation. Her eyes were as lit as fire, and she became as sparkly as diamonds under the sun as he looked at her with love in his eyes.

She was magical, and he knew life with her would never be boring. He often cringed internally when he recalled how he used to treat her. He was a damn fucking moron, and he almost lost her for good. He was flat out neglectful, and verged on worse at times, and that was being generous.

Maybe that's why he was so careful not to cross the line into abuse in their new lifestyle. He finally understood she was the gold mine of his life, and he needed to protect her. There's been nothing more enlightening of what's most important than being given a second chance he hadn't really deserved. He would not waste it. But he would protect it, and maybe even end up going overboard to preserve it, but that was preferable to not valuing her, enjoying her, loving her.

He didn't want to live the rest of his life single. He'd seen so many friends spiral out of control into divorce, and mostly, it was the man's fault. Years of neglect and ignorant laziness, taking advantage of their wives, of not giving them room to be themselves, by forever manipulating them. His entire generation seemed like they were just royally fucking shit up. He needed to be progressive and not traditional because the patriarchy didn't do his marriage any fucking favors. He was set on breaking the cycle. The alternative was microwaved meals alone on the couch, watching TV shows he didn't really care about, and hearing about her new, wonderful life from family and friends. He wanted to be her new wonderful life, and damn it, he was fucking doing it.

"You shine so brightly when you're about to have sex. I love to watch you." This was what he wanted, this very look on her face, the story of passion in her eyes.

She melted against him. "Aw, when you put it that way." Her smile lingered as the doorbell rang, inciting her excitement to erupt like the light of a match.

With a quick hop, she stepped back, allowing him to rise off the couch.

He gave her a secretive look and strolled to the front door. He spied the man through the window. The man looked to be in his late thirties. He had brown hair, brown eyes, and a goatee. He wore black glasses and was shorter than John. He wasn't fat, but he wasn't thin either. He'd be what so many called 'thick' these days. At least that's what he'd see online, but usually, the word was being used for women. He had on a white button-up shirt and three pens loaded in his chest pocket, total nerd style.

John swung the door open. "Hello, come on in."

"Hi, I'm Pierce. You got the text?" He looked nervous, which added to his awkwardness.

"Yeah, we've been having issues. Not Derek, then?" John asked with a smirk. "No matter. My wife can't watch her porn because the internet keeps cutting out."

The man's jaw dropped. And his eyes widened. When John didn't retract his statement, the man's expression turned jovial, and he grinned hugely. "Well, we can't have that now, can we?"

John laughed. "Hell, no. It's the best foreplay to foreplay on the planet."

"True that," the nerdy dude said, clearly relaxing as he entered the house.

John glanced at Laney, and she was practically salivating. She had a hankering for nerdy men, which was why she liked him, of course. John didn't see this guy as competition; rather, he was a plaything for his wife.

He'd learned that giving her what she wanted paid him back a thousandfold. Other men might come and go, but he got to be with her for life. So, why on earth wouldn't he indulge her? He actually benefited the most from the union. He just needed to be there to keep her safe, but her playtime ensured she adored him. It empowered her, gave her juicy hormones, and boosted her feelings of being sexy, which again spilled over onto him daily. He got the best sex and the best Laney because of it. And she got to come like a geyser on repeat. He couldn't wait to talk with Dom Muskie and build on that, making it even better. He believed there was always room to improve.

"Where's the goods?" Pierce asked with a toothy grin aimed at Laney.

Good. John noticed Pierce staring at his wife for a prolonged moment. He found her sexy. Perfect. John watched as her glow brightened under Pierce's hungry gaze. When Laney felt sexy, things got heated fast. That was his goal. And to his relief, jealousy just wasn't a thing anymore.

"This way, in the office, is where we have the router." John led the man into the room and pointed to where the unit was located. "Like I said, her viewing got interrupted, so it's a high priority." He was joking, but serious, so he gave the man a knowing grin. "I guess I have to work too, but her pleasure is my pleasure, if you know what I mean."

He turned to face John and leaned back, a heckle growing from deep in his belly came bubbling out. "Oh, do I get it. I love a woman open to such...visual delights myself."

"So, you're enlightened as well. Good to meet another man with such views."

"My ex-girlfriend would read smutty romance novels, and damn, that woman would erupt. I just wanted to be in the spray of her eruption, ya know what I mean. And I think you do." He chuckled as he looked at his phone. "I'd buy her any damn book she wanted. She wasn't so much into films, but the books, I'd buy her bookstore gift cards and tag along to see what she chose. We started getting really kinky after that."

John wanted to ask about how she'd become his ex, but that felt too nosy. "I can imagine," John replied.

"So, this started today, and you already tried the reset?" He glanced up to meet John's eyes.

"Yup. Both the automated line way and simply unplugging it. Nothing seems to be helping."

"I'll check it. I'm sure I can fix it and she can get back to having fun," he snickered. "I'd love to be a spy on her browsing history." He looked sheepish. "Oh, I wouldn't do that. I wouldn't hack her phone." He cringed. "Sorry, that was a bit too far." He looked crushingly apologetic.

"Oh, no worries, my man. I actually have a proposition for you, after you finish." John gave him a look that he hoped would convey something of the illicit nature.

"Oy, wow. I'm not sure what that means, but you've got the prickly hairs on the back of my neck curious."

"Good. It's really juicy and involves my lovely wife."

He perked up. "You guys swingers or something?"

"She's a hotwife," John said plainly. All the clues were now on the table. Pierce just needed to take the bait.

"Oh, really, now. A hotwife, you say. That's intriguing. I'm not sure I can focus now! She's very beautiful." He smiled, and it reached his eyes.

Hook, line, and sinker. He was hooked, and all John had to do was reel him in. "She really likes servicemen who come to our house, too."

The man jolted up straight from his bent-over position, and his eyes went wide as he met John's gaze. "I'm reading you straight up, bruh. And I'd be more than down." He laughed. "Way more. Like ecstatic. Haven't enjoyed the skin of a female in ages. Not since Maggie left me." He turned somber, then turned his attention back to the router.

"Well, I'll let that marinate and let you get to work. We'll be right next door in the living room, should you need anything..." He paused. "Or be interested in partaking."

He strolled out of the office and found Laney relaxing on the couch with a mug of something.

She smiled at him, seeming like she'd possibly heard the conversation he'd had with the IT tech.

"Mushroom coffee?" he asked with a knowing grin.

"Yes, getting ready for some fun, I hope." She flashed him a saucy look as he settled on the couch beside her.

"I believe so. Pierce seems down for it, if I'm reading him correctly." He leaned back and checked his phone. He'd texted Anderson that the technician had arrived, in case he could get home and catch the action. No text back so far, so he sweetened the pot with a text of, "Hurry".

Laney scrolled through her phone, appearing to be patient, but he knew that was false. She was likely jittery and ready to pounce at the slightest sign. She didn't look bored; rather, she looked impatient. He loved this look on her, and it made him want to tease and edge her, then make her come on repeat until she was spent and limp. Then he'd massage her to sleep. He'd become that kind of man and wondered who liked it more, Laney or him.

Not long after, Anderson bounded through the door from the garage in a rush. He zoomed into the living room with an expectant look.

"I made it?" he asked as his excited look grew with a bigger grin.

"You did. Nothing yet." John pointed toward the office.

"Hi," Laney said demurely.

"Hi, sweets." Anderson grinned. "I'm so glad I didn't miss the show."

John patted her thigh.

Anderson nodded and moved so he could peek into the office. He looked back at John and nodded, giving a thumbs-up. "Gonna change quick," he muttered as he flew up the stairs. He held his phone to his ear and pointed at it, then toward the office.

Hopefully, the tech was making progress. John looked at his phone and saw it was using the home network. The guy was successful.

When Anderson returned and joined her and John on the couch, the dude came out of the office and stared at the three of them. His jaw went slack. He looked as if he wanted to speak, but he remained silent.

"All good?" John asked. He motioned to Anderson when the tech seemed paralyzed. "Pierce, this is our third. Anderson."

"Third?" Pierce repeated as a question, clearly completely dumbfounded. "What would you need me for with him around?" He guffawed as a grin began to grow on his face. "He looks way more capable than me and you combined."

All three of them began to chuckle, so the nerdy dude joined in.

"And you two are cucks? Neither of you looks the type at all." He had an aghast expression, and his motionlessness just outside the door of the office confirmed he had no idea how to proceed.

"Oh, we definitely aren't. We'll be watching and directing you. Like a peep show for us to get her hot and pleasured. Then it's our turn to claim her."

"Together," Anderson stated firmly.

The man slowly nodded. "So, to get the lay of the land here...you two are like alphas, her Doms, and she's a submissive hotwife, then."

He knew the lingo.

"Precisely. And you are the show, my fine young man. You will pleasure her at our direction, then, of course, we'll let you get yours, too." John was so matter-of-fact and confident that Pierce seemed to shrink.

"You may have too much faith in me." He seemed to cower, and his excitement dimmed.

"Oh, no. You don't need to perform. I didn't mean it like that. I meant we just get to watch. That's the deal. You get to fuck her,

Chapter 12

"I-I feel like I'm-I'm fantasizing, but this is really happening," he said in a stammer.

"Yes, that sounds about right," Anderson stated. "I felt the same way. Once."

"What do I do?" he asked as he looked across their faces.

"Come on into the living room, all the way. You can touch her tits as a start." John gave Laney a nudge off the couch and pointed to the loveseat. "Go sit there and let him play with your tits, babe. He looks quite interested."

She nodded with a seductive smile, her arousal peaked further. She gave him a come-hither motion with her hand and walked to the sofa. Her movements were a bit exaggerated, so her breasts swayed even more than usual. She loved the idea of him playing with her tits in front of John and Anderson.

"Come sit with me, Pierce." She fell to the cushions, making her breasts bounce. She patted the cushion next to her, noticing her tits were fully nipped out.

Pierce hurried to her, but he glanced back at John and Anderson.

She stuck out her chest and waited. Pierce sat next to her. When he didn't take any action, she shimmied her boobs for him. He clearly needed a bit of guidance.

"Play with my titties. All you want." Her desire was broaching brat status. He needed to touch her and now! "Touch me."

"I love boobies." He looked sheepish as a legit giggle oozed out of him. He lifted a hand and palmed her right breast like it was precious. The man legit giggled again as he bounced her boob between his fingers.

"Go on, Pierce. You have our permission to touch her all over and fuck her, so don't hold back. Do what you want." John gave Laney a stern look, and it sent a zingy course of electricity through her clit. She had to admit, she did feel safer with her men watching. This eased the sting of the past a little bit more for her.

She also loved John telling her to engage in sex stuff, and when it was with another man, the taboo feelings from years of living in a mostly monogamous world only served to charge up the act even more. What was once taboo and even dirty was now an indulgent pleasure to live through and enjoy.

Pierce migrated his forefinger, index finger, and middle finger to surround her nipple. He pinched the gathered peak of flesh and twisted the nugget between his fingers. After a minute of that, he wiggled his forefinger and middle finger quickly across the hardened flesh to tickle her.

She felt a giggle bubble out, which she knew was coming from the way he had giggled earlier. She continued to make the little mewling giggle sounds as he brought his other hand up to reach for her other breast. She quickly shifted so he had access to both nipples. He played as if he needed nothing else. He didn't seem to tire of this simple act.

"Getting hard yet, Pierce?" Laney asked, tone loaded with suggestion. She wanted cock.

"Oh, I've been hard for a long time." He grinned at her. "I really like your titties, though."

She glanced at John and Anderson, and they both looked amused. Anderson raised his eyebrows at her as he stifled his laughter. They obviously found this guy hilarious.

He was a sort of breath of fresh air compared to her other experiences with other men. She adored his almost innocent reaction to getting to play with her naked boobs. It was a bit sweet to find a man who was satisfied to slowly just play with her and not go straight to cock in her pussy. Many men she'd fucked had already had their cocks in her by this time in and he was still tit playing.

"You can take pictures, just stay lower than my face." She smiled at him.

"I can? No way. For real?" he asked as joy infiltrated his expression. He pulled out his phone when she nodded and began to take pics of her naked boobs.

"Take a video. I'll shake them for you." She shook her chest so her breasts wiggled aggressively.

He stuck out his tongue as he videoed her. He watched his phone and he kept filming even after she stopped moving, so she started up again and continued to shake and shimmy for his videoing pleasure.

"I'd pay good money for this," he stated, practically salivating.

John rose and hurried to the kitchen.

She kept shaking for him, wondering how long she'd actually have to wait for his cock. Wondering if he'd lose control when he fucked her and would ram her hard to come fast, or if he'd savor penetration like he was the titty play.

John handed Laney a jar of coconut oil. It was the one from the pantry.

She laughed and scooped out a dollop when he extended the open tub toward her. "I've never used the cooking coconut oil this way."

John nodded his head backward.

"Yeah, shake your coconuts," Pierce said as he laughed the exact way Laney expected he would, nerdy as fuck.

She smeared the oil all over her breasts, then pinched her nips. They swiftly slipped out of her pinching.

"Fuck yes." Pierce groaned, but kept filming.

She shook her shiny tits for him until he finally reached for her.

He caressed and squeezed, his fingers easily slipping around her flesh. He filmed himself fondling her. He clearly couldn't get enough footage.

She met John's eyes as she let her disbelief show.

"You know you get to fuck her, right?" John asked with sarcasm.

Laney appreciated the urging to move things along, but she was rather enjoying this dorky dude fixating on her boobs. She'd never in her life been with such a man as him, so her curiosity was piqued about how he'd progress through sex.

Pierce nodded, and his excitement soared. "Yes." But he didn't take action other than keep on playing with her tits.

Laney reached for his cock and stroked it.

He revolted backward against the couch cushion as a "Wow!" flew out of his mouth. "Holy shit!"

"You're hard," Laney said in a low, seductive tone. "Very, very hard, Pierce. And I can't wait to feel your cock sliding in and out of me. When will you fuck me?"

He looked shocked as she kept touching his groin with force. He sat up, and the movement made her hand move off his erection. "Could I...could I titty fuck you first?" He asked it like he thought she'd refuse his request.

"Yes, I'd love that. The coconut oil will make it really good for you."

"And you?" he asked with a sharp look her way.

Laney nodded. She looked at Anderson as John walked back to the couch. She wondered if her men were bored with his leisurely actions, but they both still looked quite amused rather than annoyed. He was a lame showman compared to the other hookups thus far. Laney would definitely not forget this man, though, he was so awkward and appreciative of the smallest gestures that her heart softened for him. He seemed to really care, which was inciting an urge to pamper him. His savoring was a total one-eighty from the aggressive way most play date repairmen had taken her so far. And the complete opposite of the window guy. She assumed this guy would overall be a better lover, despite seeming like a bit of a novice with sex.

Pierce set his phone down and stood up. He glanced at John and Anderson before pulling down his pants. He looked nervous as he unveiled his cock. It swung out and was a bit longer than Laney had expected. He had a long, thin cock that curved slightly to the left. She instantly wanted it. It didn't matter how; she just wanted it.

She smashed her tits together in titty fucking style and gave him her most interested look. "Slide him right in." She leaned forward slightly. Her clit revved up as he took a step closer to her. "Screw my chest."

Titty fucking didn't feel physically good; it was all mental. She loved giving herself to his pleasure. His lewd appreciation of riding her breasts to get off would be what ultimately fed her arousal more than any part of the actual titty fucking touches.

His grin went from chivalrous to licentious as he held his cock before her mashed-together boobs. He lined up his cock at the bottom crevice and slid his dick in between her fleshy orbs. Once his cock had slid to the top and was peeking out of her cleavage, he grasped her shoulders and began to pump himself in and out. He grunted and groaned as he thrust himself.

This set her off, and her kink of getting used was getting its feed. He fucked her tits hard, making her body rock, and she got her fix. She leaned down to try to lick him, getting her tongue to graze his tip every now and then.

She was surprised he hadn't come already.

His face fell into ecstasy as he went faster. Now that his pants and underwear had slipped down, Laney observed that her men were staring at his bare ass. This almost made her laugh as neither of them tolerated seeing male ass very well. They'd have to suffer through it.

He quickly pulled out of her with a look of shock on his face. "Whew! I'd better take a break or we're done here." He heckled himself as his oiled cock bobbed.

It was impossible to ignore; her eyes were glued. "What now?" she asked when he didn't move a muscle.

His grin deepened as he pushed his hands together, about hip width apart, and thrust his pelvis.

"Insert my hips? Between?" She laughed at his innocent portrayal of fucking and released her boobs. They swung down into place.

"Oh, fuck. I could never get enough of your breasts. Ever." He shook his head slightly.

Ah, so no doubts about it, he's got quite the affinity for breasts. She smiled at him. "How do you want me?" She liked offering herself up, even after John and Anderson had given their permission to share her. It was juice to her feelings of empowerment, confirming her choice in doing this act.

"Missionary first. So I can play with your tits while I'm in you." He looked hungry for it.

"Absolutely," she said as she slid to the floor. She glanced at John and Anderson, and again was amused by their continued interest in such a slow-moving interaction. This repairman would certainly go down in the books as the most unusual thus far. She'd been toying with the idea of writing down the story of each connection to someday make a memoir, but she was also getting too many ideas with the cookbook plan and considering the sex educator certification. But she also had a fair amount of time, even after all the stuff she did to care for the house and her men. So, the seed might grow into something. It might be amazing.

She settled on the floor, and he grabbed a pillow, handing it to her as he grinned. "For your head, while mine is in you."

She released a curt laugh as the phrase 'thinking with your dick' ran through her head. He had a sense of humor, which she thoroughly enjoyed. A slow-moving, savoring, jovial, horny nerd, and he was no less entertaining than the raging bull types.

She made a deliberate display of opening her legs for him.

He settled between her, but moved to mouth her nipples rather than penetrate her.

She twisted her head in pleasure as he manipulated one nipple with his mouth and the other with his hand.

Before long, though, he was thrusting his cock against her pussy. An open pussy in front of a man was just too irresistible to stay ignored for any significant length of time. The oil was still nicely coated on him, so he slid up and down her closed lower lips and mound quite nicely.

She grasped his arms as he suckled her, twisting her head and moaning to tell him he was doing a damn good job of arousing her. Nipple play for this much time was not something she'd experienced a whole lot of. Most men wanted their cock attended to more, either with her mouth or inside her. He was again a refreshing change.

After a few minutes, he grabbed his engorged cock and threaded it between her lips, easily parting them. He pressed himself against her slit and coasted right in. He thrust with increasing power, but slowed after a short time to suck her titties again. Like a true addict, he had to come back.

He groaned like they were the best-tasting tits he'd ever had.

She stifled a grin, but then let it flare big as he gazed at her, licking his tongue all along the wrinkled nipples. She bet this man might have a milk fetish, too. That was something she'd thought about trying, and a breast pump would get her there. She had half a mind to try it. Never having given birth herself, she'd never breastfed.

But she also knew milk production wasn't about birth as much as it was about the sucking stimulation of milk production in women. She vowed to try this someday. If she tried that, she'd need to save this man's card and call him back for a titty call.

He slowly pumped himself into her body as he leisurely mouthed her nipple. He seemed content to suck while he gently fucked her.

His constant nipple stimulation had her moaning, the arousal overwhelming, though now and then it tipped into irritation. She wanted more clit stimulation, but calmed herself with the idea that this was a new sexual experience and she could learn more about her body from it. The undulations of her hunger to climax were edging her, and she was getting ready to beg. She cooled her jets as he moved to her other nipple, while his cock was gently entering and exiting her. He had his full focused attention on her nips, as if his cock in her was almost an afterthought. She could exercise her patience, with some extra effort, though she wanted to scream.

He lifted off her, allowing her to slip from his suckling. Though, he looked very happy and satiated, and she smiled. He leaned down and brought his mouth close to hers.

"Taste you this way now," he murmured.

They fell into a deep kiss, their embrace tightening as he paused his entry into her body. This man was a savorer, and he was so lovely. He was just naturally edging her with how he took his time. She was used to the men who got lost in their own pleasure and got wild and primal immediately. Both John and Anderson had a mix of this approach, depending on their mood. She had mistakenly thought this guy would lose control and ram her, then come in like one minute of being inside her. She was oh so deliciously wrong. One thing was for sure: premature ejaculation was not sexy and made for bad sex, unless a toy was handy or the man had skills.

He was the kind of lover who put the 'love' in fucking. She loved all variations of men, and she knew Anderson and John would be ravenous for her after he left, and aggressively fuck her, so this was a rare form of bliss she hadn't expected.

When he finally broke their kiss, he placed his hands on either side of her shoulder and stared into her eyes.

"I read that women need their clit touched to come. How can I do that to your pleasing?" He became sheepish, like he was hiding a secret. "I'm kind of a sex nerd. I've read lots about it."

This didn't surprise her one bit. "I like strong direct contact. I can come with penetration if you angle it up right to hit my clit, or press it with your fingers. Or I can use a toy or my own fingers in doggy." She gave him a sly smile. "However you want to mount me, Pierce, I will love it."

He liked that word and repeated it. "Mount."

"Yes," she purred. "Mount me, Pierce. I want you to." She paused and gave him a pointed, seductive look. "Mount me, Pierce. I need you to." The repetition of the word had gotten her even more wanton.

"You'd be okay with doggy?" he asked with a bit of surprise in his voice.

"I love doggy," she said quickly.

"Wow. I thought most women didn't."

"Not true. But it is true almost all women need the right stimulation of their clitoris to climax."

"I'd love to do doggy." He looked a bit giddy.

She instantly wanted to give him his fantasy, so she slid backward and quickly got on all fours. Then she looked back at him and said with gumption, "Now fuck me, Pierce. Fuck me good and hard. Feel me wrapped around you and respond. Get primal."

He grunted but met her gaze. He still looked a bit surprised.

John cleared his throat. "Pierce, let me tell you something. You can't hurt her by fucking her. She wants this, she's likely wet as fuck, and she likes to be slammed." He paused and hunched forward over his knees. "We'll be watching and stop you if we see something that warrants it. We know her well, so don't worry about going too far." He claps his hands, then swipes his palms. "Plus, she can stop you. What's your safeword for Pierce, babe?"

She pondered for a moment, unsure. Then she spotted a lost sock under the TV stand, and it triggered her word. "Shoe."

"There you have it. Fuck her like a beast and only stop if we stop you or she says 'shoe', otherwise let loose and do what you want. I guarantee she will like it."

Laney watched him as his face showed he was processing what John said.

"She really likes doggy," Anderson piped in. "She likes being dominated, Pierce. Let your testosterone and what you feel guide you."

He nodded his understanding and gripped her hips with force. Readying to enter her, he gripped her hips even firmer and scooted in place. He hovered above her, then straightened.

"Her climax, though?" he asked with concern.

"Have her be head down, ass up." John moved his hand. "Like in porn. Give her the command, then push her head down. Tell her to get her clit."

"Ah, I see. She can then reach. Got it." He grumbled something incoherent, then stated clearly, "Laney. Head down, ass up. I'm going to fuck you." He sounded a bit robotic, but still stern.

He placed his hand on the back of her head and pushed it to the ground. She allowed his press. He pushed his cock at her opening and entered. His groan as he spread her open was gargantuan. The grip of his palms and the sharpness of his nails digging into her flesh had her pinned in place. With one arm in front of her on the floor as her brace, and the other rubbing her clit, he began to ride her roughly, each thrust driving him deeper inside.

He grunted loudly like he couldn't stop it, which kept peppering in as accents between the skin smacks and her moans. He rocked her body ferociously, and gone was the gentle dweeb. He became a stallion. He snagged his aggression, and he hammered into her at such a fast pace, she feared he'd come soon, and it would all be over.

But he persisted and kept up his animalistic persona, fucking her as hard, if not even harder, than the college fence painters had. That had by far been the most aggressive play date she'd had. Pierce was proving to be the most interesting.

She grunted as she played with herself, and soon she was edging over that climactic hill and getting hers. Like falling into warm water, she launched, and her internal walls squeezed him inside her.

"Fuck," he muttered. "I'm gonna." His sounds grew more urgent, and his hips were moving with more power. Soon, he was pounding her forward across the carpet.

She figured he'd cream inside her any second, but he kept on going. It suddenly occurred to her that he had no condom on, but she figured she was safe. He clearly didn't have sex much. It was a rare occurrence when both John and Anderson were okay with such a thing, but she was grateful for it. They weren't objecting, so she was cool with it.

"Yeah, dick her down, Pierce. There you go. Nice job. Keep going," John coached from his new position of just mere feet away.

This new development was hot. It turned her on immensely to have John so close and urging Pierce on to fuck her harder.

Pierce grunted in a deep-seated growl and slammed into her even harder, inching her closer to the TV stand with each pound.

"Yeah, man. Keep it up. A nice finish, now." John moved forward and motioned with his hands. "Give it to her good. Fuck that pussy. Make it yours. You own this bitch. Get yours, get it now. Make her head hit this stand."

John got off on edging her and making her come, and the way he was acting with Pierce almost felt the same way. It was interesting that he'd take on that role with another man fucking her. She couldn't wait to ask him about it later.

"Yeah, fuck, yeah. Take my cock, ungh," he said in a relishing voice as his thrusts pushed her along the carpet. Then his groan sounded guttural as he brought his climax home. He creampied her, mere inches from her head, hitting the wood.

She felt the extra wetness inside her and wondered why John had let him come in her. He must have gotten the same impression. Perhaps he thought Pierce was such a novice that he couldn't possibly have any diseases. Risky, but she could understand why he might have assumed Pierce was clean. She got tested every few weeks, just like an adult film star, even though they often used condoms. Anderson had started the same after he'd started hooking up with Darcy. Only John didn't get tested.

Pierce fell upon her back as his heavy breathing kept raging on. "Oh, shit, that was incredible. Utterly mind-blowing. And a workout," he said with a laugh.

His cock fell out of Laney like a wet noodle in water.

They both collapsed to the carpet, panting like they'd run.

"Was so fucking good, Pierce. Thank you," Laney said demurely. "You really got me good."

"Ha! I'm the one who needs to thank you. That was the best ever. I had no idea."

She curled up on her side as she peered at him. "Pierce, when did you break up with Maggie? You weren't a virgin, were you?" She couldn't help but wonder because he bill fit.

"It's been quite some time, but no, we had sex. But I was a terrible lover. I suspect one of the reasons she left me. I came so fast, it was embarrassing. But now I have learned some techniques. I studied up on everything." He grinned as his breathing rate slowed. "I don't do anything half ass. I did my homework."

So, he was very inexperienced, just as she had suspected. But he did a damn good job of pleasing her despite that.

"I can't thank you enough. I kind of feel like I could maybe ask someone out again after that." He snickered as he traced the curve of her bare thigh. "You really did me some good today."

That made her very happy. Boosting his confidence had been an honor, plus she'd enjoyed a hefty, strong orgasm, too. Perfection.

"You've made my entire year. Entire five years."

Laney couldn't help but wonder if Maggie was an old high school girlfriend, but she decided not to pry by asking. It didn't matter, anyway. She'd given him pleasure, confidence, and a great memory in addition to getting off herself. Plus, she got to watch a new side of both John and Anderson, taking Pierce under their wings and guiding him through how to please and fuck her. Another successful play date was in the books, and she enjoyed the easygoing air in the room.

"When you said that what I'd do wouldn't hurt her, that helped. I think if I had hurt her, I'd have lost my erection. I wouldn't ever want to harm her." Pierce was a sweet man, and he deserved a good, caring girlfriend. His eyes were kind and full of warmhearted intent, the perfect aftercare from him in this situation.

"You're a good man, Pierce," Laney said. "I hope you find a new girlfriend. And now you have some ideas about how to try to please her. But remember, you must always talk about sex before and after. Only then will it be the best it can be for both of you."

He nodded. "Well, I see the time. I'd better put this tool away and get out of here before I'm late to my next appointment." He laughed heartily. "I guarantee it will be nothing like this call was."

He stood and pulled up his pants, securing the snap and tugging up the zipper of his jeans.

"Laney, it was my pleasure. I won't ever forget you." He shook his phone. "And I have the pics to have fun with to prove it."

"I enjoyed being your slut, Pierce." She writhed on the carpet, moving to her tummy and popping her ass up as she spoke.

His mouth dropped into a big O, and he chuckled, shaking his belly a bit as he rumbled. "Hadn't thought of it that way." He sighed. "Damn. Can I take a pic of you like that? Do you mind?"

"Go for it," she said, giving him her best bedroom look. "And you can include my face." The man seemed harmless enough to allow this.

He took several photos and then walked toward the door. "Call me again, anytime." He paused and turned. "Even if you don't have a problem, I'll come be your slut tamer again." He laughed gleefully at himself as he waved at Anderson on his way to the front door.

He saw himself out as John called, "I have your card and I've made a note on it. Have a great day, son."

He pulled the front door shut.

Anderson chuckled and said, "Slut tamer."

"I know, right?" John asked with a laugh.

Pierce left, and Laney's lust seethed. She couldn't wait for her men to get their hands on her, their dicks in her, and their masculine energy claiming her. She was ready to come so much she'd be doped up. The day could get even better, and she knew it would by the looks on both her men's faces. They were cocked and ready to launch her into their own pound town.

Chapter 13

"Well, that was the most interesting one yet," John said as he watched Pierce out the front window.

"I honestly kept glancing at you, wondering if you were bored," she asked with humor. "He was so slow-moving compared to most."

"Right, he really was. But he was sort of innocent. Like he was treating you as precious, and I liked that a lot." Anderson peered at her with a happy grin. "Because that's exactly what you are."

"Yeah, I agree. He clearly appreciated being with you. It wasn't just a quick getting off for him." John sauntered back into the room. "I can appreciate both ways, though," he said with a lewd grin.

Anderson stood, and Laney loved the solidarity aura of both men standing there. They were coming for her, and she had a strong inkling that they were going to claim her damn good and hard. She liked being claimed. It confirmed that she was theirs, which was how she wanted it. Sure, she got shared, but that was just for the experience, for fun, and for her to get off. What they did with her, for her, to her, that was the meat of their relationship. It fed all three of them.

"He was definitely nerdy, but in a hot kind of way. I love that he admitted to nerding out over reading about sex. A man who does that is very sexy in my book."

John whips out his phone with a determined, and jovial, expression. "Time to buy more how-to sex books!"

"I'll always second that," Anderson said in a rush. "But how about we practice how to fuck Laney first?"

"Oh, count me in," she shimmied her shoulders, which made her boobs shake.

"You've got me hypnotized by those hard shiny nips." Anderson laughed. "I feel kind of like Pierce!"

"I know, right? He was almost like examining me, but he was clearly turned on. Never in my life have I had tit sucking to that level. It actually really aroused me to have that much nipple stimulation. I was honestly rather surprised by how much." She shrugged. "Who knew?"

"Noted," John said as he took a few quick steps toward her. "Now about that video. Can you find it again? We can act it out."

She nodded quickly. "I saved it. So, yeah, I'm ready to get railed by you two." She tapped into her phone as her arousal ramped up. It only took a look from one of her men to skyrocket her lust. She was not easy; she was erotically aware. "I love the part where she's bent over the sawhorse in the living room. I always thought that was a hot, raunchy thing to do, but I imagine in real life, it just hurts." She laughed. "Another instance where the fantasy of it is way better than a thin board piercing your belly as someone slams into your backside. It kind of seems like one-sided pleasure."

"But you like that," John teased as he pulled her to stand.

"Oh, do I?" she fired back. "Get yours, I get mine."

"Always," he pulled her into a deep French kiss as Anderson slid in behind her.

She broke their kiss and propped up her phone on the TV tray so all three of them could see it. In the video, the older man was holding his hard cock in his hand, and the younger man behind the woman had a white knuckled grip on her hips. He roughly bent her over, so her face fell even with the older man's cock. He caught her and guided her mouth to his cock. What had turned Laney on watching it was how the man behind didn't immediately penetrate the woman from behind, but held her in place and then pumped her body, assisting with the rough blow job, essentially helping the older man use her mouth to get off. She became a tool before she was brought to climax. Then he spanked her for giving a poor blow job as she scrambled to do better. The final scene had Laney drooling, though, and she couldn't wait for her men to see it and try it out. The secret truth she harbored was that she'd watched this video umpteen times during solo play, and she had always come super hard. She was surging into her getting-used kink pretty heavily lately and was unsure how to navigate it, so she didn't cross over into the dark area of that. Wanting something dark playfully was a lot different from being forced to live in that darkness. Fantasy didn't have to have a real-life component.

Anderson dug his fingers into her flesh, taking a moment to rub his hard erection against her buttocks. Then, he began to push her whole body onto John's groin, her face coming nearer and nearer to John's hard cock. His firm grip was a solid reminder of how powerful he was. She'd learned long ago that she could either hate men for being the stronger sex or she could pick the right men to be vulnerable to. His strength terrified and fascinated her at once, but he was a stellar lover, man, and supporter of her.

She resisted opening her mouth for John until Anderson spanked her butt. "Open and suck, little wench."

She grinned, but obeyed as a devilish notion began birthing in her. What if she kept refusing just to see what he'd do? She curbed the notion for now, but tucked it away for the future. She really wanted John's cock in her mouth. He'd been waiting all that time, but Pierce took an eternity to taste her. Many times, she delighted in giving John exactly what he desired. Anderson too. Hell, many men, for that matter.

The grunting and choking sounds on the video were turning her on as John held her head firmly between his palms as he face fucked her. He was horny, and it surfaced as aggression. There was no question about it. If she weren't so sexual, she often wondered if her men would be too much for her, but instead, she thrived in their hefty libidos, and hers was enlarged from it. She marveled at how safe she felt, despite the whole spanking ordeal. She still needed to sort that out in her brain, too. There was a growing awareness in her that she didn't hate or feel disdain toward masculinity, but she needed to feel safe in it. Life was going on, day by day, but what happened still flitted into and out of her thoughts.

Their ministrations on her body pulled her into the present and out of her head, thankfully. She wanted to think about cock right now. She wanted to tell him to take her by the throat, but she couldn't even imagine speaking. That was impossible.

The actors in the film switched to spit roasting, so Anderson followed suit and penetrated her. She was sad that the first part was done so quickly, but figured there was more fun in copying the show scene by scene live than there was in keeping that part up. Plus, she wasn't a fan of gagging for very long, if at all.

The sound of Anderson's body banging against hers mixed with her gagging was atrocious. She loved the extremity of it and shuddered slightly as her arousal was peaking. Her loss of control at their domination sent her flying, and she fell off John's cock, his cock sliding down her chin. He still held her head as Anderson pumped himself into her like a sex starved man rooting his meat hard enough to come as fast as possible. If she'd ever enjoyed a breeding kink scene, it was when another man was holding her to take another man's hard cock and seed.

Anderson's thighs clapping the backs of hers made her face mash against John's balls.

John grunted as he rubbed his wet cock on her face.

They were losing their cadence with the film, but even the sounds of the threesome spewing from her phone were enough to stoke her climax. She was getting closer, and this time it wasn't from clit stimulation, which was rare for her.

"Fuck," muttered Anderson as he fucked her even harder. He was slipping into his beast mode, bending her body downward in preparation for his complete obliteration of her.

John followed smoothly and dropped to his knees, making a landing pad for her head.

Anderson shoved her head down onto John's lap, where John caught her and securely held her head in place.

The aroma of John's groin filled her nostrils as her face was crushed to his hard-on, pinned between his palms and thighs. Her nose was pressed to John's firm skin, and it was getting bent as Anderson rammed her. This was a new definition for being face fucked.

He grunted, then growled, then forcefully fed his cock into her so deep she cried out. He kept engaging her clit from the blows, perhaps from how hard he was hitting, and she twitched. Her climax stole her breath and voice as she exalted into the sheer peak of it.

Anderson blew out a loud breath and made a sound he often makes when he comes.

The wetness inside Laney increased, even though Anderson stayed hard enough that he kept entering her body, she knew he'd released.

Anderson gripped her hips and slid backward out of her. "Want a repeat?"

"Yeah. I want my whore's cunt wrapped around my cock like a whore sack."

She almost laughed at that one, but grinned instead. Her face felt slightly damp as Anderson spun her, so her ass faced John.

"Pump her as I kneel. We've never tried this."

Laney was certainly game to try. She'd long ago given up worrying what her body looked like in different positions, and she'd learned to hone her focus on just what she was feeling. It had freed her up to really be in her body in the moment and feel the lusciousness to the max.

She was a whore sack, and she wanted Anderson to use her on John's cock. The dirty label made it sound like her pussy was loose and slack, when in reality her internal muscles were firm and fit from so much cock and toy action. Society had it wrong; lots of penetration made the muscles stronger, not looser. Another BS theory from the patriarchy.

She mused that it would be hard for her to bounce positioned like this over John's lap, so she planned on relying on Anderson's strength to make this happen. She could squeeze her vaginal muscles around John's cock to help with constriction, but she didn't think she could bounce on him from this position. This was a three-person job.

She grinned seductively. She liked positions that required three.

Anderson smiled back and gripped her hard beneath the armpits. His grip was almost too much to tolerate. She felt John's cock tip press at her nether lips, wet and throbbing at the ready for his entrance into her. She stifled her wince as Anderson began to pump her on John's cock. His grip was a bit much, but she so desperately wanted to try the position that she kept her protesting silent. She'd tough it out just to experience this.

John had a grip on her hips and was helping with the motion of her body to milk his cock. He grunted as Anderson used her body on him. They got in a rhythm that matched, as Anderson pushed her down, John tugged her hips down, then they coordinated vice versa. It was a complex sex dance that was both erotic and kinky enough to bring her closer to her own apex again.

John's sounds helped quite a bit to egg her on forward, closer to her high.

"Squeeze him, Laney," Anderson coached. "Take his cock deep. Let him sink all the way in."

She almost laughed. She didn't have that much control, but she'd squeeze as best as she could. His cock sliding along her wet walls was a sure thing. She couldn't have stopped it in this position even if she tried the hardest. They had her pinned.

She couldn't not get royally used like this, which made it hotter. When the fill meets the wet open hole, it's going in. That's just physics, babe.

His hard cock speared her like a missile until he grunted, then curved slightly around her, his fingers digging into her hips even harder.

He was coming inside her. He quickly reached around and rubbed her clit aggressively. Within thirty seconds, she was climaxing. Her body twitched and she shuddered, her breasts bobbing as she moved. She moaned out her pleasure in a whimpering display.

When things settled, she sighed. "Mmmm. Oh, I liked that," she cooed.

"As did I," John said, rubbing her back. "Loved trying something new."

"We kind of lost our vibe with copying the video," she said, though she didn't regret that for a second. "I loved our version of what happened, though. That was hot!"

"Damn right it was," Anderson said. His cock bobbed as he moved. He was still hard.

She rubbed her right armpit. "But that grip of yours, Anderson. Whew! That's going to leave a mark!" She laughed with glee.

"Yeah, I was a bit worried about that, but it was the only way I could get a grip on you." He gently touched her arm. "Hopefully it wasn't too much."

"No. I'm fine. I would have safe worded if it had been." She could take a little roughing up for them all to get off.

"It worked best when we worked together, you pushing her down with me, and me pushing her up as you pulled. I could tell we both got in the groove, and it worked out well," John said as he leaned back against the couch.

"Yeah, I tried to work with you where your leverage was strongest, tugging her up and down. I think we created something new." Anderson made a silly face. "Though that might be wishful thinking."

"I kind of felt like a sex doll," she said with a snicker.

"A sex doll that came, too," John said with a raise of his eyebrow.

"Indeed. It was good. I thoroughly enjoyed it." She settled next to him, then Anderson sidled up alongside her so she was in the middle of the sandwich. "I've been claimed."

"Yes, you have. And rightly so. And sorry about so much gagging." John looked apologetic.

She feigned fainting, closing her eyes and draping her hand over her eyes. "I may never recover," she joked.

"Now, I don't believe that for a second," John teased. "But, it reminds me. We really need to choose a better, safer nonverbal word. You hitting my arm or leg is a good one, but you've gotten worked up and done that, and I've questioned if you were just expressing the intensity or trying to stop me."

"Yeah, that is kind of a gray one. I like the one-hand clapping one." She demonstrated by tapping her fingers rapidly on the fleshy pad beneath her thumb.

"Right, that's true, as long as your hand is free," Anderson stated with a hint of doubt.

"Maybe a backup one then? If my hands are...otherwise taken up, or something." She bit her lip. "Yeah, or what if you can't see my hand?"

"We need several signs, I guess. But watching you is the best one." John glanced at the clock.

"Only one thing left to do next. Eat. I'm starving. You two?" Laney asked.

"I'm definitely hungry. How about we order in? That way we can all chill?" John grabbed for his phone.

"Mexican," Laney said quickly.

"Perfect."

Chapter 14

L aney liked September, before it turned into October. October was okay for a bit before it got old, kind of like winter, but it just took too long to be done. She missed the hot days, the endless swimming in the pool, and the warmth of the sun on her mostly nude, and sometimes totally nude, body.

October had its good parts, but she hated to see plants shrivel and turn into crispy wisps. The parts she loved about October were warm mugs of yummy drinks, the fireplace flickering, and all the fall food. She really adored the fall food. Working on her cookbook had taken priority since the sex coach certification she signed up for wouldn't start until January. She'd missed the deadline for the fall session. No matter. She had a lot of time to occupy herself with the cookbook. And honestly, this was a better setup. She could really focus on the book before she started studying. Plus, she still had reading to do around the topic before classes started. Her favorite book so far was about living in the lifestyle, and it was helping not only calm her, but it was a sounding board for her fears. It gave her perspective. All good things. But what she really wanted was time to chat with Darcy.

Muskie and Darcy had gone on a last-minute month-long vacation to Europe starting in August, so their get-together had gotten delayed. This year, October was promising to be interesting because, since they'd be back in town, they could finally meet. The trip to Europe had been a total whim, so that had delayed getting together, which had royally sucked. It was a total bummer, but that was okay. It would happen. It had also meant Anderson was extra horny with Darcy out of town. Laney liked that part a lot. A lot, a lot. She and Anderson had sex in the mornings when John started working, then in the afternoons, when John sometimes joined them, and then before bed when John always joined them. It was a lot of sex. And she was very happy about it. She was a lucky woman. With a healthy sexual appetite, she could be called a nympho by some, but she was addicted to the pleasure and the connection, so nothing negative could tarnish her view of it. And why was being called a *nympho* a bad thing anyway? Some might say moderation is for the best; well, they didn't have the orgasms Laney did. So they could shut it.

She was healthy with her nice, big, fat, juicy libido. Perpetual orgasmic bliss was about the best existence she could think of, so all the negative losers could go and enjoy their miserable orgasm-less lives. She was seeking the good stuff. That's what life was about. That, and pumpkin bread.

She smiled as she took the loaf out of the oven. It was picture perfect. Which was a good thing because she had her scene all set up on the deck table for the cookbook. She'd made this recipe at least one hundred times across her life. It had been her mother's recipe, so it wasn't one she developed. But she wanted the top to look just right for the pictures, so this was her fourth attempt at the bread in two days. This was the one she was convinced would be good enough for a picture in the book. The natural light was right, which she'd planned to time precisely to be done when the sun rays hit the stone table with the ideal brightness. Either a bit of clouds or later in the afternoon seemed to be the best conditions, too. It was four, and soon she'd start dinner, so she had just enough time to let it cool before she had to photograph it.

The audiobook she was also listening to droned on in her ears. It was one of four books she was engrossed in, and this one made her smile as she often shook her head in agreement. There were lots of negative people in the world, and many wanted to strip rights from others just because they were different. She knew being a sex and relationship coach would be a challenge if she ever dealt with such people, but she also knew closed-off people weren't likely to be the ones seeking such help. They'd avoid help, so she hoped it wouldn't be too painful. But time would tell.

She tweaked her scene one more time as she waited for the right time to slice the bread. When it seemed ideally cooled off, she cut a slice. It came out stellar, so she placed it on a plate and carried both the loaf and the slice on a tray to the deck. She moved the bread and loaf around, then checked the settings on her camera. After a few tweaks, she started to take snap shots.

She took way too many. But that was necessary because it was often hard to tell which would turn out fantastic and which would just be mediocre. Since it was such an ordeal to find the right light, the perfect time of year for the weather to be ideal, and then to get the prepared food to be done on time and looking delicious, it was all a series of magic tricks. She snapped away and then shifted the food, changed her angle, and by the time she was done, she had over one hundred and five photos of pumpkin bread.

She laughed at herself as she kept scrolling through them in the shadow of the house. Direct sunlight made examining the photos on the camera impossible. She saw several that would work, so she was pleased.

She looked up and smiled. Both of her men were staring at her through the sliding glass door. Geez. How long was she taking pics for them to stand there like that? She waved and then walked toward the door.

They opened it.

"I love to watch you work," John said with a proud grin.

"That looks perfect. When do we get some?" Anderson also wore a proud expression.

That was the thing. They always wanted to eat what she made, but she had to make them wait until she had the right pictures for her book.

"Now you can eat, yes. I got enough pics. Too many, really," she said with a dismissive laugh. "Well, not really. You can't ever have too many."

Anderson walked onto the deck and claimed the cut piece of bread. He devoured it instantly with a huge moan. "More," he said over a full mouth.

Laney snatched the loaf and brought it inside. "Mom's recipe never fails."

The men followed her to the counter, and she smirked at them.

She giggled, then said, "I have puppy dogs following me."

She cut more slices and held the cutting board out toward them. They each took two slices, and she pointed to the soft butter on the counter.

"I love seeing you creating like this. You're such a good cook, so this is perfect for you." John polished off his first slice. "It makes me horny to watch you."

Laney gave him a saucy grin. "Oh, really, now."

"Same," Anderson repeated, finishing up his second, then third piece. He was easily lapping John's efforts with how many slices he was consuming at a rapid pace. Then, with a smile, he reached for another.

"You two going to eat dinner?" she asked in a tease.

"Yes," Anderson stated. "I'm famished. It was a hard-working day for me. What are we having?"

Laney shrugged. "I have to figure that out yet. We have options."

"Maybe a simple spaghetti meal?" Anderson suggested. He grinned broadly. "Something fast. Easy. Good."

"Ah, got it," she said with a laugh. "That works."

She set down the cutting board and pulled out the large pot. She carried it to the sink and set it down to fill it with water. As the water rushed in, John cuddled her from behind. He caressed her belly as he danced behind her, pressing his full body to her backside. Best of all, he had a turgid cock, which he ground against her.

"Oh, you are turned on. How am I going to make spaghetti with that cock pressed to me? It's quite the distraction. I might lose my mind and start to fuck you." She smiled as she looked out the window. Fall was making herself known with some of the trees turning already. It seemed too early, but it had been a fantastic summer. It would be her first full winter as a hotwife this year, and she was looking forward to all that it entailed.

"I think I can make you come before the water boils. Then I'll come while it's cooking."

She laughed. "Great plan, and perhaps a worthy challenge, but what about preparing the rest of the meal?"

"I'm game," Anderson piped up. "John didn't get to play today, and we did, so you too do your thing and then let him eat you out on the table. My only request is that I can hear and see you two."

"Deal," Laney said as her arousal began to stand up tall and proud. This was a scrumptious development to her day.

She turned on the burner and swiveled to face her husband. "My husband is a bit impatient." She gave him a flirty look with the raise of her left eyebrow. "Which is exactly how I like him. Hot, horny, and passionate."

"Oh, I'm coming in hot and horny. Might get a bit rough. Gonna fuck you hard." John guided her toward the table, and Anderson slid into the spot they vacated in front of the oven, manning his station. John's expression was ready and wanton, and quite determined.

John began to peel off her clothes with a salacious glint in his eyes.

The perks of their throuple situation never ceased to amaze her. All three of them were so happy fucking, eating good food, and their finances combined were off the charts, and she hadn't even started selling her cookbooks yet. She couldn't imagine why anyone would not want this type of life arrangement; it was making her life oh so good. Her men got as much sex as they wanted, as did she. Orgasms flowed for all three.

Sure, they had their shit to figure out still, but she was happy. And that was not something she saw coming after all those years of resentment and discontent with her marriage to John. She had to wonder if that negative history was impacting her acceptance of him on some levels, however. She admitted to herself that she was more open to Anderson doing some kinky things to her than John, and John had been her husband for several decades.

It really should be the other way around, but emotions don't fucking follow logic, for fuck's sake. This was something she needed to work out, and she knew only time and healing would dictate for her how much she was willing to put of herself into their new lifestyle. This was something she was avoiding talking about with John. He'd likely be hurt, and she didn't want to hurt him. He had changed so much that he was almost unrecognizable to his old self, so she didn't want him to feel like none of that counted. It totally did. But history is history, and it all impacts their lives now, whether they like it or not.

But they'd come so far, she hated to focus on such bad things. She wanted to dwell on the positives they had grown into. And their life with Anderson was manifesting as some of her dreams coming true. She was getting to fuck men, exploring and satiating her kinks, not to mention her men's kinks, well, mostly anyway, and she felt loved and appreciated, even prioritized. Who was she now anyhow? Life had taken on a surreal dimension she wouldn't have seen coming if she'd wished on it for a million years. She certainly didn't want to fuck it up.

John swept her off her feet, bringing her out of her deep thoughts. It was arousing to think of John fucking her while Anderson watched. Her desire for exhibitionism even infiltrated the three of them in their private fun. Anderson's taking over and making dinner were also very hot. All her life, she'd falsely believed being the doer, the over-the-top caretaker, was the way to be; now she knew the truth, that being pampered by a caretaker, especially one she was fucking, was the sexiest of all. She'd offer him some extra sexual pleasure after dinner, if he wanted it. She almost laughed. He's never ever declined anything sexual, quite the opposite.

John had more recently learned some caretaking skills from Laney, too. And it made him so much sexier; it was unreal. She'd been so independent before that she'd missed the boat on accepting any caretaking he offered in the first decade of their marriage because she saw herself as strong. She could do it, so she did. Well, that just trained John to stop offering, and suddenly, she was the sole caretaker of them both, and she was losing out big time, as she had begun to lose herself.

She gazed at John. His expression was so good, it alone was arousing her. He looked steadfast and urgent. She adored it when he got this certain zest in his eyes. He wanted her, and he wasn't hiding anything.

"I'm going to make you come so hard, you will shudder and squeak. My hand up your pussy, you'll be my orgasmic puppet."

She chuckled. "Well, there's an image," she joked with a smirk. "Fisting? No thanks, but I like the orgasmic part." In truth, she loved when he did orgasm control on her, but 'puppet' was not exactly a sexy word.

He laughed along. "How about my orgasmic pet, then?"

"Better," she said as he slid her onto the table. "Right here, right now. Huh?"

He met her gaze directly while nodding exaggeratedly, passion ablaze in his eyes. "Right here, right now," he said with pure confidence. "I mean, after all, you're naked."

His demeanor was commanding and expectant, and it was hot.

"Take me, I'm yours," she said, a phrase she now took great pleasure in repeating. She always loved it when he wanted her naked, yet he was still clothed. Maybe she'd get a cock out only fuck.

"I know, and I will."

He slid himself between her thighs and pressed his lower body to the yearning heat between her legs. He gripped her with both hands and slid her bottom forward, so that her ass was off the table. Pulling her body snugly to his, he engaged her in a deep kiss that made even her toes zing with excitement. She was ready to burst.

He held her eye contact as he pressed his fingers firmly into her thighs. He had a good grip on her; she wouldn't fall, but she also wasn't going anywhere. She was pinned between him and the table.

"You're my appetizer." He licked his lips as the saucy joke was brightened by the zing in his gaze. "I intend to eat you well, then fuck you until my cock is pumping my cum into you. I promise you, you'll be well fucked."

She cooed a deep appreciative sigh. "Dirty talk will get you everywhere."

"I know." He circled his thumbs on her thighs, pressing his fingers in too as he massaged. "I'm going to woo you into wanting me to stick my cock in you."

She tilted her head as amusement filled her. "What makes you think I don't already want that?"

"Oh, I know you do." He slipped his pants down, just enough to get his cock out, and began to thrust his erection along her vulva. "I intend to make you beg."

She laughed again and threw her head back. With a saucy grin, she said, "What makes you think I'm not ready to beg already?"

"I know you are, but there's wanton and there's hysterically wanton. I need the latter from you."

"You going to make me?" she taunted.

"I know how to. But I'm going to finesse it out of you. Curate you into my wanton sex-hungry wench. I'll have you begging for my cock like you need air. You'll be trying to hump me to get me inside you, but I'll make you wait."

Anderson snickered from his post near the stove. "Nice."

Laney met his eyes and saw he had a similar look in his eyes to John's. A threesome would be lovely, and to be ravaged by two men with such blatant hunger for her was her top turn-on. But she was John's playmate for now, and that was exactly what she desired to be for the moment.

"I'll tap you gently to drive you wild, then bring you to the vicious primal need for cock so bad that you try to attack me, but I'll not give it to you until I decide."

His statement was totalitarian, and his words made her clit lurch.

He pressed his thumb to her clitoris, and dug his fingers into her mound. He tapped her lightly, then firmly, alternating the pressure from strong to soft on an oscillating cycle.

"Oh, fuck," she muttered, pressing her fingers hard against the wooden table beneath her.

"That's right." He ground his thumb firmly to her clitoral head and wiggled it.

Her torso curled upward, and she cried out. The stimulation had her tuned into him so much that he was fully winning her attention.

"Who's your Dom?" he implored with urgency. He rubbed her clit, then lifted his thumb off her.

She gasped, missing his thumb on her sensitive spot. "You," she said breathlessly.

"Whose cock do you want inside you?" He smirked as he teased her with firmer pressure against her bean, then lighter.

She grunted in frustration. She wanted more of his touch.

"Yours," she said firmly. Her lust was mounting as she panted harder.

"Who gets to decide when that happens?"

She smiled as her breathing shifted to more labored. His little game always turned her on. "You do." Or does he? "But I need you in me now." She shot him a seductive look. He wants her to want him, which really makes him putty in her hands. Good thing it's true. "I need your cock in me," she repeated with emphasis.

He leaned over her and grabbed the back of her head. Pulling her to him, he kissed her with ardor, then broke the kiss to caress down her neck with his lips.

She dropped her head back as she relished instigating a surge of passion in him. The hard surface of the table beneath her was unyielding, but it wasn't dampening her pleasure. Anderson clanged a pan, and she opened her eyes up a tiny bit. She saw movement from him, but let her eyes fall closed again.

John continued kissing down her upper chest, his hands firm against her back, his lower body pressed unwaveringly between the divide of her legs. He sucked each of her peaking nipples, running his tongue along their firmness.

She writhed on the table as he suckled her, his mouth on her further driving up her arousal. She whimpered and moaned in response to his loving.

"Yes, more, please," she begged. Her chest heaved as he ground himself against her womanhood. She was charged up and wanted him to penetrate. "Put your cock in me, Daddy. Please. I want you in me."

He rose off her, and as he looked down, he seemed urgently ready to launch into fucking.

"Please, Daddy, fuck me."

She watched him as her words processed.

He grimaced for a split second, then the determined look returned. "Not yet," he stated. "I'll decide when I'm going to fuck you."

She pouted but secretly loved his leadership. She was aware that she adored the submissive role even more with having two men. It was like her submission was amplified. Then add in all the other men, and she was swimming in a pool of incessant juicy arousal in all the best ways possible. It was satiating. And what she loved most was soaking up their desire for her, then them being able to satiate themselves.

She never cared as much if the hookup dates made her come. They were mostly for kinks, and oftentimes they were foreplay for the main event of John and Anderson fucking her to claim her after. She had zero worries she wouldn't come soon after the sex with the repairman because it was her men's priority, their obsession, their agreed-upon right to make her climax to the max. She was first. She was their focus, and she reveled in them viewing her coming as being their kink. They were such a perfect match because she desired them to desire her, use her, please her.

Her mind swam with all the changes in her marriage as John descended upon her pussy. She needed to get out of her head once again. She focused solely on what was happening in the present as best as she could. He pressed his fingers in and rode her, then dropped down to eat her out. Ramming his fingers in while sucking her clit launched her into the gales of climaxing, and she moaned and gasped her way through her peak.

After her body stopped shuddering, he rose and grabbed his cock. He slid it into her and began pumping himself inside. The pace he kept up was slow, but steadily increasing in speed and depth.

Soon, the squelching sounds of him riding her wetness and the skin smacks from his thrusting into her filled the room.

He grunted as he worked himself in and out of her. He pulled out and swiveled his hand in the air.

"Doggy," he demanded with an intense stare that told her she'd better obey.

She slid off the table, and he spun her around and bent her over before she even had a chance to move herself. Her hands smacked against the wood as she exclaimed, "Oh!"

He entered her vagina so quickly she gasped. Then, he pounded his hips against her bottom, and her ass bounced off him in wild jiggling. Grunting and growls followed. He was set on getting his.

His cock filled her beautifully, bringing her arousal high again. He slid in and out easily, hitting all the right spots. He gripped both her ass cheeks and pressed them, and he leaned back watching his cock going in and out of her with her cheeks parted. In the past, she'd been embarrassed by him looking so directly at her anus, but this discomfort had diminished significantly in the last year, and perhaps started to become even a little sexy to her. This was quite astounding.

She turned her head and saw Anderson was mere feet away from them. He had his phone up filming and a sexy look of enjoyment on his face. They'd talked about starting an account, and she couldn't wait to see it go live. Both Anderson and John had been stockpiling and going through videos and pictures to prepare. An account to share with others would be an extension of her exhibitionism kink, and possibly others. Plus, she loved watching back the videos of herself getting fucked. It had also helped her try to shed shame about what her body looked like during sex. She'd had to reconcile the fact that how she felt didn't always mirror how she looked, though. Regardless, she found it super hot to watch. She usually wanted sex after, even if they'd just fucked.

"Nice, very nice," Anderson stated in a low voice. "Own that pussy."

John grunted, sped up his hip movements, and then released inside her.

She loved seeing Anderson's enthusiasm ignite John, and watching the men feed off each other only made her hotter. This was something she'd been noticing, and she was sure Anderson would be okay with a discussion on it, but she wasn't so sure John was yet. She didn't need to draw attention to it to enjoy it.

He slowed his pumping and slumped on her back. "Mmmmmm. I needed that. Needed you," he said softly.

She relaxed on the table. "I needed you, too." She made eye contact with Anderson. "How much did you record?"

"Most of it, but not in the beginning because I was working on dinner. We can edit out what we don't want to share with others." Anderson slid his phone into his pocket. "But it was hot." He grinned deeply. "Especially when he spread your ass to watch his cock going in your pussy."

She laughed and felt her face flush. That was a rarity. "Oh, my gosh."

John straightened up. "Yeah. That." He helped Laney up.

"You do love doing me doggy," she gushed.

"Always have."

She didn't bring up the past, and though she loved it now, that hadn't been the case back then. Sex isn't complicated until actually doing it. People needed to get out of their heads, her included.

"I had to decide I liked it." She smirked. "It took me some time to figure that out."

"I know," John said, smiling. "Your decisions often lead to our playground."

"Aw, I like that." Her safety matters. There could be no better sentence from the man in her life. "I can't wait to see where we go next."

"Same, babe. Same." He pulled up his pants and secured the button. "When do we eat? I've worked myself up quite the appetite!"

Laney purred. "I'm eating naked. How about we eat on the deck?" The idea delighted her.

"It's a little chilly out there now," Anderson called over his shoulder as he drained the spaghetti. "And good timing, you both came before the timer."

"I'll get you a blanket," John said as he strolled to the living room. "Meet you out there."

Chapter 15

"I'm so excited! I can't wait to go," Laney said above her phone, which was on the counter in speaker mode. She'd been trying on outfits all afternoon. Not that it mattered what she wore, but it gave her something to occupy her open hour while she had lasagna in the oven. They didn't need dinner tonight because they were going to Darcy and Muskie's, but she was going to take pictures of the dish for the cookbook. No matter, they'd eat it for leftovers tomorrow. She was excited about this recipe because the wine-soaked mushrooms added such a scrumptious rich taste.

"Darcy's excited to meet you, too," Anderson's voice came out of her phone.

"Are you home soon?"

"I have about an hour's drive, and it might be more with traffic this time of day."

"So, no fun before we leave then." She was admittedly bummed about that. With Anderson having the faraway job today, there'd been no afternoon sex. John was busy and worried he might not be able to leave for the dinner party with her and Anderson, so she was resigned to the fact that she might just play with herself. It had been a while since she had playtime on her own, so maybe it was a good thing. She often learned more about her body when she had only herself to focus on.

"I'm afraid not. We'll have to leave right when I get home. I'll change, then we can head out."

"We might have to drive separately from John. He said he has a lot to do before he can go."

"Well, that sucks for a Friday night."

"Yes, it does. He needs tonight. He needs a decent break to have some fun."

"Yep, for sure. I'm going to listen to a podcast the rest of the way home. I'll see you soon."

"Okay, drive safe. Love you." She fingered her silky beige top.

"I will. Love you, too."

She was deciding between the shimmery top with black slacks or her new dress. Her new dress was sleeveless and showed a good amount of cleavage, but she had a shawl to keep the October chill off her flesh while she was outside. Inside, she was likely to be warm enough, as long as they didn't keep their house too chilly. She scoffed. Well, for all she knew, this difficulty in deciding on an outfit might be all in vain because she might end up being naked most of the evening anyway. She loved dresses for quick, easy access to her hot spot, plus she'd feel sluttier. Dress it was.

She slipped it over her head as she filled with giddiness. She smoothed her dress down, then hurried from the room; her excitement made her jump. The potential for three dicks in her and a bonus pussy had her so jittery and wired that she completely forgot to grab her favorite sex toy. Bringing it had been at Muskie's instruction. Getting orders from another Dom she barely knew was titillating, but only because Anderson had vetted him.

She hurried back to the room. She had placed her rose toy on the bedside table last night to charge it after their three-way fun. It was nowhere near time to go yet, but she was in a rush. Her nerves were firing with anticipation, so moving slowly was very difficult to accomplish.

She took pics, then sat on the couch with her camera, scrolling through the pictures to occupy herself. This also helped her hold off on playing because she'd decided to be riper for tonight by not playing alone.

She had to choose one pic for the cookbook for the lasagna dish. The laptop would give her the best view, but scrolling on the camera at least let her spot which ones might make the final cut. Sometimes she was surprised when she viewed them on the laptop, though, because they often came through differently than on the camera. Some were unexpectedly blurry, and some just didn't strike her as she had expected. So, the camera perusal was always just a preliminary peek. She settled on a few top faves, then went to grab her laptop. Since neither of her men had appeared in the living room, she'd move on to the next step and download the images.

After she'd downloaded, eyed, and chosen the final pool down to three, John finally appeared.

He smiled at her as he approached. "You look so sexy, honey. I adore you in your new dress."

She melted from his words. In past years, the first things out of his mouth were always about him or his hard day. Now, they were almost always about her, what they were about to do, or what she was wearing. This she held close to her heart because it had been the first steps on the road to improve their marriage, which honestly had been dangerously on the rocks. As a result of his change of behavior, their intimacy was set on a good path, too. It meant she was more important to him than all that other noise, and prioritized her over his needs and the goings on of the day. She wasn't a diva; she didn't need to be put first, but him making her his top priority changed their marriage, because she felt more special than ever. And now, their marriage recently had been more incredible and wonderful beyond all her wildest dreams. So, their little recent blip she hoped was nothing more than a small hiccup. They certainly could discuss things way better than they used to. Back then, they often shoved everything under the rug that they could. It had gotten so bad, she had expected she'd be single by now instead of loving her life with John.

"Thank you. I'm loving it." She dragged a finger down the exposed flesh of her cleavage. "And all the skin I get to show."

"Ah, and I can't ever get enough of that, too." He sat next to her and placed his hand on her bare thigh. "Nice length, as well."

He smiled at her with hungry lust, and she returned his lusty grin.

"I know, right? I agree. I feel so sexy in it." She pressed her lips together as she flicked her eyes upward. "And how was your day?"

"Brutal. But done. Thank goodness. I was worried I'd have to drive separately from you two. But I see he's not home yet."

"Nope, he must be hitting traffic."

He leaned back, and she noticed he'd popped a partial boner.

"You do like my dress, don't you?" Her arousal was peaking at noticing his, and she hadn't even planned on any sexy stuff before the party actually happened, but before she could stop herself, she was reaching for him. "A quick suck, perhaps?"

He looked relieved. "Ah, babe. That would be incredible. I could really use the stress relief. I'm so thrilled you asked."

"Direct me." She gave him a serious look.

He grinned as his lecherous mood slid across his face. "Suck my cock, slut."

As she leaned over his lap, her breasts falling forward, her desire for him erupted. She shifted to see if her breasts would fall from the dress, but they didn't. But that didn't matter because a second later, John was cupping her breasts and slipping them out of the dress. He pulled her straps down, so she was topless.

She gave him an appreciative look and adored the fact that Anderson would likely walk in while she was giving John head while half-nude. She unzipped his pants and pulled his hard cock out, now at a full erection. His cock was packed, and it looked incredible. She consumed the head of it into her mouth and began to bob. She loved how her tits bounced as she gave him head.

He played with her breasts and nipples as she sucked him off. "Ah fuck, that's so good. Such a good girl, my slut, my wench, my dirty girl." He grunted. "Feed you."

His words got her bouncing on him even stronger.

She heard the garage door slam, and her lust skyrocketed. She knew Anderson would soon catch sight of their interaction, and that was extra hot.

John groaned and put his hand on the back of her head. His body lurched into a curl forward, and his cum burst into her mouth. If she hadn't just done her makeup, she'd have followed her urge to spread his cum all over her face. But since she was already prettied up, she just swallowed his jizz instead.

"Oh, just the kind of scene I love to come home to." Anderson sounded horny and appreciative. "I could use some of that, but I'm going to hold off for the evening."

John's face was full of relief. "Yeah, I may have ruined things, but damn, it was a rough day, and I needed that." He caressed her hair as she lay her head in his lap. "Thank you, babe."

"My pleasure," she cooed. Her first taste of cum for the day, and it was already the evening. "I wish we had time, but I also want to get to their house." She rose to a sitting position, but didn't fix her dress.

Anderson moved in front of her and fondled her breasts. He made direct eye contact with her as he played, pinching and pulling her nipples. "I'm highly tempted, but I'm going to stop here, or I won't be able to stop." He reached for her straps and started to cover her up. "I hate to do this, but Darcy and Muskie await. I'll go change, and then I'm ready to go."

They were only fifteen minutes later than they said they'd leave when John backed the vehicle out of the driveway. The app said the ride was to be about a half hour to their house, and it was agonizing to wait. The drive couldn't go fast enough for Laney. She felt like a little kid with how excited she was.

"I am just jumping out of my skin!" she exclaimed as she squirmed. She'd built up the night so much in her brain that it was feeling like a big event rather than just a get-together.

"I can see that," Anderson said with a chuckle from the captain's chair behind her. "You are going to have fun, I guarantee it. Darcy and Muskie are the best. I can't say it enough."

John turned down a street as the app dictated the route. The homes were decently sized; some were bigger than the previous ones. The lawns were meticulously kept, and the trees and shrubs were well-shaped. The fall colors decorated the deciduous trees, and the street looked like a festive fall painting. The chill in the air had been replaced with warmth, and Laney was quite happy about her choice of dress as she rolled down the window.

"Smell that fall aroma. I miss summer, but this is just beautiful." She gazed at the trees as they made their way down the street. It seemed to Laney that many of the homes were probably homes to families because many of the driveways were peppered with bikes and brightly colored toys.

She had once wanted children, but after trying for several years, she accepted that they weren't meant to have kids. They had fallen into a bad place in their marriage by that point, too, so Laney had not tried to push having children harder. She knew from friends that having kids only made divorce even harder. But years had gone by, and her resentment of John had built until it died a bloody death. She shook her head, realizing the need to get out of reflection mode or she'd not be able to embrace the fun evening ahead.

"There it is," Anderson said from the back seat. "The one with the two big red trees."

The house was stunning with variously shaped stones decorating the face of it, and the siding was a dark gray. Brightly colored burnt orange and red mums lined the walk up to the house. The double and single garage doors were closed, making it look like no one was home.

John parked the vehicle, and they all got out.

Anderson led the way, and Laney grabbed his hand from behind, which prompted John to grab hers. She liked that. They were going to walk into the house as a threesome, a walking symbol of their new relationship. Laney wondered how long it would take before she shifted from thinking of the three of them together as new versus just being them.

Anderson opened the door and entered.

"No doorbell?" Laney asked with surprise.

"Nope. They told me to always just walk in. They are very open people and don't put on a show for anyone."

Laney liked that.

Upon entering, no one appeared.

"Hello, we're here," Anderson called, his loud voice booming in the large entryway.

The floor was a dark hardwood with a lighter wooden starburst symbol in the center of the planks. The walls were covered in paintings of people embracing, and one was a beautiful nude woman in a flower garden, with a stream flowing through it. As Laney peered further inside, she saw a painting that appeared to be an orgy.

This made her smile. This was a sign they were her kind of people.

The aroma of cinnamon and apples hit Laney's nose, and she sighed. "Well, that smells good."

Darcy appeared first, zipping down the hallway. She had a huge smile on her face. She was just as gorgeous in person as in her photos, well, maybe more so in person. Her hair was curled and flowing down her back, bouncing in waves as she moved. Her shiny hair and bright eyes added to the rosy color of her cheeks. Not only was she beautiful, but her movements seemed effortless and graceful. She was curvy in a lush but fit way, and her maroon colored dress highlighted her blond locks quite nicely. Her cleavage was as obvious as Laney's. As she reached them, she threw her arms up at Anderson and squealed.

She gave off an aura of sweet, friendly innocence, significantly adding to her sex appeal. Being that she was just an inch or two shorter than Laney came as a surprise, but she shouldn't have assumed Darcy would be taller than her either.

"You're here! I've missed you so much, Anderson." Her voice was smooth, pleasant, and feminine.

"Ah, hon, and I've missed you, too, terribly, so," he stated, then pulled her into an embrace that quickly launched into a kiss.

They were entwined deep for a full minute before she broke it.

"Whew! Wow! That got me going." She shifted her gaze to Laney. "You must be Laney. I've been dying to meet you."

"I've been dying to meet you, too, Darcy." The woman was a bundle of energy and wore her openness in her eyes.

"I am so looking forward to tonight. I've been beside myself. The time has been taking so long." She pulled Laney into a hug. She giggled. "If we're gonna fuck later, we can hug now."

Laney chuckled and allowed herself to be tugged into Darcy's arms. Darcy's golden hair smelled floral. When they stepped back from each other, their eyes met. Laney sensed goodness. The kind of good feeling that meeting a new friend was supposed to give.

"I've been so excited, and so impatient, too. I've heard so much about you and, honestly, your pictures don't do you justice. You're beautiful." Laney didn't take another step back. "Stunning."

"As are you," Darcy cooed. There was a seductive gleam in her eyes that enticed Laney.

"Come on in," said a man with dark hair, a goatee, and a few tattoos on his arms. Muskie was tall like Anderson, with a muscular build. He wore dark black washed jeans and a shirt Laney expected a biker would wear with intricate art that included a disguised skull in the center, paired with tennis shoes. He had a chain hanging out of his jeans pocket. His brown eyes were warm, but he didn't seem soft. He seemed self-assured, the kind of confidence that bathes everyone nearby. "I'm so very happy to meet the other halves of Anderson." He smirked good-naturedly. "We've heard a lot about you. It's great to finally meet you in person."

Laney almost shivered. The man oozed dominance as if it were cologne wafting off him. It made him sexy, dangerously sexy. Where he was this way, Darcy was all bubbly and feminine and soft. They seemed like they complemented each other.

"Let's move into the living room, shall we?" Muskie led them through the doorway to their right and then waved his arm. "Our house is your house."

He moved over to a heavy-duty-looking leather recliner and plopped into it. The leather creaked as he got situated. "I think the first thing up is Darcy and Anderson would like to fuck."

Laney smirked. Wow. He didn't mess around. Darcy had disappeared, but Anderson seemed as if he was getting into place for something. Perhaps this was their routine when they got together. Whatever it was, Laney was intrigued.

Darcy appeared from the kitchen with a tray of drinks. She stopped moving and twirled. She had changed into a little dress with a poofy skirt that had multiple layers, but it didn't fully cover her buttocks. The front of the tight-fitting dress gave her dangerous cleavage so much so that her breasts looked like the perfect sandwich for a titty-fucking cock dive. Even though the dress was tight, her breasts still bounced as she walked. She had put her hair up in a ponytail and slid on some ridiculously high heels.

"Ah, our waitress is here," Muskie said in a cool, low tone.

Ah, they were slipping into roleplaying. Laney was up for watching the show. She was usually performing, so to be a watcher was quite a new thing. She was excited to be the observer. She hadn't had sex with Anderson yet today, but it had been much longer for Darcy.

As Darcy moved around, she glanced at John, and he looked amused. The pretty woman carefully walked in her dagger-like heels, only almost toppling once. She bent over to offer a drink to Muskie. He took the drink, then gave her ass a swat, which made her almost drop the tray. She hurried over to Laney and John and offered them each a drink. Darcy's expression was pleasant and full of congenial servitude. She was perfectly in character. Laney wondered if Muskie expected her to swat Darcy's ass, too, but she took the red and orange one and simply smiled, without giving her a spank.

"Thank you, Darcy, this looks delicious."

Darcy looked pleased, nodded, and then moved on to John. She lowered herself, and John took the brown drink. "Is this a Guess What You Are Drinking game?" His drink had a dark red maraschino cherry skewered by a sword toothpick laying on the ice.

"Yes, our waitress has chosen for you. She is sort of a cocktail chef, one might say. But, if you don't like it, you can spank her." Muskie cocked his head to the right, then took a swig of his drink. Then he smiled.

Laney's eyes shot toward Muskie. Was he fucking serious? And isn't that just a bartender?

John simply laughed, but Laney was concerned. Was this consensual? She imagined it must be by the look on Darcy's face, but this didn't sit well. She wasn't going to be comfortable watching that without more information.

"She likes it," Muskie said with emphasis, but nonchalant.

Darcy nodded, then gave a sassy smile.

"I'll consider that," John said with a snicker. He was playing along just fine.

But Laney wasn't. However, she felt a little more at ease.

Perhaps it was her own life coloring this; she wasn't into kink shaming, but she had to check herself and cool her jets. Half the kinky stuff she'd done, an outsider might have thought she was being abused, but she'd fully consented. She'd never been on this side of things, but then again, she'd not been around other kinky women much. This was clearly something she needed to change, but the surprise of all these discombobulated feelings was suffocating her.

She stood up and hurried from the room. She had no idea where she was going or if she was even allowed to go through the rest of the house. Glancing around, her panic started to rise.

"Babe, you okay?" John called from the living room.

She didn't answer but began to walk and kept going. She spied a bathroom down the hall and dashed into it. Her heart was beating so fast, and she wanted to cry. What the fuck was this? She had done so much kinky stuff, and on her own accord. She was shocked at her own worried reaction, and nothing had even happened. It was just suggested. Being triggered meant something, and she needed to examine it, but now was not a good time for that.

She used the toilet, wiped, and then stood to wash her hands. She stared at herself in the mirror. The bathroom smelled like lavender, and it was calming. She simply stood and took slow breaths in and released slow breaths out. This was reminiscent of a panic attack she'd had in the past. She didn't want this to go that far.

She powdered her nose and then prepared to leave the bathroom.

The sounds of smacking hit her ears as she opened the door. It was unmistakably someone getting spanked. She froze in place and considered what to do. She could go back to the bathroom, go to the living room, or run out the front door and not stop. Two of the three would alarm everyone, but she had reached the point in her life that she didn't give a fuck. Her sanity was more important than anyone's opinion of her.

She puffed up her chest and walked toward the living room. As she entered, she saw that Darcy was over Anderson's lap getting spanked, and pretty aggressively. Darcy was squirming, and then she squealed. The multilayered skirt stuck up in the air, and her tits had been pulled out so they bounced as Anderson hit her. Her butt was already red.

Laney froze. If these people were so focused on consent, they'd already lost in her book.

"Take a seat, Laney," Muskie ordered. "The scene already started, but I would like to apologize for not orienting you to it. This is fully consensual between Anderson and Darcy. They have done this many times, as have I."

"It's the topic," John stated with a knowing expression.

"I can speak for myself," Laney shot back. Her anger was mounting fast, and she was afraid she'd say something she regretted. Rage was threatening to erupt in her. Her blood teetered on the brink of a boil.

John gave her a nod and fell silent.

Laney glared at him, though he had already turned his head.

Muskie cleared his throat. "Anderson, we've fallen into a situation we should have prevented, could have, but we were too comfortable. Let's pause."

Anderson looked up, and his expression shifted from intense and angry to surprise.

"Can we just talk about the scene for a moment, and orient our guests?" Muskie didn't sound angry, but he was firm.

"Sure," Darcy said as she stood up, turned, and then sat on Anderson's lap.

That was where Laney liked to sit. She was jealous, and she hadn't expected to be. Anderson was getting something he must have wanted, but she hadn't provided the kink to him herself. However, he had spanked her before, but this was more hardcore. She hadn't even known he wanted to spank hardcore. She felt lost, not having known this about him.

"We've broken our first rule, which should have been stated first. Never make assumptions. Darcy, please tell Laney about your spanking kink." Muskie took a sip and stared at Darcy.

Darcy leaned back into Anderson, snuggling against him.

Laney's body was stiff, yet she had the urge to flee again.

"I love being corrected and humiliated in front of others. Spanked, especially. Titty spanked, too. And most definitely pussy spanked, and hard. All hard. Well, soft, too, but especially hard." She shrugged and was unapologetic. "I adore it from a man who respects and loves me, though I can also get satiation from a random man with these kinds of acts, as long as Muskie or Anderson are present to watch over me." She giggled. "Well, that's not entirely true, but at least nearby." She shrugged again. "Or a field away, or something."

The men all chuckled.

Laney wasn't accustomed to feeling shocked, but that's exactly how she felt. But she wasn't a prude.

Anderson had prepared Laney with all the stories about Darcy with BDSM, being chased and hunted in the woods, and even being rigged up and group pleasured, so why the hell was she reacting this way? She was starting to feel embarrassed. Or wait, was she really this much of a novice to the kink world after all she'd done? It didn't fit together, and she yearned for it to. She desperately needed things to make sense.

"I got carried away with our usual routine," Anderson said. He made eye contact with Laney, and he looked sorry. "I don't usually go this hard, but she was asking for it. You were in the bathroom for that part."

"Watching a scene is different from being in one," Muskie stated plainly.

That made sense. Her breathing rate started to slow.

"Even someone like me can get carried away and forget. With all the experience I've had, the stories I've heard, but I still shouldn't have assumed," Muskie said. "My apologies, Laney. That was something I should have properly set up." He looked apologetic. "Guess I'm too comfortable in my own home." He gave Laney a compassion filled glance.

Hmm. If even he still made mistakes...

Laney nodded. Was she overreacting? Regardless, she was the elephant in the room. An elephant who had recently been spanked hard. She felt like a hypocrite. She wasn't supposed to feel like this; she was kinky as fuck, too, dammit!

"Darcy, do you consent to being spanked and spanked hard by Anderson, John, me, and even Laney, if she desires?"

"Yes," Darcy said strongly. "I'm one hundred percent in." She was tranquil as she snuggled further into Anderson's lap.

"Who is your Dom?" Muskie asked politely.

"You are, and Anderson is second." She smiled at John. "And John can dominate me, too. I'd enjoy that."

It suddenly occurred to her that Anderson was second dominant in two throuples, but no one called him a beta. Was second dominant even a thing? She jerked her head. One thing she'd learned from the books she was reading was that there were no rules in alternative lifestyles other than the ones agreed upon consensually by those involved. But Anderson seemed like a full dominant, not a beta. But what she, John, and Anderson did was working very well. They didn't need to fit into a box.

"It's complex. This is not unusual, Laney." Muskie had a kind expression.

She didn't like being singled out.

"How about we start with a sex scene rather than impact play?" Muskie suggested.

"Sure, I got my spanks already anyway," Darcy said with a raise of her eyebrow.

Laney's body relaxed, but she was still on edge. When John reached for her thigh, she jumped and recoiled.

"Whoa, yeah, wow. Okay, hey, babe," John said with alarm. In a calm, reassuring tone, he continued, "Come here, babe. Can I hold you?"

She stared at John. Her struggles with reconciling their past with her present felt right at the forefront of her brain. She had to admit she was dangerously on edge. Being in John's arms was comforting, though those old feelings of being held by him and not being comforted flitted across her brain. They hadn't made themselves known for quite some time. Unease was flooding her, and she desperately wanted it to stop.

He kept his arms up and his eyes warm.

"Laney, would you like to watch Anderson and Darcy have sex?" Muskie leaned forward with his elbows on his knees. His face was full of compassion and concern. "We don't have to do that right now."

She knew all the things Muskie had done to Darcy, well, many at least. She wondered if that was why she was reacting this way.

She settled against John and took a long time to answer. Her comfort level was returning to baseline, thank goodness. Being pressed into John's side hug was helping, as was gazing into Anderson's loving eyes. She finally nodded once she felt secure.

"Yes, I would." That wasn't a lie. It hit her like a ton of bricks that this was a form of debriefing mid-scene. Watching a kinky scene should also be consented to, and they had just started in without discussion. But she could move on past it.

"Okay." Muskie leaned back, looking pleased. "The one thing we need is honesty. Always. Honesty ensures safety. My home is a judgment-free zone for all. In fact, wherever I am present, I deem a judgment-free zone, and I will defend that. Laney, please feel safe in using your safe word even when you're just watching. Do you need more discussion on this? I'm happy to discuss anything. And we should."

Laney melted further into John. She was being singled out; however, she was also the only one reacting in alarm. Her nerves were finally settling, and her panic was fizzling out. Darcy didn't look remotely scared at all. She looked eager. Her own reaction still had her jarred, but this correction and immediate attention to her reaction gave her a relief she was surprised by, too. She had thought she was full-on kinky with all the shit she'd done, and she still thought she was, but she'd never watched another woman experience heavy kink before, other than on films, and then to have it be administered to a woman by a man she was in love with was a shock. Would she react this way if John spanked Darcy, too?

She had no fucking idea.

"I understand, and I am good," she stated with confidence. She believed it, for the moment at least. Muskie had made her feel better with a few powerful words, and she was feeling safe, not shamed. Her respect for him swelled. This man was a true leader. "I'd love to watch you two fuck." She relaxed further into John, and he kissed the top of her head. And just like that, her emotional dumpster fire was soothed.

He pulled her closer and rubbed her thigh. She sensed the urge in his eyes to talk about all of this later. She loved that she didn't dread that. Even more, she loved that she went from triggered to feeling safe. That made her hopeful.

Chapter 16

After a quick few swigs of their drinks, Anderson and Darcy rejoined their bodies in an embrace. Their eyes were bright with passion and excitement.

"I'm always happy to fuck you, and I've missed it," Anderson stated as he caressed her hair, then dragged his finger across her cheek, all while keeping eye contact.

"And I've missed you terribly. All those European men were great, but they weren't you."

Laney could understand that statement. Anderson was special.

They fell immediately into a deep kiss, their hands urgently mauling each other. They were hungry for one another, and their groans and grunts as they felt each other up bloomed as evidence. With Darcy's top already bare, Anderson kissed down her neck in a clearly destined path to suck her nipples. Laney wondered what it would be like to taste her there. She watched as Anderson savored her peaked tips, and her arousal began to climb. Arousal was her comfort zone; it had blissfully become so.

This was a show, but more than a show, it was watching two people enjoy each other, who also wanted to share the experience with others. She reached for the bowl of popcorn Muskie had placed on the coffee table before her and John. She began to munch away and offered John a piece, which he smiled at, then took into his mouth from her fingers.

She was now genuinely excited; the shift from how she felt earlier had almost brought her to tears a few moments ago. She sighed with relief and suppressed the urge to cry, which she knew they'd all admonish her for, but she did it anyway. This was all so new to her, and her safety and trust were growing. The growth she'd experienced made her feel like she was amongst friends again. It's amazing what a little clear communication can do. It was like magic.

Anderson slid his hands into Darcy's dress to cup her bottom, then he grasped her dress and slid it down her body. She stood before them fully nude. She had a sexy, curvy body with heavy, teardrop-shaped breasts that looked big enough to be assumed to be fake, but were clearly big naturals. She was hot, there was no doubt about it. Laney was curious about their age gap; it didn't seem to be much now that she'd met Muskie.

Anderson was devouring her breasts, and she was moaning her appreciation. She glanced down at John's crotch, and he was clearly swollen from arousal. She was going to find it very difficult to restrain herself and not touch him. Her motive to do so was to fully be an observer until she joined. But it was gonna hurt to just watch. Her fingers twitched.

John snickered. "It's hard to just watch, isn't it?" He looked entirely too amused.

She pouted and couldn't suppress her smile. "Yes, it totally the fuck is."

"Good, I like you a raging, horny wanton slut." He grabbed a handful of popcorn and shoved it in his mouth. "Edging is in full swing over here."

Muskie looked their way and grinned.

She felt sassy. She wanted to protest and engage her loud, bratty mode to join in, but she simmered herself down. It was easier to hold back and let them have their time together, knowing they'd missed each other. She wanted to give them time to reconnect, and honestly, she hadn't thought she'd get to watch it. So, this was exciting.

Anderson was mauling Darcy's body heavily as he seemed to be losing control, and she was desperately trying to undo his pants. She was having trouble and couldn't slide them down after she undid the button because he was so aggressively groping her. It was almost comical how she was failing.

She grunted in her impatience. "Please," she pleaded.

"Not yet," he responded adamantly.

"Please," she begged.

He looked even more determined and said louder, "No. You're coming first. You know the rules, now stop."

He was firmer with her than he was with Laney. It was extremely surprising to see the differences in Anderson. She instantly wondered if that was because Darcy liked that or if Anderson did. She was fascinated and kept her eyes glued to them.

Anderson pushed Darcy back and then flipped her body over in a flash. She cried out in surprise. He spread her legs from behind. "Lift that ass up," he commanded.

Anderson dove in between her thighs like a man hungry for pussy. He smashed his face into her, and she writhed, crying out in pleasure as he ate her out from behind.

"Oh, fuck. Oh, fuck. Oh, fuck," she muttered as a chant. Her moans increased, and her body twitched, which made her boobs flop.

Anderson did not let up; he seemed to go at her harder.

Laney was ready to touch her pussy and rub her clit. She squirmed in her seat, trying to slow her arousal. "Shit," she said under her breath.

John and Muskie made eye contact, and both chuckled. Clearly, she hadn't whispered that low enough. But then she realized she liked them knowing she was getting turned on. The plan had been for her to engage sexually with Anderson and Darcy at some point, and John and Muskie were holding off, but she hadn't thought to ask John if that meant she couldn't do anything with him. And she desperately had a growing urge for Muskie to fuck her. She wasn't used to this kind of waiting and restraint. She was beginning to understand brat on a whole new level.

"I like seeing you like this," John teased under his breath.

"Oh, you do, do you?" She couldn't hide her impatience one single bit.

"You know I like to see you lose control and go crazy," he whispered into her ear, then nibbled it.

"Fuck," she muttered and squirmed. If getting her hot and bothered to the point where she went crazy and impulsively did something, if that was the grand plan, she wasn't going to be able to resist it. She was fucked.

Darcy's body shuddered, and she yelled out while clutching her hair. He had her securely pinned, yet she thrashed under his hold. She bucked and let out a primal scream, her head was thrown, and she twisted back and forth in agony. Oh, it was sweet agony. She slapped backward, trying to reach for his head, but he kept going, and her body convulsed through another peak.

"Fuck," Laney said as she squirmed.

Both John and Muskie glanced at her with full amusement.

Laney twitched as she forced herself to stay seated.

Anderson finally released Darcy, and she would have crumpled to the floor if Anderson hadn't maintained his grip. He gave her a moment to recover, then, after assessing her for her own control over her steadiness, he entered her.

She yelped and moaned as he slid all the way inside.

Laney knew that delicious feeling oh so well, and her pussy ached to feel Anderson do that to her, too. It couldn't happen soon enough. She was tempted to hop on top of John and demand his cock. She'd happily bounce on his while she watched them fuck.

Anderson began to thrust harder into Darcy, making her ass jiggle violently. The sounds of their bodies smacking together filled the air.

"Oompha, uffda, onneyspa," Darcy muttered gibberish.

Muskie rose from his seat and walked to a dark wooden chest in the corner of the room. He opened it and pulled out a ball gag attached to a leash. He took his time as he made his way to Darcy. When he reached her, she opened her mouth and aggressively nodded, making eye contact with Laney. Muskie placed the ball into her mouth, secured the ball gag's collar on the back of Darcy's head, and then handed Anderson the attached leash.

Shit. Laney would not allow this. She watched in fascination as Anderson took hold of the leash and yanked Darcy's head back. Muskie stood close by watching them both. It wasn't wasted on her that her trust level of Muskie was now higher.

Anderson worked himself into her rougher as he held the leash taut. Her large breasts rocked quickly across her chest. Muskie placed his hands on her shoulders, and Anderson fucked her even more aggressively.

Saliva streamed out of her mouth as she made obscene sounds. Within a minute, her body convulsed again. Like a chain reaction, Anderson grunted, and his body jerked. He was coming, too. Anderson kept pumping into her, but at a much slower rate.

When he stepped back, Muskie removed Darcy's ball gag.

She collapsed to the floor in a panting, chest heaving, disheveled mess.

Anderson lay beside her and spooned her from behind, planting kisses all over her head and caressing her arm.

It was such an intense scene, and to see the sweet aftercare from Anderson made it so moving. Laney was full of emotions. It had been a thing of beauty made even more beautiful by their intimate snuggling. And she was super grateful Darcy had been considerate enough to indicate her consent for her. There was no question that Darcy wanted it.

Laney's whole body relaxed. And it felt damn good.

John's happy glance at her was also reassuring.

"Wow, that was incredible," Laney whispered. One thing she knew about herself, though, was that she'd never want a ball gag. She'd be gagging the entire time and likely end up vomiting, and she had no desire to have vomit be a part of her play times. She likely wouldn't even be able to climax like that. But to each their own.

Darcy and Anderson both looked spent.

Muskie turned to John and Laney. "How about we have an appetizer while they recover?"

John stood. "That sounds great."

Laney followed her man into their kitchen, her mind still a little stunned. "That was hot, but I could never," she said.

"No?" John asked with a bemused expression.

"Nope. No ball gag ever, for me."

"Darcy easily gets off when she endures extremity during sex. It gives her intense orgasms because she fully abandons control of her body, so she reacts to whatever is happening without restraint. She loves it. She can just let go, and it amplifies her orgasms." Muskie offered them cheese and crackers from a platter.

Laney took a few slices of cheese and a few crackers. She placed them on a little plate and leaned her belly against the island. "I couldn't do that. Maybe other things, but that I couldn't do."

"It's good you know your limits." Muskie nodded at her. "It can take a while to figure it all out."

"Yeah, we're slowly figuring it out. My trouble is I worry I'm pushing her. I worry when I feel I've gone too far. I don't want to slip into something that harms her or ends up feeling like abuse." The worry was all over John's face.

"Yeah, exactly. We should talk. Anderson said you had some questions." Muskie didn't look annoyed at all; in fact, he looked cordial and pleasant. "Maybe we can talk later while Laney is occupied."

"Oh, don't mind me. I can go back and sit with the sleepy love birds. Maybe Anderson and I can fuck if he's recovered. I'd really like to try playing with Darcy, too."

"Oh, we want to see that," John stated quickly. "Will you wait for us, please, babe?"

She nodded. "Yeah, of course. But I don't want to stop you two from talking. I can go on my phone for a bit. I think I'd like to know you two are talking." She wiggled her body. "That's kinda hot."

Muskie grinned and motioned for John to follow him.

Laney piled up her plate and headed back to the living room. Both Anderson and Darcy almost looked like they were asleep. She made herself comfortable on the couch and watched them. A myriad of thoughts drifted through her brain. She loved watching Anderson fuck Darcy. It had been really hot. She could totally imagine how Darcy felt, minus the ball shoved in her mouth, and it had brought her almost to a braingasm to watch. There was a twinge of jealousy, but mostly, she had just wanted to join them. So, she was really looking forward to her turn. She was the fifth wheel at the moment, and she was used to being the star.

She chuckled at herself. This was okay. And a new experience was always welcome. She honestly couldn't wait to hear what Anderson thought about controlling Darcy with the ball gag on a leash. She'd had a leash on before with sex and not tolerated it well. She just couldn't handle anything externally on her neck like that. She'd gagged the entire time, crumpling to the floor. It had not gone well, and she'd indicated to John she never wanted to repeat it. She liked the idea of being controlled by some sort of leash, but that way around her neck didn't work for her. It must be her anatomy, but whatever, there were many other things to use for control where straps didn't have to be across her neck.

The other two men were taking forever. But downtime was not a bad thing with how intense things just got. Laney scrolled on her phone for ten minutes more before Anderson stood up.

He smiled at her and joined her on the couch. His cock had softened. He pulled her onto his lap and kissed her.

"What did you think?" he asked softly as he caressed her cheek.

"I think you're a sexy beast, as usual." She smiled widely at him because his gentle gesture warmed her heart.

He laughed lightly. "You've never seen me do such a thing. Did it bother you?"

She shook her head. "No. I'd never want that ball gag, though, or even a collar around my neck. I tried it once and it didn't go well."

"Yes, John told me about that."

She always found it hot when she heard that Anderson and John talked about her when they were alone. They were a team, and her sexual pleasure was their top goal. "I'm so lucky to have you both, you know that?"

He cuddled her to his body and kissed the top of her head. "Sweetie, I'm lucky to have you."

This was exactly what she needed to hear. Knowing Anderson fucked Darcy was a whole lot different from watching the reality of it. It had been hot, but this was exactly what her heart needed. Time in his arms and affirmations from him made her feel perfectly right about her world.

After a few minutes of silence, Anderson asked, "Are you still interested in playing with Darcy and me after she wakes up? It's okay if you're not."

She sat up and looked him in the eyes. "Oh, I can't wait to. But John and Muskie are talking, and they want us to wait for them." She smiled devilishly. "They want to watch us."

He laughed. "Of course they do. We will wait. She's napping anyway." He eyed up her empty plate. "Are there any more left?"

She climbed off him and pointed to the kitchen. She led him past a sleeping Darcy on the floor. "Lots more."

After Anderson's snack, they made their way back into the living room. Shortly after they returned, Darcy woke.

"Hi," she said meekly. "That was soooooooo fucking good." She stretched on the floor, making her breasts fall flat against her chest as she lay on her back. "I'm ready for round two."

Anderson laughed. "Me too, but we're waiting for John and Muskie. Want a snack?"

"No, I like to fuck on an empty stomach, as you know." She grinned deeply. "Are you joining in this time, love?"

Laney nodded. "I'd love to."

"Good, I can't wait to make you scream," Darcy said in a smooth tone.

"I never have from a woman."

"Then you are in for a real treat," Darcy said with salacious eyes. "And I'm chomping at the bit to get at you."

The fire and passion in her eyes were a total surprise. Laney had only ever been the lucky recipient of such an intense, hungry gaze from men.

She gave a little short laugh. "I'm so ready to begin."

"As soon as they are back, we will. I'd never start without Muskie here. He absolutely loves that shit. He really likes to see me go crazy sexually, which is why he loves to watch me with new people and do new things. He always knows I'm a sure fuck with him when he reclaims me. It's the excitement and newness of me playing with others first that sends him straight to full Dom mode. And damn, does he fuck me good-good-good every time, too."

Anderson nods heartily. "No lie. I've watched."

Laney always loved a similar phenomenon she'd often experienced with John, well, and Anderson, too, but she'd never thought much about how her doing exactly what she wanted also revved up John's arousal. He always said he just liked it when she was getting pleasured, but it was true; he was also getting more turned on. She loved to objectify herself, and she was learning that John may have the exact same kink. How lovely.

"Just when I think I understand things, I learn something new or a different way to look at it all." Laney smiled pleasantly as Darcy settled onto the couch next to her.

"Oh, that never stops. Every situation I'm in, every new kink we try, sometimes in just a different way, I'm learning something new. I'm incredibly surprised, pleasantly so, that we also learn more about each other's kinky selves, too. And the reason we also learn more is that our sexuality isn't stagnant. It's fluid, constantly changing, just like everything else in our relationships. We experience new things, so we never wake up exactly the same person we were. It's literally impossible." She smirks. "But we were created to keep learning and adapting to our environments." She tilted her head to the right. "Variety is the spice of life."

That made perfect sense. Now that she and John were open and accepting, that process was no longer hindered by harmful things such as jealousy, control, and neglect. Sure, she loved John's control in sexual situations, but beyond that, she abhorred it. She was already learning from Darcy, which felt a bit odd considering she was younger. But in many ways, Laney was more immature than Darcy. She'd lived a whole lifetime already in the lifestyle more than Laney had. In truth, Laney was a baby adventurer in it. As was John. So, they'd make mistakes, and she also acknowledged that she had to be forgiving, too.

"So, you aren't 24/7?"

"Well, yes and no. It's more topic-driven for us. Maybe more like 17/7." She laughed. "I've never quantified it before, like he doesn't dictate my day. If I want to go grocery shopping, he doesn't tell me what to buy, when to go, or how much to spend, for example."

"Got it. So, not like full control or a full dictator."

She shook her head. "No, but for sex, yeah. But I granted him that, and he earned it and continues to earn it. He also knows I can yank it away. If I couldn't pull my consent at any moment, it would be abuse."

Laney nodded. She needed to hear this. This wasn't meant to be lecture time, but she was gaining a greater understanding just from a casual conversation with Darcy. Anderson remained silent and simply watched them with a curious look, but he also showed a loving, understanding expression.

Sitting between the two of them yet being much older than them, she felt a bit clueless and lagging. This was not usually the case, so it felt odd.

Darcy patted her thigh. "You'll find your niche in the lifestyle. You, John, and Anderson, you three together will. Just remain open to things, and never ever stop communicating. That's the key. And be honest. Always be honest." She tipped her head. "And don't hold back. A hidden comment or fear can fester and turn into resentment."

"Oh, I know about resentment." Old feelings began to flood Laney and choke her. She needed to stop that train. And fast. She had baggage she was ignoring, but at least she admitted that. Such thoughts were only going to kill her mood, however. "But that's old news. And history to not be repeated."

"There's always that, too." She had an innocent calmness about her, and it came off also as an easy confidence. It was a surefire manifestation that was as sexy as fuck.

"I have a lot to learn," Laney shifted in her seat.

"That's okay. I'm still learning, shifting, and modifying. We aren't static as humans. It's just a fact." Darcy placed her hand on Laney's. "Don't be afraid to make mistakes. If you do and you talk it out, it can easily help you be alright with whatever happened. If you hide from it and don't mention it, don't discuss it with your dominants, it's a future step already closer to a problem in that area because you're already operating from some negativity that has you poised closer to the trigger at the get-go."

Laney snorted. "I haven't thought of it that way before." But she's right. "Like you are already closer to your trigger."

"Precisely." She sighed. "Don't set yourself up for failure."

Anderson cleared his throat. "Yeah, we have a few topics we need to discuss, but I think John also wanted to talk about it with Muskie."

Darcy nodded. "Yeah, he's a good one to talk to about being a dominant. He's been mine for years and years." She smiled a kind smile. "And he's not only talked with others, but read books. He takes it very seriously."

"I think I need more books." Laney slumped back into the soft couch.

"Well, I have suggestions for you. And one is a blog." She hopped up. "I'll be right back, and I'll make you a list." She disappeared into the kitchen.

"Wow. I didn't expect this." Laney was feeling low. She thought she had this submissive hotwifing thing figured out. She's been having so much fun, and it had been going so smoothly until John overstepped.

"We'll get this figured out, sweets. Don't worry."

She sighed and snuggled against him. "I just wanna fuck and orgasm, that's all."

He squeezed her. "And you will."

Chapter 17

Laney snuggled into Anderson as Darcy wrote on a piece of paper on a clipboard. Anderson was massaging her thigh as he held her tightly to his body. Being up close to him was comforting, and thoughts of all their interactions flitted about her brain. Their doings weren't fraught with negative history. Did she feel safer with Anderson than she did with John? She didn't like thinking about that, but she couldn't avoid it either. The truth was staring her in the face. She had thought she could just move forward with their new life, but whitewashing the past wasn't a long-term solution either, and basically, it wasn't working.

"Here, and if you finish those, I have more." She handed the paper to Laney. "I'm a reader." She wrinkled her nose.

"Me too," Laney said as she took the page. All the books she already had stacked on her nightstand, and now she had more? And they were all so pertinent to her life, she wanted to read them all instantly. "Thank you. This will take a while."

"And that's okay. No one is done growing. I accepted this long ago and gave myself grace." She leaned forward with her hands on her knees. "And I also learned to give Muskie grace."

That's what she needed to learn to do with ease. She simply nodded at Darcy and folded up the paper. She walked to the entryway and slipped it into her purse. Muskie and John's voices filled the hallway, and she zoomed back to the living room, wondering why she was rushing away so they wouldn't catch her there.

She slid in between Darcy and Anderson and reached for her drink. She needed more liquid courage to shed the dark mood plaguing her. The bottom line was she loved John and Anderson, and they loved her back. The three of them were all open to discussing things without blame shifting and with acknowledging their actions, even wrongdoings, and they all wanted to work for a compromise with consensual collaboration. That was a setup for success, even if bumps and dips came along the way.

After John and Muskie joined them in the living room, and everyone was refreshed with a drink and snacks, Laney's mood lightened, and she felt comfortable again. The get-together had been an emotional roller coaster so far, but knowing the two men wanted to watch the three of them fuck was lighting her lust on fire. This was the mood she had expected to be in while at the party, and it was a relief that she was settling into it.

"I'm starting to feel the urge," Laney said with sassy boldness. Her fresh feelings of being horny were very welcome. "I could use an orgasm."

"And I can give you several," Darcy said as she made eye contact. Her expression was flippant, and her eyes were playful.

"I'm hard and ready," Anderson said with abundant energy, and a sweep of his hand over his hard cock. He slid to the edge of the couch. "You two sexy women do this to me. I'm more than ready to start anytime. On your lead." Anderson was his usual sexy self, his hands twitched, and then he stood.

Darcy placed her hand on Laney's cheek and caressed it, then slid closer to her. "I want to kiss you. Have you ever kissed a woman?"

Laney shook her head. "No."

"Do you want to kiss me?" Darcy asked with a sly grin.

"Yes, very much so." Laney's desire was popping, and the thought of kissing Darcy was both intriguing and terrifying. What if she liked it a lot? Then what?

"That's wonderful because I'd love to kiss you, too." She pulled Laney closer and threaded her hands into her hair, collecting her near enough to dive into a kiss. "I want you to know I find you very attractive, sexy, and beautiful. And it would be a great honor to settle between your legs and eat you out until you're thrashing and screaming."

Laney scoffed and curled her body into a self-hug. The thought of all of that was truly exciting, and she savored the zingy emotions flooding her body. She'd been fantasizing about this very moment for a long time.

Darcy held her head and went in for a deep kiss. The touchdown of her lips was soft, but sure. They melted together. Darcy was gentle yet hungry, very active with her tongue. It was softer and more sensual, almost slow, yet savoring, and not so intrusive. However, the passion was clearly there; it wasn't lackluster by any means. To her utter surprise, she liked kissing a woman.

They nestled their bodies together as close as they possibly could as they deepened their kiss. Darcy's breasts pressed against her were very arousing, and feeling her body was even more of a turn-on than she'd expected.

Darcy's groan ignited her, and she moaned herself. The heat between them was ramping up at lightning speed.

Anderson settled behind her. Once his hard cock was pressed to her back, her desire for them both peaked.

"Fuck," she said as Darcy kissed down her neck.

"Fuck that's hot," John said with relish.

Hearing the arousal in his voice propelled her even higher in her hunger. He liked watching them, and that made it even hotter.

"Very," Muskie stated. "I've been waiting for this."

"Same," John said in a thick, lusty snarl.

Anderson caressed her sides and hips, then moved his hands to fondle her breasts. He slid his hands between the crushed, together bodies of the two women. He played with both of their breasts as he released his own ravenous groans.

Darcy began to lick and suckle her right nipple as Anderson fingered her left one.

She squirmed in place and undulated in response to their touches.

"Need you both," Laney said in a cooing voice.

Anderson thrust his cock gently against her lower back as Darcy pushed the fabric of Laney's dress down to her belly.

"Oh, nice," Muskie said with enjoyment.

"She has fantastic tits," John said appreciatively.

"Fuck yes, she does. Whew." Muskie released a slow whistle. "Mmmm."

Laney smiled as she rolled her body with their grabbing, allowing the pleasure of both Anderson and Darcy's hands touching her to flow through her. Arousal was easy for Laney, as usual; she wore her eroticism close to the surface, but this was a whole new level of wantonness. To be the center focus of two very sexual beings was launching her right into a heightened state of sexual elation in a flash. This might be a bigger bliss, more than she'd ever experienced before.

The pace of their foreplay was slow but steady as they played with her body. Darcy's hands and mouth traveled her front as Anderson's hands roamed both her backside and her chest, his mouth often finding spots on her neck and shoulders to kiss.

The mouth smacks and moans filled the room, making Laney immerse herself in the moment with great enjoyment. She was rolling on waves of never-ending pleasure.

Darcy slid back and waved her hands toward Laney. "Scoot her back, Anderson."

He immediately responded and tugged Laney to lie back. He pressed her to rest her head on his lap.

With his cock resting on her head, she glanced backward and laughed with glee. "Well, this is a new view of your cock tip."

Anderson snickered, and lusty chuckles burst from the other three. He lightly pumped his hard dick upward, making his cock mess up her hair.

Darcy gave Laney a determined look and settled into place between her spread thighs.

Laney quivered in anticipation as Darcy lowered her open mouth to hover over her pussy. Her hot breath blasting her lower lips drove Laney wild. She grunted out of impatience as she waited for Darcy to touch down. If she was going for angst in Laney, she was succeeding.

Finally, Laney pleaded, "Please, Darcy."

Anderson groped her breasts as he gazed down into her eyes. He looked horny as fuck, and she adored it. Normally, that look would accompany strong attention from him, but he was holding off for Darcy to make a move.

Darcy smiled at her with a devilish expression. She blew air along her slit slowly. Laney squirmed and grunted.

"I want it," Laney whined. "Please."

She dragged the tip of her tongue up the line dividing her lips, then did a full tongue slurp in the same path.

Laney clutched at Darcy's hair, pressing her fingers into her scalp as if to urge her to do more.

Darcy repeated the movement as she dug her fingers into Laney's thighs.

Laney shifted as her tease sent her resolve sprawling. She gasped as she twisted between them, her orations flipping to whimpers.

What the fuck were they waiting for? Laney's impatience emerged as a bratty groan.

John and Muskie chuckled.

"I know that sound," John said with strong emphasis. "She wants it."

"Yup," Muskie said. "And Darcy will give it to her. Come on, honeypot. Do your thing."

Laney wondered if she had been waiting for Muskie's guidance. But regardless, it didn't matter. She just wanted to come, so however Darcy was probed to begin, she was happy about it.

Darcy wiggled her tongue into her sealed flesh and explored Laney's uncovered sensitive spots, moving her tongue everywhere but up to her clit.

Anderson continued to pinch and play with her nips, twisting them into harder nuggets.

Laney couldn't sit still; she was on fire, and she wiggled, reacting to each of their touches. She couldn't wait for more; the uprising of need in her was getting unbearable. She glanced at John and Muskie, and they looked interested, their eyes glued to the threesome. Laney had enjoyed multiple threesomes with two men, and this would prove to be completely different, she suspected, and she was so ready for it. If variety was the spice of life, having a woman licking her clit was the current top spice of choice because she was working her over damn good. Darcy consumed her clit in a fast, open-mouthed attack.

"Fuck," Laney slurred as she twisted in a full body response to Darcy's suction and tongue action.

Laney bucked as Darcy pressed her most sensitive spot. This got Anderson playing with her nipples even more aggressively. Having his fully erect cock still pressed to her head was driving her crazy. She could smell Anderson, and she wanted more.

Darcy pressed her face into Laney's crotch with greater force, digging her fingers into her flesh with a stronger grip than she'd expected Darcy to have. Her suction increased, and Laney cried out even louder.

"Yes," John cheered. "Oh, that's it."

"Keep it up, hon. She's launching." Muskie hooted then clapped. "Nice. Really nice."

Laney couldn't keep her sounds subdued, and she let her emotions sing in her sounds of pleasure. The encouragement from the two Doms was lighting her up almost as much as the touches.

"That's it, Laney. Let her take you. Yeah, just like that. Nice. You're getting there," Anderson coached as he cradled her head in his lap. He kept stimulating her boobs.

She smiled inside. He knew the multiple-point touching would send her flying. He'd done it to her himself many times.

"Come on now," he urged. "Let's get you there. I know you're right at the cusp. Let it take you."

Darcy doubled her efforts, and Laney broached her apex. She burst into that no-return zone, and her orgasm roared. Darcy had edged her well, and her flight into its height was big. Really big. This was promising to be the kind of orgasm where Laney tended to rip her clit sucker off because the blissful intensity was almost too much to bear. Both John and Anderson loved those climaxes the most, as did she. Oh, the fucking sweet agony!

She rode the monster dopamine blast and smacked Darcy's head. She wished she could also swat Anderson's away. Her explosion was building, and it was promising to be ginormous.

"Oh, fuck, fuck, fuck, fuck," she muttered in a strained voice as her back arched instinctually. She was losing control of her body, and the onslaught of the climax hurled her into ecstasy. This is exactly what she's been waiting for. She let her sounds rip as the contractions radiated out from her vaginal walls, and her body crunched up. The exquisite enduring of her big peak was scrumptious. Her muscles clamped, then opened over and over again as she felt herself opening and closing on repeat through about eight contractions before they settled. The grip the sensations had over her was wild and primal, and exactly what the female body was designed for. It was fucking genius.

"Aw, fuck. Shit." She twitched through the aftershocks that jolted through her pussy.

Darcy released her suction and rested against Laney's leg.

"Excellent," John stated happily.

"That looked damn good," Muskie agreed. "Nice. Very, very nice. Well done."

"It was," Laney cooed. Those kinds are incredible. Wild, but incredible. I don't always get them that strong."

Darcy tickled her fingers around Laney's vulva, and she responded with a jerk.

"I know exactly what you mean." Darcy was smiling with a knowing in her eyes.

"Oy, still so sensitive." She played with Darcy's hair as she continued to gently stimulate her.

"That's the sign to ramp this party up," Anderson declared. "Ladies, asses up, heads down in the crack of the couch. I'm mounting for a double ride, in immediate succession. Get close."

Laney and Darcy giggled as they got into place. Darcy sidled right up to Laney, so their hips and thighs were touching.

"I want to feel him ramming as he's riding you," Darcy said in a lusty tone.

"Oh, that's a good idea. I'm in, and yes, please," Laney said as Anderson caressed her sealed off hole. She couldn't wait for him to be in her.

He entered her lips and pressed his fingers in for a few pumps, then lined up his cock at her entrance. He gripped her hip, then penetrated her swiftly.

"Mmmm," cooed Laney. "Give me every drip of that precum."

Laney turned her face toward Darcy and stared directly into her eyes as Anderson bottomed out in her, spreading her out to make room for his full cock. Her eyes rolled. He began to thrust and as he hit her G-spot, she groaned. Darcy's eyes were wanton, and Laney reached for her hand.

They held hands, looking into each other's eyes as best as they could, as Anderson rocked her body from behind. The loud skin smacks of the backshot pounds sent waves of pleasure through Laney. She wasn't expecting to come, but she was getting close.

"Harder, Anderson. Fuck her harder," John instructed urgently.

The usual direction from John never ceased to arouse Laney further, and she was ready to launch, but Anderson pulled out and side-stepped to Darcy. Her lip slipped into a pout. As Anderson entered Darcy and began to pound, Laney enjoyed the rub of Darcy's gyrating hip against hers. Soon, Darcy's eyes were rolling, too, and Laney had the urge to help her come; she would have to break her position to do it.

She started to creep toward a position to reach for Darcy's clit, but Anderson spanked her butt.

"Don't move, I'm coming back," he commanded.

He moved quickly into position behind her to assert that he wasn't kidding, and entered her body quickly.

"No one is coming yet, I'm just edging you two," he instructed. "I want to see you two trib to come."

Muskie clapped and hooted. "Good call, my man. Good call. Give us that show. Whew!"

Laney liked being pushed into this and savored it in such a way that they were going to catcall and watch them with lecherous eyes. But she also liked playing for the male gaze, which she was learning Darcy did, too. She hoped she'd get to see the other men come, but that wasn't likely. However, she might get to hear them, and that was good, too.

Darcy's sounds were hot as she played with her own clit.

"Don't come yet, hon," Muskie instructed. "Hold off."

"I know," she said breathlessly as she continued to work her fingers.

"Obey," Muskie warned.

Her body started to twitch, and she yanked her hand away from herself with a shout of disappointment. "Fuck," she muttered.

"It will come," Muskie reassured. "Take your time. Make it big. It will be so good, honey."

She nodded and whimpered.

Laney knew that tempting feeling all too well to just disobey and dive into the ecstasy of that lush dive. She often wondered if she could mask the signs of her climaxing, but in the end, that was wishful thinking, and everyone would know what was happening. She'd then face the punishment knowing she got hers without direction. But she also loved obeying and following the guidance because it often amplified her orgasm as well. So, it wasn't a lose-lose situation, but an intensified one.

After a few more rounds of pumping himself into each of the women, Anderson stood back.

"I think you're both primed and ready to explode. Let's see you go at each other." Anderson walked over to take a seat near the other two men and sat his naked ass in the chair. He immediately started to stroke his hard cock.

Laney looked at Darcy, and they both giggled.

"Guess we're up," Darcy said happily. "Let's do this."

"I'm so in," she smiled back. "I've never done this, so I might be terrible."

"Hey, just do what feels good. That never fails."

That was the truth.

Laney grabbed her hand and asked, "Where?"

"How about some pillows front and center?" Muskie asked, pointing to the space on the carpet in front of the three men's chairs.

He hopped up, as did John, and they promptly created a nice pillow-encased stage for their women to play in.

"Oh, I like this," Laney said, leaning back on the big dark blue pillow and running her fingers across all the bumpy fabric within reach.

Darcy scooted over to her and spread her legs. "Let's scissor, sister. Pussy to pussy."

They fell into a kiss against that big pillow, and their hands began to roam, feeling each other up, squeezing, and fondling. They were both making such delicious sounds.

Laney could hear the men stroking, and she opened her eyes for a peek. Sure enough, all three of them were beating their meat. "Well, fuck that's hot."

"I know, it's fucking amazing. I love it." She dove into kissing Laney's nipples, taking each into her mouth.

Laney stopped her. "Can I?" This was her first taste of a female nipple, and she didn't want to miss out on it if they started up scissoring right away.

Darcy leaned back with a smile. "Be my guest."

"You have such gorgeous breasts. I'm dying to taste you." Laney moved with trepidation, but with deliberate movements.

She hovered over Darcy and then cupped her right breast. She giggled as she jiggled it. "Oh, this is the first time I've ever touched another woman's breast." Her boob was heavy, and Laney smiled big as she bounced it in her hand. Well, no wonder men loved this. She loved making her jiggle. She gave it a playful slap, and Darcy squawked, then laughed.

Laney pinched her left nipple, then tugged it. It was at peak erectness. Darcy groaned out and began to touch Laney's breasts.

"Maybe we can both play. I can't resist touching you."

The women fondled each other's breasts as the men groaned and made sounds of appreciation.

Laney leaned in with an open mouth and took Darcy's nipple in. The flesh was a firm nugget that she ran her tongue around. She began to suck and pull her nipple in deeper. She didn't slow down, but suckled harder, causing Darcy to moan and arch her back. Laney played with her other nipple, and soon Darcy was writhing heavily. She liked suckling Darcy's titties very much.

"Fuck I love that," she said in a sultry tone.

"Yeah, it's pretty fucking fun to suck a woman's nipple. You've got me pretty fucking hot."

Darcy pulled Laney off her breast and kissed her on the mouth.

She broke the kiss for a moment. "But now I need your mouth on mine," Darcy demanded, then kissed her deeply again.

The two women's bodies were pressed together, and when Darcy rolled, Laney ended up beneath her. The men hooted and clapped; apparently, they liked Darcy's bold move of dominance. Darcy kissed Laney's neck and suckled her hard nipples. But then she didn't stop, there, she kept kissing her way down Laney's body to her pussy mound. Then she sat up and spread her legs.

"Spread 'em, sweet pea. Fuck me," she demanded in a cool, seductive way.

"My pleasure," she said, copying Darcy's body position. Laney reached for Darcy's pussy and tickled her fingers along her slit. "I really like doing this," she said demurely. "Watching you react." She wiggled her fingers along Darcy's flesh, then poked her finger at her slit. She pressed her finger in and gasped. "Oh, my gosh!" she exclaimed.

The men laughed at her in delight.

"I'm enjoying this so much," Muskie said.

"As am I," John followed.

"Hot as fuck," Anderson agreed.

Laney kept playing with Darcy. Pumping her fingers in and out, then inserting two fingers and curling them to find her special internal spot.

This was addictive.

Darcy bounced as Laney played, sounds of pleasure increasing. The louder Darcy was, the harder Laney went.

After a minute, Darcy grabbed Laney's hand and slid her pussy closer to Laney's.

"Let's fuck," she repeated. "Come on. I want your juices on my pussy."

"I'm pretty sure they're already there," Laney said, amused.

"From you, not from a cock. Let's do this, babe."

They lined up, and Laney kept eye contact with her as they began to gyrate against each other. The sounds of their wet flesh sliding along each other were arousing, and the thought of her pussy flush with another woman's heightened things for her. She moved her hips like a dance with Darcy, her arousal jumped, her heart rate and breathing rate skyrocketed, and she was getting ready to climax really quickly. Darcy ground her clit against Laney's, and Laney dropped her head back as a groan of yummy sexual anguish fell from her mouth.

Her sound sent John off, and from the sounds he made, she knew he was likely climaxing. It set off a chain reaction as Darcy took her turn to peak, then Muskie hollered. The only one left was Anderson.

"Can I join?" Anderson asked quickly as he rose.

"Yes, come," Laney said with a come-hither motion of her hand.

He settled in between the women, and they both fell upon him like a cloak, kissing, sucking, cupping, squeezing, and fondling.

Darcy pushed him back and readied to slide onto his cock. "Ride his face, love," she instructed with a head nod Laney's way.

Laney obeyed and positioned over Anderson's face. She began to slide around his open mouth and nose as she heard Darcy bouncing on his cock behind her.

Anderson shouted into her pussy as his body clenched, and his arms wrapped her thighs tightly. His body shuddered as he consumed Laney's clit. He grunted with a mouthful of Laney, and she came with a shudder once more.

Darcy collapsed first. When Laney glanced her way, she looked spent and was panting heavily. She lay back on the big pillows while her breathing remained labored.

Laney crumpled down as well, and the three of them didn't move.

"Holy fuck," Laney mused between pants.

"Yeah, that," Anderson said with a happy grin, he was heaving much less than the two women. "I couldn't have held off for much longer."

"That was a rush," Darcy said in a dreamy, subdued voice. "So, fucking good."

"Absolutely stellar." Muskie sounded pleased. "Proud of you all."

"Loved it. It exceeded my hopes for Laney's first experience with a woman." John made eye contact with Laney. "What did you think?"

She laughed and draped her hand over her mouth. "I fucking loved it. I'm ready again anytime."

"Same, I loved it, too. Thank you. And thank you, Anderson, John, and my man. That was one epic set of sexual experiences. Fucking top-notch raunchy satisfying shit."

"Seemed a bit vanilla for you, though," Laney said, meaning it to sound like a question, but it came out as more of a statement.

"Oh, bah, hell no. I love the full gamut of sex, so this was just as exciting and enjoyable. Plus, I, too, really enjoyed your virgin reactions to being with me. Your face was priceless."

Laney laughed, mostly at her own novice nature. "I was surprised by lots of things. Pleasantly surprised. I wasn't sure, but now I am. I love pussy," she declared as she threw her arms up in the air.

This elicited laughter, and it filled the room.

"I do believe our food is about to arrive. We decided to order in rather than try to cook with all the sex we had planned. So, let's put our parts away and enjoy dinner."

"I am famished," Laney stated.

"Oh, I'm ravenous. I hope you ordered a lot." Anderson stretched, his expression unapologetic.

"I know you, Anderson. I ordered extra," Muskie said with a knowing glance back at Anderson.

"Thank you, all of you. My first time couldn't have gone any better." This was shaping up to be a way better evening than it started out. And that was a huge relief.

Chapter 18

"I'm going to bathe you, feed you, then fuck you." John held her face between his hands as he looked directly into her eyes. His demeanor was fierce, his love was evident.

His words thrilled her. That's exactly what she wanted for her anniversary date. Anderson had gone to Darcy and Muskie's for a sleepover, and though they'd invited him to stay and do their anniversary date with them, he wanted them to have alone time to celebrate something they alone had created. Sure, he was in their relationship now, and they could have their own anniversary, but that didn't erase John and Laney's. That had made perfect sense, so Laney had kissed Anderson and happily watched him leave with his overnight bag in hand.

Laney was happy to be excited about her anniversary, because in the distant and even some more recent years, that had not been the case. She'd dreaded it, in fact. So, this bright beacon of a desire to celebrate her marriage was a beautiful thing.

"You have my full attention and my full excitement with that."

"Good," John said as he pulled her into an embrace. "All of what I have planned will be edging you for when we fuck. And I intend to fuck you good and hard until you're screaming, orgasming, and pushing me away." He kissed her on the lips. "I'll be pinning you down and hitting your clit relentlessly. You might have to beg or use your safeword to get me to stop."

She giggled. "Well, that sounds like a very fun way to use a safeword."

"Sit." He released her and pointed to the couch. "There's your drink, enjoy that, and I will prepare your bath."

She settled on the couch while keeping her eyes glued to his. This was very exciting. John was going to pamper her, and he wanted to. A few years ago, she'd have thought someone was insane if they told her John would be like this. But here she was watching him unfold right before her eyes and repeat his caretaking of her. Bliss didn't even come close to how she felt. His words of intention already had her feeling pampered.

She heard the water running for the bath as she took a sip of the rich, bold wine. It had the perfect hint of berry that she loved. It was a full-bodied wine and quite delicious. John had dinner in the oven, so she didn't even have to cook. This was the first anniversary of its kind in their marriage. And she loved it. John cooking? Caretaking? Promising so many orgasms, she will scream? Unheard of.

After a few minutes, John called from upstairs. "Come up, babe. It's ready."

She carried her drink and started for the steps.

"Bring the bottle," he called.

"Sure," she responded.

She grabbed the bottle by the neck and ascended the stairs. The wafting of a bath bomb hit her nostrils as she entered their bedroom.

"Wow, that smells incredible. Is that the island scent?"

"Yeah, Island Goddess. I bought one yesterday because I know it's one of your favorites."

"You really are amazing me."

"Good. That's intentional." He took the wine glass and the bottle from her and set them on the counter. "Strip and hop in."

"Are you getting in?"

"No, I'm bathing you, as I said. Then we eat. Then we fuck." He gave her a very satisfied, eager grin. "Not deviating."

"Well, I can't tell you enough times how much I love your plan." She was all lit with tingles and joy inside.

She stripped off her dress and entered the bath. The bath bomb was about fizzled out, so the aroma was fresh and filled the air. Scented water and scented air were certainly luxurious.

She shifted in the water, instantly enjoying the relaxation of the hot water. "Oh, that feels incredible."

The water around her body was an instant ramping up of the pampering.

John kneeled beside the tub with a washcloth and a bottle of liquid soap with the same scent as the bath bomb.

He smiled and held out his hand. "Your arm, my goddess?"

She placed her arm closest to him in his palm. He drizzled the soap along her skin and began to rub her with the washcloth. He stood over her and soaped up her other arm.

Then he stood and reached for something on the counter. "This toy can be submerged. Not too deep, so it wouldn't work in the pool, but in the bath, it will." He winked at her. "I held it under water earlier, and it still worked." He leaned over and dipped his arms into the water. "Spread your legs, babe. I'm going to make you come in the bath."

She smiled and spread her thighs apart. "Did I mention how wonderful you are yet?"

He grinned back and slid the little toy inside her, which basically looked like a little sperm itself. She smiled at her raunchy imagination.

"I remember this toy. It's been a while since we've used it."

"Yeah, and I remembered reading it could be submerged in water, so I searched for it."

He dried his hands and arms off, then picked up his phone. After a few taps, the toy sprang to life inside her with vibrations.

"Mmmm, that feels *wow* already." She twisted her head slightly back and forth on the bath pillow John had affixed to the top edge of the tub. "I'm digging this pillow, too."

"Get ready for more pleasure." He ramped up the toy higher then drizzled more soap over the top half of her body.

He rubbed the soap into her neck and chest, then lingered on her breasts. With the washcloth, he teased and tugged at her nipples, the rough texture making her breath catch. With the toy buzzing inside her and his attention on her breasts, heat built fast, she was already creeping close.

He cleaned her belly and then sat up straight. "Flip over."

Laney turned over. It felt so good to have her full front immersed in the hot water. He rubbed her back and then her ass, even taking time to clean her pucker. He worked his way down her legs and then massaged the soap into her feet. It was an odd feeling to have him do something to her that was so ordinary and commonplace as washing her, something that was usually a mundane, everyday task she did herself. He was making it sensual and erotic. The caretaking action of his plan was unmistakable, and she literally felt taken care of in a way she'd never felt before. She wanted to explain it, but the warm water had her so soothed that she remained mute. Maybe she'd tell him later.

"Flip back," he instructed in a subdued tone.

She obeyed. "Mmmm. This is so good. You're so good to me."

He began to work the washcloth into her mound.

The toy inside her was titillating, and the exhilaration was delightful.

"How's that buzz treating you?" he asked with an expectant, amused expression.

"It's got me really hot."

"I can tell. Just where I want you." He pressed the washcloth to spread her lips open and rode it up to her clit.

She squirmed and mewled as his touches electrified her. "Oh, fuck yes, that feels so good." She grabbed his arm as he pressed the rough-textured cloth to her sensitive spot. "Mmmmm."

He rubbed and pressed, and the waves of pleasure filled her, making her back arch. "Yes, babe. Feel that. Let it fully take you." He worked his hands even faster. "Take that ride."

"Oh, Daddy," she cooed. "I'm close."

"I know," he murmured. "Come on. I want my cumslut to come and come hard. Come on, babe."

He kept stimulating her until the urge took its grip, and there was no turning back.

"Oh," she said as she moaned.

"Yes, that's it. Now come, babe. Come for me."

She relinquished any hindrance and let the orgasm sweep through her body. Her torso jerked and twitched as she allowed the sensations to consume her. She let the sounds of her pleasure fly, and with the cradling of the warm water, she let the full climax run its course.

"Perfect. I love it," John said appreciatively. "Next, I'm washing your hair."

"What?" she asked in surprise. He'd never wanted to wash her hair before. She nodded at him. "I'd love that."

He let some water drain and turned on the faucet, guiding her so her head rested beneath it. He coaxed her under, then massaged shampoo into her scalp, working it through her hair in slow circles

"Mmm, that feels so damn good," she cooed as he pressed her to lean back. "Like I'm at the spa."

He continued to massage her scalp, then helped her to position herself underneath the faucet again. He rinsed her hair and then squeezed the water out.

"You've never washed my hair before."

He looked at her with love in his eyes. "I should have."

Then he coated her hair in conditioner and let it sit for a few minutes. He handed her the wine glass and sat back to gaze upon her.

"I love to look at you," he said. "I never told you enough before, but I do. I love it. I can't get enough. You're a beautiful woman, babe."

She rolled in the water slightly, making it ripple, as his compliments soaked into her, making her feel so sexy and so loved.

"Thank you for allowing me to wash you."

"I never knew a bath could be so sexy."

"You're sexy."

He took her wine glass and turned the water back on. "Let's rinse out the conditioner."

He caressed her hair and rinsed her strands. His touch was careful, and his eyes were loving. It was such a common thing to do that he'd made it extraordinary.

"I love taking care of you," he said softly as he caressed her cheek.

"It was strange having you do something for me that I do mindlessly for myself every day. You made it sexy." John continued to astound her.

"Good. Now let's get you all dried off so we can eat. I think the dish is about done cooking."

He helped her out of the bath and rubbed the towel all over her. It felt like a light massage.

"I'd love to fuck you right now. You smell so good. But I'm going to hold off and do things in the order I planned. But know that it's really hard for me not to fuck you right now." He snickered. "Like really hard."

She glanced at his groin and noticed his big bulge. "I can see that." She reached for him, and he jumped back. "And I like it."

"Oh, don't do that or I won't be able to resist fucking you."

She gave him a sassy look. "That's the point."

He grabbed her hand and led her to the bed, where he had her robe laid out. He placed it on her without a word, then took her hand in his again, smiling the whole time.

"Our dinner awaits," he announced with a pleasant expression.

After gathering the empty wine glass and the bottle, they went downstairs.

The table was already set for dinner.

"When did you do this?" She was amazed that she didn't notice him doing it.

"I did it earlier."

He pulled out her chair and scooted her in, then filled her wine glass. She was used to making dinner, so this was a special treat indeed.

"I can't wait to taste it," she cooed.

"I'm not a cook. But I tried." He set the lasagna in the middle of the table, cut it, and scooped out a piece for her, then for him. He then grabbed the salad from the fridge and joined her at the table.

"Let's eat," he stated as he handed her the basket of garlic breadsticks.

"I might have to ask you to cook more often."

"That's usually you or Anderson, so I wanted to give it a try myself."

"It looks really good. I bet it's going to be awesome."

"Hope so."

Over dinner, they talked about her progress with the cookbook, their plans for the weekend, and finally, what toys they'd use after dinner.

"I'd like to try that crazy wiggly one again if we can find it."

"Oh, the one I coined 'crazy dick'?"

She laughed. "Yeah, 'crazy dick'. That's it." It was a rearranging of the guts kind of toy.

"I think I know where it is. When I went looking for that other one we used in the bath, I saw it."

"Hopefully it's charged."

"Right." He rose from the table. "I brought your rose down, so you go on the couch and use it. But don't come. I'll enjoy listening to you."

"I should help clean up, though. It'll go faster."

He grabbed her forearm and looked directly into her eyes. "I'm not interested in fast. I'm interested in pampering you. Now do as I say and go edge yourself."

She blinked as she processed his words. This was new. But she liked it. Old John would have wanted to clean up as fast as possible so he could lie on the couch and veg out.

But old John had not made an appearance for quite some time now, at least the old bad parts.

She settled on the couch and placed the buzzing rose over her clit. As usual, within a minute, she was ready to come.

"Pop it on and off, babe," John instructed from the kitchen. He reminded her, "But don't come."

She did as he said, and it helped alleviate her urge to climax. If she wasn't careful, she'd lose control and blast into her orgasm.

"Take it off and place it on each of your nipples, then back to your clit."

She loved him telling her what to do with the toy. Having him guide her was so freeing and exhilarating because she was free to experience it without any effort. This was the dominance she sought.

"Hold it firmly for thirty seconds. Go!"

She held it strongly within herself and almost rocketed into her climax.

He shouted, "Off."

Her arousal began to dip immediately. "Shit."

He didn't appear before her, but his voice boomed, "Again."

She gasped but did it again and almost lost control once more. Panic seized her. She was going to climax, but by breathing through it, she succeeded in stopping her climax.

"Again," he repeated sternly.

This went on for several minutes, and each time it was harder and harder for her to stop her climb.

"Off."

"I almost couldn't stop it," she whined.

He chuckled. "I know. And I love it. I'll be right there. Leave it off now." He paused, then said, "It's my turn."

She remained motionless on the couch as her chest heaved. She gasped as her body calmed down. "Holy fuck, that was super hard not to come."

Her robe had fallen open, so her body was mostly nude.

He sauntered into the living room with an excited expression. "That's the sight I was hoping for."

She returned his smile. She knew he'd been waiting for this as much as she had.

"You first. I'm making you come, then I'm fucking you hard. A selfish hard fuck and I'm going to spurt my cum up your quaking cunt."

She adored his dirty talk and couldn't wait for him to fuck her hard and use her hole to come. She'd happily let him use her body like a toy. It didn't take much to reach her satiation of that kink.

"Yes, please, Daddy," she purred.

He settled in beside her and put her right leg between his body and the couch. He grasped her thighs and tugged her closer to him, allowing her other leg to rest on his thigh.

"How's my girl?" he asked with a proud tone.

"I'm good. So good."

"Good," he said, taking the rose toy from her. "Nothing fancy, but I'm making you come first, whatever else we do."

"I already came in the bath."

"True. But that doesn't count." He turned on the toy to the third constant level and pressed it firmly against her bean.

Her body lurched upward in response to the touchdown, and before long, she cried out. It was getting extremely difficult to stop her climax. This toy was her magic tool. He pulled the toy off and urged her to straddle his lap.

"Let's try something else. You're too close."

As she sat upon him, she molded her pussy along his hard cock.

"Mmmm," he said. "That feels nice. Love your pussy on me."

"Wait until you're inside," she said with sexy confidence.

"Oh, don't I know it." The anticipation on his face was a huge turn on.

She ground herself against his hardness as they fell into a deep kiss. Their lips smacked, revving up her lust for him more as they kissed.

He fondled her backside, rotating his hands up the back of her robe, down to squeezing her ass cheeks.

She danced on his lap, wiggling into his touches.

He kissed down her neck, and she dropped her head back with a sigh. He nibbled down the mound of her breast and onto her nipple.

She held his head as he suckled her, his hands pressing firmly to her back, making her breasts pop out.

"Fuck me, I need your cock in me. I want it." She mashed her hot, wet spot against his erection encased in his pants. "Making a wet spot," she said with determination.

She slid her hand down his pants and caught his precum, sliding it down his shaft.

He groaned as she worked her hand inside his pants. He scooted forward and stood, helping her stand up.

He sent his pants to the floor and removed his shirt while she tossed her robe across the couch cushion.

They embraced and kissed, their nude bodies smashed together. He broke the kiss. "Bend over," he instructed.

She loved his suggestion, well, it was more of a command. She quickly bent over.

"Hand me your rose," he stated next.

She snatched it and reached backward to hand it to him.

He turned it on and pressed it to her clitoral head.

"Fuck yes," she slurred as she swayed to the sensation.

He slid his cock along the crease in her buns and rode her cheeks vertically up and down, sliding along her crack. He remained curled above her back so he could still press the toy to her. It didn't take long, and she swelled close to her apex.

"Close, aren't you?" he whispered against the flesh of her back.

"Yes," she said in a strained soft voice. "Very."

"Then come, babe. Come again for me."

She was so happy he had decided she'd been edged enough. She released control and soared into her ecstasy. Her body responded with jolts, and she let her sounds spill freely.

He dropped the toy with a grunt, urgency in the way he seized her hips and drove against her. Then he fisted his cock and slid into her in one smooth stroke, both of them groaning.

She loved her clit orgasms, but having a cock enter her was also so scrumptious. The thrill of it never ceased to amaze her.

He began slowly but quickly sped up his thrusts. Her breasts were flopping, and her mouth fell slack as she was overcome by the sensations.

It was a simple doggy fuck, but it was the best.

True to his word, he just pounded away relentlessly until he growled, gasped, and then crumpled over her back. His cock was still inside her as he gently rocked himself in and out while softening. The extra fluid inside her confirmed it. Her man had come.

The rose continued to buzz on the couch as they remained cloistered together. After a short time, he lifted himself off her, then helped her spin to face him so he could hold her.

He kissed her on the lips and stared into her eyes. "I love you more than life itself, and I'll forever be grateful that you gave me another chance to be a better husband."

This melted her insides, and she was suddenly extra grateful for their second chance, too. The afterglow of fabulous sex and his love filled her. "And I want to be a better wife. We can always do better." She didn't want to blame him; she wanted to just keep their movement flowing in the direction of a good, happy, and satisfied marriage. If life could become this good, she was intrigued by how much better it could become if they kept trying. If they didn't stop. All the negative shit seemed to vanish as he held her, and she felt calm. Happy. Satisfied.

He stretched them out on the couch, silence folding around their embrace. One hand found his phone, and soon music filled the space as they cuddled.

"Best anniversary ever," she said into his warm chest.

"Best ever, babe. Love you forever."

"I love you forever."

She spied the 'crazy dick' toy on the edge of the couch sticking out from beneath a pillow. She grinned. "You found it."

He grabbed the toy and turned it on. It danced wildly and he grinned back at her. "Now it's time for this."

It was the most unhinged toy she'd experienced, and she was so ready for another round of fun. "Bring it," she stated with confidence. "I'm ready."

"I'm going to be ruthless." And his eyes showed how true his statement was.

"I sure as fuck hope so." She squeezed his bicep as her excitement once again began to rise.

Chapter 19

"I am reading up on spanking and dominant-submissive dynamics, consuming a few books Muskie recommended to me." John sounded conversational and thus Laney tried to remain calm.

She had just walked into the kitchen and heard John talking, so she hadn't meant to eavesdrop. She marveled at his authoritative tone, even when he was referring to his own learning. She was super glad he was researching even beyond his discussions with Muskie. A quick glance toward the living room told her Anderson and John were still talking over beers. It was a regular thing for them now to chat over happy hour, but the words she'd just heard were not the usual happy hour talk. She moved closer, careful to stay in sight, so John and Anderson knew she was there. She dug through the fridge for salad supplies, making plenty of noise on purpose.

"After talking with Muskie, I finally understand myself better. I have an aggression streak in addition to a dominance one, though not entirely sure I'm sadistic. But I'm learning healthy defined outlets for all this, plus, I now know I don't want a full swap with Laney. I can't handle not knowing what's going on, not knowing if she's safe and being treated the way she wants. I feel unsafe. I take it very seriously to protect her, and I know now that's why I reacted the way I did." He sighed as Laney joined them on the couch. "I'm not proud of myself, but now I understand my motivation behind that rash spanking. I was out of control, and I don't want that to happen again. Ever. I'm not okay with that." He fell silent. "I have to admit,

I'm still glad it happened because it brought us to the cusp of a set of boundaries we haven't set yet." He patted her arm. "For both you and me."

She nodded as his words sank in, but she remained silent. *It's silly to think he can control everything.*

Anderson tilted his head to the right with a raised eyebrow. "I can totally understand wanting to keep her safe. I do too. But for me, I came into this with you two already doing your thing, so I guess I've always deferred to you, as her primary Dom, as it should be. But I'll always have her safety as a top priority, too." He looked skeptical. "And are we really in full control of everything? Is that even possible?"

At times, they were teasing the very edge of danger itself. She was glad Anderson said that.

John raised his right hand. "True. And I appreciate that. I actually appreciated you stopping me that day. Not at the time, mind you, I was pissed," he paused to smirk, "but that proved you have her safety as your top concern, even when it comes to me. This has all made me a better dominant for you, Laney." He paused as a look of worry took over. "Do you feel that spanking changed us? In a detrimental way?" He rubbed her thigh. "You've been so silent. What are you thinking?"

"I'm processing it all." She kept her expression as calm as possible as she considered their words. On the one hand, she was an independent woman. She was strong and smart, and she considered herself to be street smart. She didn't like the feeling of thinking they needed to watch her all the time, like she was a child. On the other hand, what they were doing in their lifestyle now could potentially turn dangerous for her if no one were watching to keep her safe. Men were not to be automatically trusted. She tried to shove off the bad feelings she got from them, saying she wasn't capable of watching over herself and making decisions. That's not what this conversation was about. It was about her safety in a world where some men are monsters, and no one can tell who is a monster until they are losing their shit.

"I can see your wheels are turning," John stated in a voice that was understanding and supportive.

"I've said it a hundred times. I want to make my own decisions. And even if this doesn't always feel like that, I understand we're playing with fire. Things could get dangerous, and the fact is, I am a woman, and I'm not stronger than most, well, maybe, almost all, men." She knitted her brows as determination filled her. "But I can do a mean kick in the groin!" She crossed her arms over her chest.

Both men laughed boisterously, which made her smile and relax her body.

"I think God did that on purpose to even things out between the sexes. There's a sense of humor there. You are stronger overall, but you have one weak spot that we can easily bring you to your knees by with a swift kick."

"I don't think you're wrong," John said with humility and amusement. "So, we are on the same page? No playing with anyone else alone? Either Anderson or I need to be present."

"I agree," she said with a nod. It was the reality she couldn't deny; she was at risk without them there.

"And we also need to discuss spanking as a punishment. I would do that if I needed to, especially if you repeat playing on your own. And it's about your safety, and asserting my dominance as your protector, not about me wanting to hurt you. It's just an effective way to assert all of that." His face turned serious. "Plus, it really solidifies my dominance in an easy-to-do act that I could do anytime, anywhere."

"I can buy into that, somewhat, but I'm still out on deciding my boundaries." She really liked the idea of him doing something that would solidify his dominance. But was that the way? She didn't know. And she wasn't deciding on something that big right now.

He shook his head. "We don't have to finalize things, just keep thinking about it." He cleared his throat. "Just wanted to say that spanking is also about a reset. And it is an effective redirection. It kind of cleans the palate, so to speak. Muskie gave me some guidelines to think about, and he said to remind you that you always have your safeword, even if I were to punish you with a spanking."

Anderson leaned forward. "That's exactly what I've learned from Muskie, too. Plus, and I'm sure he talked with you about this, not only is spanking boundary defining, and a resetting of your dominance and caretaking of her, but it can set a trigger in her brain and make the redirection more..." He paused to consider, "instinctual after the physical act of being spanked. It's like the body remembers even when the mind might falter." He chuckles. "Plus, it fixes Darcy's brat mode."

John looked amused. "Ah. Right, yeah, exactly." He smirks. "I stub my toe while walking barefoot. I remember the pain it caused, and I may not walk barefoot in that location again, or maybe I automatically flinch and be more careful." John looked pointedly at Laney. "I'm not used to you being so quiet."

"I don't think I know yet..." She paused and eyed both men directly. "I'm not saying no, I'm not saying yes." She dropped her eyes away from them both. "I have such kinks of correction, domination, being controlled, and even humiliation, as you both know, but the reality is it may not be a kink I want to live beyond role play. But don't pressure me. I can't say yet because I'm unsure." She slid into a demure state, and it left her feeling odd and totally not like herself. That felt like a sign she should pay attention to. "Though, don't get me wrong, I value and love your leadership."

John nodded. "That's fair. This can be an ongoing discussion until we clarify everyone's boundaries and come to a mutually agreed-upon compromise."

"Sounds so business-like, when it's nothing of the sort," she said with a light chuckle. She needed things to lighten the fuck up.

"Negotiation is negotiation," John responded matter-of-factly. "No matter the realm."

"I want sexy talk, not business talk." She pursed her lips and partially closed her eyes, feeling a bit bratty. But her men indulged her, so she liked being honest. She'd have to talk with Darcy more in-depth about all this.

"It can be both," Anderson declared. "That's up to us."

"But, I'm curious, what makes you think you know what I should be punished for better than me?"

John and Anderson both laughed.

"Fair enough, my love. Point taken." John's expression grew humble. "Maybe we make it about a violation of set rules and boundaries that we agree upon then."

"Or kinky play," she mused with a flirty gleam in her eyes.

"Indeed, I like that," Anderson stated quickly.

"Well, dinner isn't going to make itself." She stood up and left the men, wondering if they'd keep talking with her in earshot. She wasn't a child, and she didn't think her instincts were weaker than theirs; sometimes, she felt they were sharper.

AFTER DINNER, WHEN everything had been cleaned up, she announced she was taking a bath. Alone. Both men eyed her curiously as she zoomed up the stairs. She had an ulterior motive, and she intended to fully carry out her plan. She grabbed the monitor from the dresser and set it at the top of the stairs. Then she dug out the spare receiver and put it in the bathroom with her as she started the bath water. She was spying on them, and it wasn't honest, but she needed to know some things. She imagined that if John found out she was listening in on their private conversation, he'd suggest she get spanked. But this was her life, too, dammit!

John's voice came through the monitor loud and clear. "I've realized I've been selfish about this lifestyle. Too often it was about what I got from Laney. The sex, yes, but also the devotion that came from what I let her do with other men, with you. But I can't ignore my own needs either. There has to be a balance. The bottom line is, I want her empowered, overflowing with pleasure and joy, so much that she feels life couldn't get better, and then together we'll make it better. I want to amaze her, lift her up, let her shine. She's not my prisoner, not my slave, not just my muse. She's the love of my life, the one I almost lost because I was too damn selfish for too many years. Midlife woke me up. Harshly."

"I think it's a dance and a conversation that never ceases. And being fluid and non-judgmental is the only way." Anderson made sense, as usual.

"How are you so wise for your years? If I had been like you back then, where would we be now?" He chuckled. "I still have a lot to learn."

"As do I, but honestly, hanging with Muskie has really helped me understand so much about life, love, sex, and relationships. It's been invaluable for me to spend time with him." A heckle spurted from his mouth. "So, no, me going over there hasn't always been just about fucking Darcy, but let me tell you, that's been fucking incredible!"

"Right? I can only imagine. She's absolutely beautiful and sexy as fuck."

"Well, you could do more than that, you know. Imagine, I mean. Even Laney said she'd be okay with you fucking Darcy."

"I don't know. I kind of only want Laney." He fell silent for a moment. "Can't explain it. It's just a thing."

Laney smiled. Then she felt guilty for listening. She went to turn it off but then couldn't bring herself to do it.

"Fair enough. Laney's an everything-good-about-sex kind of person, and then some. I can understand your perspective. But damn do I love boning Darcy, too." He released a flurry of laughter. "I can't get enough of either of them."

John scoffed. Laney imagined he was shaking his head. "You know what Muskie said that affected me the most was how the line between abuse and being a dominant is that an abuser seeks to control, whereas a dominant seeks to lead, yet power exchange is a form of control, but with consent. And I want to lead Laney, not control her, other than in power exchange play, of course. And that's why I've been so hyper about all this. I want to get it right." He paused. "Keeping her safe with control is not what it should be. I'm not her keeper, she must have a say in her own life. I'm not a dictator and would never seek to be one." He sounded a bit frustrated.

"Yeah, that's exactly right. Her submission to us is a choice, her choice. If our leadership isn't consensual, it's harmful. She needs a safe and empowered space, and honestly, so do we. Which also means, she freely makes her own decisions without fear of repercussions."

"I regret it, ya know. I let my anger lead me. I mean, it was the fear for her safety, but I was also very angry that she put herself at risk like that..." John paused. "I'm not proud of myself for that. I know. I keep saying this. I just need to figure out how to move on."

"But still, we can't lose sight of the fact that it's all still her choice." Anderson fell silent before he spoke again. "We can have rules in place that she agrees upon. But spanking for punishment, that recourse almost has to originate with her, not us. We can provide it, if she seeks it."

"Yeah, that's exactly the right approach. I'll not bring it up again unless she does."

"I don't think that's right either. We should talk about it."
Anderson was always so persistent with communication.

John sounded amused. "I'm stuck in my old ways sometimes. I'm
an old fart. It's hard to unlearn shit," he said. "But with reflection and
contemplation, I think I can get where I need to be." He laughed,
which turned into a scoff. "With a few fuck ups along the way."

That was it. She was heading down and confessing. She didn't
bother moving the monitor.

"Fuck ups, is that like cock up my pussy from a standing fuck?"
Laney asked as she practically floated into the living room. She was
grinning from ear to ear. "Because I like the sound of that!"

"How was the bath?" John asked.

"I didn't get one. I was listening to you two." She felt guilty
and didn't mask it. "And now maybe I do deserve a spanking." She
slumped on the couch.

"You listened to us? Just now?" John looked surprised.

"Yeah, I used the monitor. I'm sorry. I should trust you both.
And I do. I was just worried, I guess."

"Well, I'm not going to spank you amidst this conversation, but
yeah, not what I'd call your best move." John looked disappointed
in her, and part of her craved a spanking from him. Maybe it would
make her feel better for doing a slimy thing.

"I know," she said gloomily. But part of her was glad she'd heard
their conversation.

"Hey, babe, why don't you go get that bath anyhow. You need
something to calm your nerves." John patted her arm.

Did John want that calming to be a spanking rather than a bath?
She shook off the thoughts because she couldn't begin to assume
what he wanted. She stood motionless in the living room. It didn't
matter.

"I agree with John. No spanking, and you go take a bath. We
forgive you for spying." Anderson looked like he meant it.

John didn't protest Anderson's statement, and that made her feel calmer. She let them each hug her, and she went back upstairs to the bath she never got in, wondering what to make of all this.

Chapter 20

The next day, John had some news. They were taking a vacation, with Darcy and Muskie on a cruise. A sex themed cruise. He had arranged for Darcy to pick up Laney for a day of shopping. He reasoned with her that he had time alone to talk with Muskie, and now she needed time with Darcy. She had agreed to spend the day with Darcy and was excited about it.

"She's here," John called from the front window.

She'd never had issues with John's direction, but for some reason, his watching out the window for Darcy to arrive bugged her. The desire for him to back off was choking her.

"Thanks," she said, not wanting to say anything else to stir any negativity. "Love you, bye." She hugged and kissed him, then zoomed out the front door.

Her feelings had her mind boggled. Why the fuck was she annoyed at John? Her brain was clear as mud, and she had no clue how to clear it.

She slid into the car, and it was an immediate shift to calmness. "Hi," she said to Darcy with a swipe of her hair off her shoulder. "Thanks for picking me up."

"No problem. When John called, I was excited about spending time with you. And, of course, the shopping. I love shopping!" She smiled. "And can you believe the cruise!"

"I am so excited I could burst. And I do love shopping, too. I haven't done it with another woman for quite some time, so I'm really pumped up." Swirls of thoughts about potential new and exciting adventures spiraled in her. The thought of cultivating a friendship with another woman in the lifestyle sounded wonderful. She had read that many people living in the lifestyle tended to only surround themselves with others living the same way and old friends fell to the wayside, and they were much happier being surrounded by non-judgmental people. That made perfect sense to her, so she was quite happy about developing a close friendship with Darcy.

"I am so excited about our vacation plans, too. I can't even tell you how excited I am. There are no words! It'll be epic." She backed the vehicle out and turned up the radio. "You want any certain kind of music?"

"No, this works." She waved at John, who was waving from the window. "He's hovering."

"He looks happy. But, being totally honest here, you didn't when you walked out the door."

She called it as she saw it. That's one thing she'd come to realize about Darcy in the short time she'd known her.

"Yeah. I'm usually fine with him orchestrating things, but for some reason, it annoyed me today when he was watching for you to arrive. I really have no explanation why." She shrugged.

"Maybe something you two are going through? I won't pry. But I'm here if you want to talk. Muskie and I were once where you and John are now."

She sighed. She really did want to spill her guts to Darcy. But how honest should she be? "Yeah. Well, we're trying to figure out our limits. And it's kind of hard. The problem is, something that turns me on also sort of offends me in some ways. And I can't figure out how to reconcile it."

"Ah, yes. I've been there. It's tough. Really tough. But give it some time, and that will tell you. And keep talking about it. Don't hold back. If you hide things from them, you'll end up with resentment, and your true Dom/sub relationship can't grow in any kind of resentment. In fact, it will kill it."

She startled, then nodded slowly as she looked out the window. Feeling hesitant to share, she toyed with the buttons on the door.

"You won't shock me; I promise you that." She gave a little curt laugh. "That's not possible."

"Okay..." She paused. "John got mad at me for fucking a young man without him and Anderson there, and he punished me by spanking me as discipline. But we had only ever done spanking playfully as a kink."

"Oh, yeah. That's not good. Let me guess. You hadn't talked about it, so you felt violated. But at the same time, it turns you on a little because he's your dominant and you like to submit to him. So, you're feeling anger and resentment toward John for doing it."

She met Darcy's eyes. She had loads of compassion in them. "Yup. You got it." She shifted in her seat. "And he apologized and said he overstepped. But Darcy, I didn't even say my safeword." She stopped talking for a moment. "But I thought about it."

"Hey, that's okay. Sometimes we don't respond the right way because we're conflicted. But that's why we debrief and discuss it afterward."

"The thing is, John said he made a mistake, but that he was only concerned for my safety and didn't want me to get hurt. And that's somewhat noble."

"Right, but that doesn't erase your feelings of him taking the liberty of doing it."

"Yeah. He said he never wants me to feel abused, but that he felt like that bled into it, so he's struggling with that." Laney paused. "But at the same time, his correcting me and dominating me turns me on." She dropped her head in her hands. "How am I supposed to get my head around all this? And now it's affecting how I feel about John.

Things have been going so easily, and it's been so wonderful. But this is becoming a roadblock."

"You need to keep talking about it until you come to a place of comfort. Whatever that ends up looking like for your boundaries. And Anderson is a fantastic mediator, so use him."

Laney nodded. "Yeah, he really is. He has already been helping. Geez," she threw her hands in the air as tears threatened to spill. "I just didn't see this coming."

"It's not always smooth sailing, but you can get there. New things will bring waves." She cleared her throat. "I've been in this situation before. When I break our rules, Muskie spanks me. After you all left, he punished me hard because I'd broken a few. But we've already worked through this, and I had consented. The spankings reset me. I want them. They reaffirm Muskie's dominance and keep me on the path I choose."

"Whoa, I didn't see you do anything offensive at all." Laney was aghast, feeling a bit scared by what she said.

"It wasn't anything offensive; I just broke a few of our agreed-upon rules. And I deserved the spanking. It was a correction and a disciplinary action that I both craved and wanted from Muskie. I fully trust him and have zero resentment toward him. We have it very, very explicitly defined. We even have a written contract."

Laney shook her head. "I can't fathom it."

"You will. It's not that you need a contract, too, but you just have to keep on talking to John, and don't ever stop. As long as he's not some sort of hidden, or like, covert abuser, you will reach a place of comfort, trust, and love that you both agree upon. And it's so freeing, Laney. It's really incredible. I assure you. It's a fantastic way to live."

"I envy your spot." She slumped in her seat. "But I don't see myself getting there."

"Look at it this way. Every step has glory in it. And you're never done negotiating. It will be ongoing for the rest of your life together, and rules can change. However, John seems open to discussion and self-reflection. That's imperative. This is more of a test and a working out of a plan of how you will navigate waves in the future. How you handle this one will set the pattern, mood, and ease for future bumps."

She scoffed. "Geez, no pressure at all." She fell silent for half a minute. "The problem is, I don't know what I want. But I don't feel like he knows better than me what's good for me. I want a say, or maybe even full control in some areas."

"And that's okay. That's information. And you must communicate that to John to move forward."

"I have told him, but since I'm still unsure of where I stand, it's all still a little murky to me. And I just feel uncomfortable." A resurgence of tears threatened her calm. "I'm sorry, I'm losing it."

"Don't be. It's perfectly normal. And hey, it's human nature. People hide things. You need to get comfortable with not hiding anything from John. But that has to come naturally. Look. Let me say this. For instance, if he were a narcissist, you couldn't have even had the conversations you've already had. So, I think if he's open to hearing you and acknowledging that he went too far, he will understand, and you can get to a good place again. Just don't expect it to always be easy, because it's not."

"It's been easy, though. Until recently." She glanced at Darcy to make eye contact. "You make it look easy."

"Yeah, but you can't compare. We've lived as a Dom and sub for years and years. You two are super new."

All of that made sense and was helping her to feel better. "That really helps."

"The other thing is, get used to not knowing. This will come up again. It took me a long time to make up my mind that I wanted Muskie to discipline me. It wasn't an overnight decision. And like you, it had just been kinky play during sex or role play for us at first."

She turned in her seat to face Darcy. "But how do you accept that he thinks he knows what's better for you than you do? Why does he get that final say?"

"Well, for us, it's more about the fact that we have set rules, and a plan of consequences when I break those rules. And these have all been agreed upon ahead of time for us. If we broach new ground with it due to an incident, we talk about it first to figure out how we will proceed. Everything is talked about first and agreed upon. There's no rash judgment or wild spanking that goes on, unless we set that up for a scene." She grinned. "Which we have done, and it was so fucking hot. I would highly recommend it if you like impact play and being dominated."

Laney nodded aggressively. "Ah, I see. I can imagine that being hot, yeah." She slapped her thighs. "But what if Muskie breaks rules? You don't spank him, do you?"

She laughed. "No, he's my dominant. I'd never spank him." She shook her head. "That's funny though."

"Okay, but what gives him the authority to spank you?"

"I gave him the authority. But he has consequences, too; if he violates our boundaries and rules, it's just not a spanking that I'd administer to his bare butt." She laughed again, like it was hilarious.

Laney tapped her finger on her thigh. "Okay. I see." She fell silent as she processed everything Darcy had said. She didn't need to know all their details to understand.

After a few minutes, Darcy spoke, calling her out of her processing. "Do you understand what I mean? Does it all make sense?"

"It does. And I don't think I could ever give John full authority to decide what I should be spanked for and whatnot."

"You're not cut out for 24/7. And that's okay."

"As you said before you aren't 24/7, right?"

"Right. We are close, but not all the way. I still decide many things. But for sex, it's Muskie's call, but he also knows my boundaries, my yes's and my no's. He doesn't violate them. He's very careful and intentional." She smiles. "He stays in control very well, except for in areas or defined scenes. We've agreed that he can exercise loss of control. But, even then, I still have my safeword."

"Interesting," Laney said as more calmness settled upon her. Maybe that's just what John needed, too. "The rule is there are no universal rules, except the ones you two agree upon. But your safeword is still your safety net."

"Exactly. And he has one, too." She pulled the car into the parking lot of the mall and drove down the aisle. "And we literally talk to death. And I mean to death. Like we over-talk about it to excess, and then we talk about it again, and we know we will, because invariably, something happens to alter it, and we need to re-negotiate." She parked in a spot and turned to Laney. "Nothing is done. Life is fluid. Relationships are fluid. The best thing you can do is go into this with the mindset that nothing is really set in stone. You'll constantly be modifying your relationship. New things will happen, new feelings will emerge, and accept that negotiation is never done. It's now a part of your relationship and a part of your life that will never end. It's a forever state. And that's not meant to make you feel unsafe or unstable; it's the exact opposite. In fact, it's meant to help you feel safe in the knowledge that John will always have your safety in mind, and you will have his. You've got each other's backs, and change will be ongoing, but that's okay because if you can always talk about things, then you can always talk about things. You know? And, he will listen to you and consider, and you will do the same for him. It's when people are in relationships with those who can't talk about things without blowing up, or they shift blame, or deny accountability, rewrite history, feel attacked when you express how you feel, don't listen to you, or they don't fully accept you. Or, they don't accept that things will change and keep changing. Then, in those cases, if you are experiencing any of that with John, I'd advise you to leave him."

Laney dropped her jaw. "Wow, I hadn't thought about any of that." This was a bit shocking to hear. "I don't think John does any of that." Her brain felt fuzzy again. She must not apply past John's behavior to the new version of John, but she wasn't quite sure how that was possible.

"He'll make mistakes. You'll make mistakes. It's how you deal with them that matters."

Laney nodded and felt a clearing of some confusion. "That helps. I can't expect him to be perfect, but when it hurts me, it's hard to let the mistake settle."

"Which is why you need to talk the absolute shit out of it and not stop." She smiled kindly.

"Makes sense. Thank you. I feel clearer-minded than when I first got into the car."

"Yeah, I could see it on your face when you got in, and I see where you are now. Be patient with yourself and with John. Ya'll have a full past to reconcile as well, before the lifestyle, right?"

"Yes," she said with a sigh. "That's a problem, too. And to be honest, I've kind of just glossed over that because our forays into the lifestyle have been so wonderful. But I can't fully go blind to the past bullshit. I know that. I've kind of been indulgent and just moved on without really moving on, and it's coming to bite me in the ass."

"You'll get there. I have faith. And we'll be here to guide you. It sounds like what John did stirred up some of your old mistrust and set you back, when before you were moving forward."

Shit, that made perfect sense. "You're wonderful. You know that? And how is it that you're younger than me and saying this?" she scoffed, feeling a bit sheepish

"It's not only about age. I've already lived through where you are now. It's simply experience." She grabbed her purse. "Let's keep talking, but I'm dying to grab a coffee in the mall. Then we can sit at a table and keep talking. That sound good?"

Laney opened her door. "It sounds perfect."

"I love talking about this stuff. And, oh, and that brings up another thing I wanted to say. Don't shoot for perfection; it won't come. It won't stay even if you feel it for a moment. It's a myth. Instead, shoot for whether you are feeling safe enough for what you're currently doing, then do it. If not, stop and reassess."

LANEY BOUNDED INTO the house with bags in her hands and a smile on her face.

"How was the shopping trip?" John asked from the couch. He appeared calm and relaxed.

"Hey, sweets," Anderson said with an equally happy look.

"Oh, it was so good! Darcy and I scored some great outfits for the trip. I cannot tell you how excited I am about this cruise. We're going to have so much fun together! I didn't even know this kind of cruise existed."

"Yeah, I'm pretty excited, too," John said with gumption. "I'm so delighted to see you looking so refreshed and happy."

"I'm so ready to go," Anderson cheerily agreed. "And I don't need to buy a single thing." He grinned widely as he shifted on the couch.

"Same," said John.

Laney took a step back. "I've walked in at a bad time, haven't I?"

"No. But we were having a serious talk. And I want to tell you some things, if you're up for listening."

She cringed internally. Things have been so heavy lately. But, she simply nodded and sat in the loveseat across from John and Anderson.

John looked apologetic. "I know I'm human. And I'm allowed to fuck up, too, but I don't want my fuck ups to irreparably harm you. I'd never forgive myself if I did that, yet I know I've already done it. That's on me."

"Your spanking of her like that did come from love and concern," Anderson gently reminded him. "For you," he said, looking directly at Laney.

"We need to talk about this further. I need better outlets, too. Which I learned can also manifest as BDSM acts we all consent to. Play is play, and play can look like punishment, but real punishment has to be explicitly laid out and consented to, and I believe it has to come from your desire for it, not mine. Not that we won't all be held accountable for our agreed-upon rules and boundaries." He sighed, looking taxed. "But I need to master my control, so for now, I'm going to table the spanking for discipline, and seek your guidance on anything like that for the future. I promise to try and not act rashly like that ever again."

Laney slowly nodded. "I appreciate that. I've learned a lot from talking with Darcy today, too. She and Muskie have reached their consensual existence with regards to that, so it was really great to listen to her." Her expression turned contemplative. "And I have no idea where I fall on that gradient yet. But I do love the punishment role-playing fun. I am one hundred percent sure I'd like to continue doing that with you two."

Anderson looked proud. "We'll get there, we just need time, discussion, and ongoing debriefing, because as we all know, our kinks can also shift and change." His expression changed from serious to playful. "But back to the fun topics, did I mention that I'm really excited about this cruise? Did I say I've never been on one?" he asks with a knowing laugh.

"Oh, only about fifteen times," Laney said with full amusement twinkling in her eyes. "I'm so excited, too, I cannot even convey how much. I was perusing their workshops and classes, and damn, I want to take every single one of them!" She was happy to talk about the issues in their relationship, but also quite happy to move on to the cruise topic.

"Well, sign us up, babe! Or I can. We have to do that before we board? Or can we add some once we are on the cruise?"

"I think we can once we're on the ship, but that's only if they have spots left. The travel agent told me they get those classes fully booked more often than not."

"So, servicing the workmen is going to switch to servicing the cruise ship crew," John stated with a hearty laugh.

"Perhaps. Well, I'm not confining myself to just the staff, though!" Laney blurts.

"I love your sluttiness," John said as he crossed the room to sit on the loveseat she was on. He pulled her onto his lap. "This new life of ours is about fulfilling fantasies, and I aim to try for every one of yours. If I don't share it, I'll find a way for you to still have it. Safely. Consensually."

"Ditto," she said as she cuddled into his embrace.

Anderson piped up, "Same. I'm in." He joined her and John on the loveseat and then collected her feet in his lap. He began to massage her soles as he spoke, "I'll never tire of giving you pleasure, nor taking my own from your hot, sexy body, mouth, pussy." He grinned devilishly. "All the parts."

"Use me!" she declared. "And I'll use you. As it should be, otherwise, why are we even in a relationship?"

"Agreed," John stated as he held her closer.

Laney was thrilled that John finally saw things in a way that nurtured their marriage. It felt like a long time coming, even with all the hotwifing she'd been allowed to do. This was a whole new level of support, exploration, and a promise of complete satisfaction for all three of them.

And going on a swingers' cruise together felt like the perfect way to begin fulfilling all of that. She really was a lucky woman.

The End...for now! Stay tuned for book 3 when this sexy throuple goes on a sexy cruise!

About the Author

R uan Willow is an award nominated open door spicy romance author, sex blogger at https://ruanwillowauthor.com/ , sexuality and spicy romance fiction podcaster at the Oh F*ck Yeah with Ruan Willow Podcast, and an audiobook narrator/voiceover actor. She is also published on Medium, Frolic Me, and Theo Reads, plus in several anthologies. She loves spending time with family and friends, interacting with fans, cooking, sharing/chatting with and educating people about sex, reading, travel, being outdoors, swimming, learning about sex, podcasting, and more sex. Did you catch all the sex? She's giggling right now thinking about you reading all about sex. She values openness and talking about the natural act of sex. And. Yup, she loves to laugh!

Pen Names:

She writes general erotica/erotic romance/erotic rom com/ menage as Ruan Willow, hotwife erotica as Ruin Willow, taboo erotica as RuAnn Willhoe, and R.U. Ann for open door romantasy/ erotic horror/paranormal fiction.

Ruan has been nominated for Best Erotic Writer by the ASN Lifestyle Magazine Awards 2025.

Thank you!

Thank you to all my family and friends who support me. I wouldn't be where I am without you. You are all the magic and the light in my life, the love that grows in my love. I am honestly thrilled and humbled by the supportive people in my life. Love you!

To Fans:

Thank you for purchasing and/or reviewing this book!

I peddle fantasies for the purposes of your enjoyment, entertainment, and expanding your sexuality and openness. Always remember that no fantasies are bad. You should enjoy your sexuality and your fantasy life as much and as often as you can.

Thank you for reading my book! I write for myself and for my fans. My fans are my main focus though, but of course, I want to like what I write too, and I thoroughly enjoyed writing this story.

In writing spicy romance, I'm always excited for the erotic journey! I'm personally on a path of sexual empowerment, enlightenment, and enjoyment. Thank you for reading this and I'm honored to be a part of your journey as well. I strive to spin stories where the characters get to enjoy lots of pleasure, and I hope you have also gotten pleasure from reading this book. Enjoy your own journey!

I am where I am because fans have responded to me and my content, so I owe everything to you! Thank you! Thank you! Thank you! You are a blessing in my life, and you give me more joy than you will ever know. I love interacting with all of you and I will never give that up.

My stories are open door romance, so they have a generous amount of sex in them, as I believe our relationships should have as well in real life. I hope you enjoyed this novel for what it is, literature that is in the spicy romance genre where sex is a part of the plot, storyline, and character development. It is very different from a closed door romance, and there are different levels of heat in the genre as well. Explore them all! I personally love open door romances because I want the full story of the relationship, not a partial one.

If you'd like more of my work, please see below for my list of published works on the following pages, visit my sexuality/sexual health/wellness podcast, find my audiobooks, visit my website, my Patreon, visit my profile on Medium, and my linktree with all my links at https://linktr.ee/RuanWillow

Thank you for purchasing this book, I'd love to hear your thoughts in an honest review on the site where you purchased the book from. I'd absolutely love it if you shared my book with others. It warms my heart profusely when I see someone who has taken the time to review/share my book. Love you all very much!

All my best, yours truly, with overflowing love from a full heart,
Ruan Willow

Spicy romance author, sexuality/spicy romance podcaster, and book narrator

Ruan's other books
and novellas:

All books:
https://books.ruanwillowauthor.com/
Collections:
Howife books:
https://books.ruanwillowauthor.com/hotwifebooks
Spring Break and Stranded with Her Best Friend's Brothers Collection:
https://books.ruanwillowauthor.com/
springbreakandstrandedwithherbestfriendsbrothersseries
Servicing the Work Men, Her Filthy Hotwife Adventures Series
https://books.ruanwillowauthor.com/
servicingtheworkmenseries
The Sex Challenge Series
https://books.ruanwillowauthor.com/thesexchallengeseries
The Getaway Series: age gap
https://books.ruanwillowauthor.com/ruansgetawayseries
Taboo books
https://books.ruanwillowauthor.com/
taboospringbreakandstrandedwithherbestfriendsbrothersplus6men
Check out the Audiobooks:
https://books.ruanwillowauthor.com/
audiobooksnarratedbyruan
Standalone by R.U. Ann:

In Scarlet's House, in ebook
https://books.ruanwillowauthor.com/inscarletshouse
In audiobook
https://books.ruanwillowauthor.com/
inscarletshouseaudiobook
Arching Hunger Series (open door HEA Romantasy)
https://books.ruanwillowauthor.com/archinghungerseries

ANTHOLOGIES AND AWARD Nominations
Ruan has stories in the following anthologies:
He Will Obey (which was AWARDED THE 2020 SILVER PIGTAIL IN BEST ANTHOLOGY CATEGORY
The Femdom Coven (nominee for 2021 Golden Pigtail Smut Awards)
Inside of Ruan Willow (also available in an audiobook)
(this audiobook was a nominee for the 2021 Golden Pigtail Smut Awards)
Decadent Erotica An Anthology **3rd Place Winner in the 2022 Golden Pigtails Smut Awards for Dark/Taboo Category**
Nominations for the 2023 Golden Pigtail Awards include:
Servicing the Trash Man, My Filthy Hotwife Adventure
Dressing Room Domme
Anthology Ruan has a story Hearts and Flowers, Whips and Chains
Nominations in 2025 for 2024 books
Narration of Emma's Policy (finalist) (book no longer available)
Ruan has been nominated for Best Erotic Writer by the ASN Lifestyle Magazine Awards 2025.

ANTHOLOGIES: SEASON'S Teasings: Snowbound Seductions (finalist) and the charity anthology Not So Guilty Pleasures 45 Filthy Stories for a Cause (no longer available)

Ruan was nominated for Best Erotic Writer by the ASN Lifestyle Magazine Awards for 2025.

OTHER ANTHOLOGIES:

Halloween Anthology: Trick or Tease II

Christmas/Holiday anthology: Season's Teasings: Snowbound Seductions

Summer Teases II

The Best Bi Erotica of the Year, Volume 2

OTHER LINKS/URLS:

Ruan Willow on Goodreads Ruan Willow Goodreads Author page[1]

Ruan Willow on BookBub https://www.bookbub.com/profile/ruan-willow

Sign up for Ruan's newsletter: https://subscribepage.io/ruanwillow

ARC copies are usually on BookSirens and StoryOrigin App. Check those sites for FREE ARC of books and audiobooks.

---

1.   https://www.goodreads.com/author/show/21312130.Ruan_Willow